TO DIANE AND CARA,

WITH LOVE AND GRATITUDE

"*Closing Time* is terrific. It presents a world that sounds and feels like the one we live in, crowded with engaging characters who have things to impart about love, violent death, anger, and sacrifice." — Thomas Perry

"What sets [this novel] above the crowd is the wonderful sense of place—few books give you such a vivid portrait of Manhattan—and the poignant relationship between our hero, Terry Orr, and his incredible daughter, Bella. *Closing Time* is a fine, heart-wrenching debut from a very talented writer." — Harlan Coben

"[A] chic modernist tale. . . . The wised-up, hollowed-out characters . . . may have the sickly look of people who do business under lampposts, but they are vital citizens of Fusilli's gorgeous nightmare of a city."
—*The New York Times Book Review*

"Downtown New York is beautifully captured in all its idiosyncrasies . . . [a] powerful and melancholy debut."
—*Detroit Free Press*

"With a voice as unsentimental and gimmick-free as it is sharp and knowing, Jim Fusilli writes about New York, about atonement, revenge, and finality, about children and parents. That he does this in the context of a crime novel points out both the vitality of the genre and the talent of the writer." —S. J. Rozan

D0103095

continued . . .

CLOSING
TIME

JIM FUSILLI

BERKLEY PRIME CRIME, NEW YORK

CLOSING TIME

A Berkley Prime Crime Book / published by arrangement with the author

PRINTING HISTORY
G. P. Putnam's Sons hardcover edition / September 2001
Berkley Prime Crime mass-market edition / October 2002

Visit our website at
www.penguinputnam.com

ISBN: 0-425-18712-8

Berkley Prime Crime Books are published
by The Berkley Publishing Group
a division of Penguin Putnam Inc.,
375 Hudson Street, New York, New York 10014.
The name BERKLEY PRIME CRIME and
the BERKLEY PRIME CRIME design
are trademarks belonging to Penguin Putnam Inc.

PRINTED IN THE UNITED STATES OF AMERICA

10 9 8 7 6 5 4 3 2 1

I LOVED YOU WHEN OUR LOVE WAS BLESSED
AND I LOVE YOU NOW THERE'S NOTHING LEFT
BUT SORROW AND A SENSE OF OVERTIME.
—*Leonard Cohen*

THE INDIVIDUAL WHO TAKES REVENGE
USUALLY DOES NOT KNOW WHAT HE REALLY WANTS.
—*Friedrich Nietzsche*

Mei Carissima:

A little adventure, perhaps. An opportunity.

Around midnight, Diddio stopped by, looking for company after a show at Irving Plaza, the Mercury Lounge, the Peppermint Lounge, somewhere: Who knows where he goes? I spent some time with him, poured him a beer, got him settled in front of the TV, went up to check on Bella (sleeping in the center of her big bed, still making little fists, thumbs tucked into her palms), and headed out to run, cell hooked to my elastic waistband, as she demands. Through the chilly night air, I went along West, heading north. A little breeze off the Hudson, flickering stars beyond the low clouds. Nice.

I had nothing on my mind but what's always on my mind—the petti di pollo con arucola your father served that first glorious day in Foggia; an April afternoon in Gramercy Park, as we glowered at the somber faces of Goethe and Dante and Milton on the Gothic facade of the

National Arts Club; your Italian lullabies, sung sweet and softly to Bella, Davy and, as I waited in the vestibule, to me; how happy we were when somebody finally stole that old piece-of-shit Ford Jimmy Mango foisted on us: memories, as I've said before, that are more vivid now than in the days after they first formed.

Anyway, I reached Little West 12th and decided to turn back—three miles would be enough for the night. Shuffling in place until the traffic light went green, I crossed West Street and headed toward the meatpacking district, the old Gansevoort Market, cobblestones glistening eerily under the violet streetlamps, as delivery trucks sat idle against vacant loading docks. As I was deciding whether to take Washington, Greenwich or Hudson, to run through flatbeds angling in at the post office depot or weave my way around people pouring out of the dance clubs to flag a ride, I saw a livery cab resting at an odd angle, its front end tilted toward the curb, its rear too far out for it to be parked; and I noticed vapor rising from its tailpipe, as its ponderous V8 growled. I drew closer—I'd stopped running now—and I saw the driver, his head back, shoulders lax as he sat awkwardly on the broad front seat.

I opened the driver's-side door cautiously to let the dome light shine and, in the dull glow, I saw that the driver—a black man, maybe 60, 65 years old—was dead. His nose had been battered, and blood had poured across his lips and along his chin to his thin neck; and I leaned in and saw that his skull had been cracked open above the right temple. Blood saturated the right shoulder of his dark shirt and coated his hand as it lay crumpled on the seat.

As I started to pull away, I noticed, on the floor of the backseat, one of those steering-wheel locks, the bar-like kind: *a perfect weapon, I thought; surely capable of shattering someone's head.*

So I had this thing sussed out, Marina, in seconds—old, black livery-cab driver killed by a rogue fare; the cops would bury this near the pit of hell—as if my meager experiences as a P.I. have given me a level of insight. I pulled out the cell and I started to call Tommy Mango and stopped. He'd treat it like a stain on the cuff of his white-on-white shirt. So I called Luther Addison. Twenty minutes later, he arrived with two patrol cars in tow, all official, no solicitous bullshit, and I gave him a statement and, before I know it, he blows me off: "There is nothing you can do here."

I tried to say something. I was thinking about saying something.

"You stumbled onto this," he said pointedly. "Could've been anybody."

He knows what I'm trying to do, tesora. What I'm trying to learn.

But he turns and he walks away, toward the billowing steam, the sparse crowd gathering on the cobblestone.

At least I got a ride home, from a mute uniform who favors musky cologne.

I walked gingerly into the house: Diddio asleep on the floor in front of the sofa; Bella watching Bogart's "The Treasure of the Sierra Madre" on Bravo.

"You're not sweating," she said. "Why?" She wore her floppy flannel nightgown, a ratty beret and bowling shoes without socks.

I nudged Diddio onto the couch, cut the TV and chased Bella back upstairs.

"You might as well tell me," she said as she bounced into bed. "I'm only going to ask you again in the morning."

As I went into our bathroom to shower, I'm thinking about the gypsy cabbie—Aubrey Brown, 63, lived in East Harlem—and I'm still thinking about it three hours later, as I sit here in the study and write to you.

Diddio, I just remembered, is in my spot. I've got to sleep in our bed.

Did I tell you I still stay on my side?

Of course I did.

Sorry it's gotten sloppy tonight—shifting verb tense, for one, and clumsy transitions; and a sentimentality only you understand. I'm running low, too tired to edit; angry at Addison; and I'm thinking now about our long walks down Fifth as the park began to blossom, your sister's bountiful garden in back of your father's house, the scent of your hair, the green flecks in your brown eyes. You.

And Aubrey Brown, and how Addison ushered me away.

Theory must give way to action, Marina. At some point, learning surrenders to application. The time when I can ignore opportunity has passed.

And it matters not what anyone else thinks or says.

A presto, Marina.
All my love,
T.

ONE

WE WERE WALKING DOWN Greenwich Street, in the moments before twilight, on our way home.

An hour earlier, Bella announced that we were having grilled hamburgers for dinner, and I shrugged in agreement and threw on my short coat over a torn t-shirt and jeans. We'd been living on Italian food; the refrigerator freezer overflowed with containers of *pesto con gorgonzola, lasagne con melanzane* and the like, prepared by our housekeeper Mrs. Maoli, who seemed to believe I'd allow Bella to waste away without her cooking.

The canvas sack Bella now carried was as full as mine, but, with a glint of mischief in her eyes, she had packed hers with paper products, Boston lettuce, two Portuguese rolls, a copy of *Seventeen* magazine and a lightbulb. I had the canned goods, a half-gallon of skim milk, five pounds of potatoes and a softball-sized red onion. As she lifted her sack at the Food Mart checkout, she quoted John Stuart Mill: "Each to his own ability, Dad." My daughter is very clever. "I know," she once said. "I'm too smart for my own good." Apparently, I sometimes forget that she's younger than she seems.

"Dad, I heard a good one today."

"Yeah."

"Did you roll your eyes at me? Don't," she warned. "My information is solid."

"Your information is rumor."

"Be that as it may," she replied. "But Mrs. Maoli believes me."

Of course your surrogate *nonna* believes you. She fed you, changed you, nurtured you while Mama was painting, while I scribbled my nonsense.

"Ready to listen?"

I shifted the heavy sack up into my arms. "I'm a giant ear."

"Cynic," she charged. "But, if you listen to me, I'll forgive you."

We reached the corner of Beach Street. With very little traffic on a late Sunday afternoon, we crossed easily heading south, as a few yellow cabs went toward the World Trade Center. On the other side of the wide, pothole-scarred avenue, a young man with Aztec features, his black hair pulled into a long, glimmering ponytail, struggled with three impatient dogs. A tall, auburn-haired woman in a midnight-blue suit, white silk blouse and pearls frowned in anger as she checked her watch and craned her neck to glare uptown. In the air was the scent of the river, and I could smell the dusky potatoes and the paper sack I had in my arms.

Bella said, "Now, Dad, Little Mango told me his uncle saw Isabella Rossellini at the TriBeCa Grill and she was drunk and screaming for Martin Scorsese to be a man and come out and fight and Robert De Niro had to calm her down and then Scorsese's mother had to come over and she was wearing a housecoat and she put her arm around her to calm her down and she started sobbing, saying 'Mama, Mama' and the cops came and it was wild." She didn't breathe; she gasped. "And I don't know how they kept it out of the papers. But it must have been wild. Mango said it was really wild."

Little Mango was the son of Jimmy Mango, a neighborhood wiseguy, and the nephew of Tommy Mangionella, a hard-ass policeman. It was a toss-up as to who was crazier, Jimmy or Tommy the Cop.

"So?" she asked.

"Very vivid."

"Wild, huh?"

"Bella, I heard the same story when I was a kid. Only it was Ava Gardner looking for Frank Sinatra at the Copa and it was Dolly Sinatra who did the calming down."

"Could happen twice."

The TriBeCa Grill was, in fact, part-owned by De Niro, who I've seen in the neighborhood but never in his restaurant. I said, "Mrs. Scorsese died a few years ago."

"Maybe it was someone who looked like her."

"Yeah, maybe it was Ingrid—" I stopped myself, and exhaled slowly. "Diddio would've said something." Diddio is a rock and jazz critic who loved brushing up against celebrities. "Nobody said anything about a brawl."

"You can be so naïve sometimes," she huffed. "They can keep it quiet, Dad. They're rich."

I was preparing my reply when I looked up and saw her skidding toward us, her arms waving, a frantic, near-maniacal expression on her round face. Purple jacket open and billowing behind her, she bore down on us, shrill-shouting out our names, flapping, flouncing.

"Yikes," Bella whispered.

It was Judith Henley Harper. Judy had been Marina's

agent. I wasn't sure if Bella remembered her, though she never seemed to forget anything.

"Terry! Terry Orr!"

Hugs; air kisses, cheek-against-cheek, as she arrived. Bella flinched, but was gracious.

"Gabriella, oh my god in heaven! Dear, how old are you? You must be, what? A teenager, at least."

"I'm twelve," she chirped.

"Twelve years old, my goodness." She turned to me, and went on her toes to touch my head just above the ear. "Your hair's a little longer, Terry, no? Very becoming. The slightest hint of gray, not too, too much; is it? I like it. I approve. Though what are you? Thirty-two-ish? A little early for gray, maybe. Maybe."

She stepped back to examine us, giving me a chance to look closely at her. I figured Judy for about 55 years old, though her exuberance, her butterfly gestures, bright eyes, made her physical age irrelevant. She was a ball of energy, under short hair that was either blond or silver, depending on the light, that she combed with her fingers. There was a time when I would've welcomed her company, when I would've invited her to join Marina, Bella, Davy and me for tonight's dinner.

She adjusted the pale-violet frames of her glasses and returned to Bella. "And who do you look like, dear? What I mean is, you don't look very much like your father. Nor do you look at all like Marina. But you'll be tall, like your mother. Not as tall as your father, thank goodness." She grabbed Bella by the chin and squeezed. "You have your own beauty, dear Gabriella. Very cute. Lucky. Yes."

"Thank you," Bella managed. She adjusted her faded denim jacket.

Judy made a sad, sympathetic face. "So, Terry, really, how are you?"

"I don't know, Judy." I shrugged. "Fine."

"I think about her, Terry. She was gifted. No doubt about that."

"Yeah, you were good to her, Judy."

She waved her hand, dismissing the compliment. "Her work sold itself, Terry." She smiled. "And would continue to, if you'd let me."

I shook my head. "I told you, Judy—"

"Now, now, Terry. Don't get huffy."

We had four of Marina's paintings in our home, four of the seven that remained in the family. They were land-scapes of the environs of the Foggia region of Italy, where she was born and had been raised: the sea-arch of Vignanotica; the cliffs of the Gargano coastline; the view east from the church of San Giovanni; and Lake Occhito, near Campobasso. Her father, who still lived in the province, had two street scenes Marina had done here in TriBeCa, and her sister Rafaela had a portrait of her son, Marina's godson, a work that was the least characteristic and by some accounts, the most interesting.

Judy knew I would never sell these remaining works, but I suppose I didn't blame her for trying: She's no mere mercenary, but she's not in business to amuse herself, like some of her effete peers whose rich husbands set them up with a few paintings in a well-appointed yet soulless gallery. Judy presented Marina's first major exhibition nine years ago, and from her small storefront in SoHo, she sold 46 paintings and a dozen or so sketches, making certain that the work of Marina Fiorentino was well known not only downtown and around Manhattan but throughout the art world, arranging shows in London, Seville, Paris and Florence. (For her efforts, she'd pock-eted 15 percent of the $18.5 million those sales netted.) To this day, Marina is the subject of articles in art maga-zines, and a TV documentary she's featured in turns up every now and then on PBS, on MSG's Metro channels.

Last year, Bella's web search on her mother produced more than 5,800 hits. Later, after Bella went off to bed, I repeated the search and found that some 3,000 of them were about her murder. I didn't read any of them. I know that story better than anyone else.

"Terry, did I hear right? Have you been working as some sort of private detective? Is this true?"

Bella interrupted. "He's doing research for a new book. On, er, Samuel Jones Tilden."

And with that, Judy became animated again; her voice jumped an octave, her hands darting as she spoke. "Good for you, Terry. You're writing again. God knows we need you to keep writing, Terry. The world needs books by Terry Orr."

I nodded amicably, or at least what passes for amicably for me now, but I was thinking that social amenities had been exchanged, obligations met and fulfilled, and now it was time to go. I started to inch forward.

"Terry, listen: I want you and Gabriella to come to an opening. I want you to come. I insist. Tomorrow night. Sol Beck. You know Sol Beck." She paused. "Do you know Sol Beck?"

I said no.

"You'll like his work. Very natural, *après* Hopper. A touch of darkness. New York without hope." She smiled. "He'll sell."

"Judy, you know that's not my thing—"

"We'll come," Bella chimed.

"Gabriella, good for you. Good. Seven o'clock. You know the drill, Terry."

"Judy," I said, "I—"

"Gabriella, you can bring a boyfr— No, I guess, at twelve, maybe not yet, although who knows these days? These days: You could be married for all I know. No, I suppose not. Your father probably scares the boys away.

How does Mr. Muscles do it? Stomping around like Frankenstein? Big angry face?"

Bella looked up at me. "He's cool with my friends," she said, "mostly."

"Anyway," Judy continued, "you just make sure he comes. Terry, don't make me hound you. You know I can be a terror." She waited a second and put her hands on her hips. "Terry, you're supposed to say something right about now."

"Well, you are a shark, Judy," I said. "It's your gift."

"From you, Terry Orr, I take that as a compliment." She went on her toes again and I got another set of kisses. Bella did too. "Seven o'clock," she repeated. "Gabriella, nag him into it, okay?"

"I will."

And Judy bounced off, her low heels click-clicking on the cobblestone as she crossed Beach.

A young, paint-splattered couple emerged from the warehouse behind my daughter. The man, who was no older than 20, wore a circular ring through his eyebrow. His girlfriend, the long expanse of her stomach exposed by a short, cropped t-shirt and jeans that began beneath her hips, had a tattoo of a snake that ran up to her pierced navel.

I looked at Bella, who smiled broadly, comically.

"You shouldn't have done that."

"Oh, Dad, it's good for you to go out. To someplace other than the Tilt."

"Bella, you know better," I added gently.

She slumped and said softly, "We don't have to go."

"Yes we do. You made a commitment for us."

"Sorry," she murmured, her eyes locked on the concrete at her feet.

"All right."

We started toward North Moore. I looked ahead,

toward our house, and I was not unaware that she was staring up at me.

THE NEXT EVENING I was at the kitchen table, lost in a thick brief Sharon Knight had messengered over from the Manhattan D.A.'s office. I had long ago gotten beyond the stilted language of these things, the impossible syntax, the disagreeable self-importance that characterized documents written by lawyers, and now I was able to make sense of them on the first pass-through, then get to understand the real point of the matter. Beyond the reams of obfuscation, legal briefs had a certain elegance, and they revealed precisely what was at stake in a case. Typically, it was either money or revenge or both. With an increasingly wavering dispassion, I was learning the system, as I had to, thanks to Sharon's aid and Addison's obstruction.

"Dad?"

I looked up to find Bella at my elbow. She was dressed in what could only be described as neo-hippie: a purple, floral ankle-length dress, the green-and-red bowling shoes and her all-too-familiar denim jacket. The thing on her head was not so much a hat as a velour throw pillow. Giant clip-on hoop earrings dangled almost to her shoulders. She was wearing my watch as well as her own.

She asked, "Are you going to change?"

I was still in a tattered UNLV t-shirt, well-worn sweats and running shoes. "I'd better."

"I'll wait," she smiled.

Ten minutes later, after I had changed my shirt and dug an old brown corduroy blazer out of the back of the closet, we were outside, under the distant stars, thin clouds, the silver rays of the moon, as we headed toward SoHo, toward Judy's.

Bella said, "We should take a cab. We're already late."

We approached a large green Dumpster on Harrison. Just beyond it, an Asian man in a starched white uniform sat on a wooden crate and read a newspaper. The scent of bok choy, snow peas, water chestnuts and MSG wafted from the screen door of the cubbyhole restaurant behind him.

She said, "We told Judy we would be there, so we should be on time."

We turned onto Hudson, passing Chanterelle, for my money the best restaurant in Manhattan. For a moment, I thought about the seafood sausage, the squab with lentils, the turbot, the cheese tray, and the Opus One Marina had sprung for on my 30th birthday.

"Don't be so agitated," I advised.

Bella said, "I'm not agitated. I'm just talking about the time. I'm a kid. I have to be on time."

"Five minutes doesn't mean much."

"You can be late by two seconds, you know. One second."

We turned north on Hudson. There were several ways to get to the Henley Harper Galley from our place. I decided to head over to Franklin to West Broadway to Canal, then on to Greene. Bella, I knew, was still thinking about a cab.

We walked in silence to Franklin, observing the small parade, the indifferent clash of men in Brooks Brothers suits with stout $20 cigars; unruly boys in lime-green, long-sleeved t-shirts over hooded sweat tops and baggy jeans; high-gloss women in Gaultier and sapless, doe-eyed girls in old Doc Martens and thrift-shop rejects. To me, TriBeCa was a place of uncertainty now, of permanence and transition; of graceless wealth and timeless abjection; of coexistence: where seemingly abandoned warehouses stood above empty streets, and where other seemingly abandoned warehouses were in fact blocks of luxury apartments carved out of vast, unwieldy lofts. It was a place where people in blue chalkstripe formed a slapdash line and waited for a table at a 12-seat storefront restaurant that served Thai or Pakistani or Rumanian and, until the man with the goatee from the architectural firm that built the million-dollar apartments dined there, was known only to the rumpled man who read a Schoenberg score through bifocals held together with a safety pin, to the matronly woman in the tattered gray smock, the former model who decades ago ran with Ginsberg and Kerouac, who listened to Ferlinghetti on red vinyl, who slept with Neal Cassady. There was a Gothic quality to the neighborhood, and the cast-iron colonnettes, stone gargoyles, the Italianate palaces, the ornate metal canopies, the broad-shouldered textile buildings were redolent with a sense of history I could feel and admire. And yet there were shadows, and broken windows, razor-wire, wide cracks in the pavement, and failure and loss. And there were the ghosts, apparitions that materialized without warning, whenever they chose to, on barren cobblestone streets, in the graffiti-splattered alleys, under the frail trees in Duane Park, at the Tilt, at Wetlands, when I pass Chanterelle.

A gaggle of teenaged boys played handheld video games on the steps of a brownstone. Rusted fire escapes loomed overhead, and a cracked hydrant dribbled water into the gutter. In the distance, the Empire State Building was crowned with a white light that seemed to waver in the mist.

"Did you go to see Dr. Harteveld?"

"No," I replied.

"You haven't seen Dr. Harteveld in three weeks."

We reached TriBeCa Park. A man with matted hair and dirt-crusted feet was sleeping on a cardboard mattress he'd placed on a bench. Under him lay an old, forlorn dog.

"She's your doctor."

"She's *our* psychiatrist," she corrected. She was disappointed in me, for not seeing Dr. Harteveld, for not being ready for the Beck opening, for not writing about Samuel Tilden.

"Bella, I'm walking as fast as I can go without losing you."

She stopped. "I'm not nagging, Dad," she said, "and no cab is okay by now. I think Dr. Harteveld's good for us, that's all. It's good for us to talk to her. She'll like this, that you're out. With people."

I said nothing. She was under my skin now, and I am prone to resist that, to resist pressure, as quickly, as fiercely as I can; a red light and heat, fury—though not ever with her.

"Dad?"

"You see her when? Friday? I'll see her Friday."

As we reached Canal, the green WALK sign beckoned and we crossed in front of a FedEx truck. "You promise?" she asked.

"Do I have to promise?"

She skipped ahead.

"Come on," she shouted. "The light's changing."

GREENE STREET WAS quiet, surprisingly so, and the bright lights from the large bay windows of the Henley Harper Gallery shone across the cobblestone to the other side of the dark, narrow roadway. Inside, the crowd was larger than I'd expected, and it was a blend not unlike what I remembered from Marina's exhibitions: neighborhood artists in denim peacoats, poseurs in black, a handful of local craftsmen, men and women who might've been in rock bands, scruffy journalists, two photographers busily clicking away, business suits, tall, empty-eyed women of unimaginable posture and beauty, friends, competitors. Judy and her assistant Edie Reeves were known to invite a flamboyant, bald-headed transvestite named Dominick to their openings, just to add a bit of contemporary color. But he was not in sight, and I realized I was disappointed. Dominick was easy to talk to: He was a man doing his job and, surveying all that spun around him, he was not impressed.

"Wow," Bella whispered as she surveyed the crowded room. "This is very cool."

She was no more than seven at the time of Marina's last opening. She couldn't have been older, since Davy hadn't been born yet. Maybe she had forgotten what a SoHo opening was like.

"You like this?" For me, I was in a room overflowing with phonies, with people I could live without.

"I'm the only kid here," she answered gleefully. "I'm going to look around. Okay?" And she was off, squeezing by a small circle of people and disappearing into a veil of cigarette smoke and well-practiced ennui.

The steady din, the hissing chatter, covered the music Judy had chosen for the event. I declined a glass of white wine and went to the brick wall on my right to study the first painting of the exhibition.

It was entitled "D. Rich Co." I recognized the rooftops and top-floor fire escapes of a row of buildings on Worth, not very far from either here or my home. The exteriors of the actual buildings were remarkably preserved, and from the angle Beck had selected, they looked no different than they would have 75 years earlier. On one of the fire escapes was a vapid woman who stood languidly, staring nowhere, remembering. Resting her elbows on the metal railing, she wore a slip that hung formlessly to her knees. One thin strap had slid from her shoulder.

The sky above the rooftops, above the tired, heavy-breasted brunette in the slip, was without spirit. A water tower hovered in the distance.

I liked the work. The woman stirred my imagination: The Baby Doll Lounge was on the corner of Worth. Did she work there? Had she, years ago? And its sense of surrender, its joylessness, was all too familiar to me. I wondered what she had lost.

At the same time, though, I realized that "D. Rich Co." was the most transparent rip-off of Hopper since Hitchcock co-opted "House by the Railroad" for the Bates residence in *Psycho*. Judy could have chosen the music of Bernard Herrmann, rather than Charles Ives, as the score for the evening's event.

"Terry Orr. Dear, dear Terry," she shouted breathlessly. "You came. You came."

I turned to find Judy. She was dressed casually: an oversized, wheat-colored silk blouse over black slacks, her glasses dangling on beads around her neck. Her wineglass was empty, a smudge of lipstick on its rim. She was bubbling.

"Kiss, kiss," she said, as she brushed her cheeks against mine. "It's a good crowd, Terry." She gestured for me to bend down, so she could whisper. "Can you smell the money?"

"No Dominick tonight, Judy?"

She shook her head. "He's booked uptown at the Public Library. But I got us a Rolling Stone. Did you see him? Ronnie Wood? And his wife: My God, she's fabulous." She looked around the crowded room. "Did you say hi to Edie?"

"I haven't seen her," I said.

A lean woman, fiftyish and in a red military jacket, with wide eyes and impossibly white teeth, came by and greeted Judy with prototypical overexuberance. Judy listened with apparent enthusiasm, nodded often, beamed, affected surprise, then sent her off into the gathering with a hearty laugh and a promise to call "sooner than soon."

"That woman hasn't paid for a meal since 1985," Judy grunted, with a frown. Then, instant brightness: "What do you think of it? Beck, I mean. The work. His work."

"Well, I—"

"Exactly," she interrupted, still shouting. "Have you met him?"

"No, but it's not—"

"Come on. You'll see Edie too. She's knows you're coming."

She grabbed my hand and yanked me toward her. We bumped through the cackling crowd, across the polished, hardwood floor, toward the back of the room.

Sol Beck was about 35 years old, with a balding pate that had once borne red hair. His skin was pale to the point of translucence. About six feet tall, he stood with a slump, and he exuded a sense of discomfort, of shyness, that was painful to observe, even at a distance. He fingered the buttons of his nondescript suit and toyed with his thin black tie as he listened respectfully to a lecture from a man I recognized as a fatuous critic who wrote for a local rag that was dumped in Laundromats and takeout joints.

Standing at Beck's side, listening without nearly the same level of acquiescence, was a stern yet striking Asian woman. She wore a simple, sleeveless dress and had a black silk jacket draped over her shoulders. Her perfect black mane hung well down her back.

Next to her was Edie Reeves, in a white blouse, short black skirt, her long legs in dark hose and heels. She brushed her black hair off her thin, angular face as she listened to a round man in a tweed suit and bow tie.

"Sadler. Shoo, shoo, shoo," Judy ordered.

The critic, Sadler Boyd, feigned injury. "I was merely telling our boy Sol—"

"You were flattering him. Then you were going to turn to Edie and say you intended to write a glowing review. Then you were going to remind her that we hadn't yet ordered our quarter-page ad for next week's edition, which, coincidentally, *coincidentally,* was going to contain your review of Sol's opening."

Edie took in the exchange and cast a furtive glance at the Asian woman, who watched stoically.

"Judy, you make it all sound so vulgar," Boyd replied. "Edie, rescue me from your mentor."

Judy said, "Sadler, if you go right now—I mean, *right* now—I'll pay for a half-page."

Boyd smiled and slunk off, bowing at Beck, the young woman, at Edie. I didn't get a bow. In here, I didn't exist.

"Sol, did you shake his hand?" Judy asked.

He nodded. "Yes."

"Count your fingers." She turned. "Lin-Lin, these things you need to know. You have to protect. *We* have to protect. Say yes."

The young woman nodded without smiling. Edie peered at the glossy floor, as if she'd been chastised.

I felt slightly embarrassed by the exchange. Edie was the one I spoke to in Judy's office when I needed to pass on a call about Marina's work. Over the years I'd known her, she'd been transformed into a junior Henley Harper; though considerably younger and a raven-haired beauty, she had Judy's natural instinct for business, if not the fine-tuned bullshit detector. After handling a few losers after first coming to New York, she was grounded now and determined to get ahead.

Judy said, "Sol, Lin-Lin, I am introducing you to Terry Orr. You should know him. He's a writer. Very fine. History, New York, all that."

We swapped greetings. Lin-Lin bowed slightly, causing me to do the same. Beck took my hand, but did not meet my gaze.

"Terry," Edie said, her clipped British accent noticeable even on two syllables. She leaned in, kissed me on both cheeks, and left behind a trace of a tangerine fragrance, which was not unpleasant.

"Maybe you know him. Do you?" Judy asked. "Sol?"

Beck's eyes wandered. "No," he managed.

Edie said, "He was married to Marina Fiorentino."

"Oh," Lin-Lin exclaimed. She prompted Beck. "Sol."

Beck reddened. "I knew Marina," he said. "She helped me."

Lin-Lin added, "We're very sorry for your loss."

Judy put her ebullience aside to address Beck and his companion. "You two have got to get out of this corner, all right? Edie, move them around the room. I mean, Sol, shy is shy, but for Christ's sake, listen. You hear that sound? *Ch-ching:* The cash register opens, the money falls in. And you work as you want for the rest of your life. If you doubt me, ask Terry." She looked at me. "Terry, forgive me. Sol, if this was Marina's night, she wouldn't be hiding in the corner, and every work would be sold by tomorrow afternoon. I mean, a little personality; could it hurt?"

Chastened, Beck shook his head.

Judy leaned in, grabbed his cheeks and kissed him flush on the lips. "Sol, we love you. Go make the doughnuts, okay?" She tugged at the sleeve of Lin-Lin's jacket. "And you: You want to be a mover, be a mover."

Lin-Lin nodded, then glanced at her delicate wristwatch.

"And Edie," Judy continued, "a little less for the client, a little more for the clientele. Right?"

"Right, Judy," she said. She smiled broadly at me, nodded meekly at Beck and Lin-Lin, then followed Judy as she disappeared into the crowd.

We stood in awkward silence for what seemed like minutes, the sense of discomfort broken only by the appearance of a tray of grilled Portobello mushrooms and another with champagne in tall flutes, delivered by young women in tuxedo shirts and bow ties. Behind them, a young man with a shaved head and a salt-and-pepper goatee waded in and asked, "Have you seen Judy?"

"She went that way," I offered.

"There's a phone call for her. The man said it was urgent," he added. He looked left and right, then went off.

Across the room, the Rolling Stone was having his photo taken with a man with a flawless tan. The toothsome woman in the red army jacket was trying to squeeze into the frame.

"May I ask a question?" Lin-Lin said. "Does Judy represent your wife's estate?"

She'd begun to inch away from the station Beck had made for himself in the corner of the room. I followed, reluctantly, as did he, shuffling, slumping.

"Yes," I replied, "but there's not much happening now. Judy generates some publicity but it's all winding down."

Suddenly, the music stopped and the crowd began to quiet. From across the room, I could hear Judy shouting, trying to get everyone's attention.

"Now, now, quiet, quiet," she said, then repeated it. She clapped her hands. "Please. Please. I have to make an announcement."

When it was as quiet as it was going to get, she continued. "Believe it or not, I repeat, believe it or not, I just got off the phone with an asshole who says there's a bomb in here. A *bomb*."

Her announcement was met not with panic or concern, but with a peal of laughter.

"No, I'm serious," she said. "I've called the police and they told me everyone has to get out, and right now. So, let's move it. Let's go."

Not a single person budged.

A hoarse shout came from across the room. "Nice touch, Judy."

She drew herself up, her face tightening. Her reply was terse, delivered firmly. "Ladies, gentlemen. Asshole says there's a bomb in here; I believe him. I advise you to get out."

I turned. Beck looked as if he was going to faint. "Lin-Lin," he mumbled.

"Yes," she answered. "Immediately."

Without a word to me, she walked toward the door. Beck followed.

The crowd began to funnel casually, lazily toward the front exit and down the steps. And then I thought maybe I ought to get Bella and go as well. Maybe it was more than a prank. Maybe there was a bomb.

I turned and, looking over the crowd, spotted her at the far corner of the room, on the other side of the brick divider, across from where I'd been. She seemed confused, as if she was trying to decide whether she should be frightened. I knew that, in a moment, she would be, and her brave smile would fall away.

As I nudged toward her, she gestured to me quickly. I stepped up, moving with a purpose, pushing against the wave. But I had little effect on the crowd, which would not be ruffled by the threat of a bomb or by a harried man. Their faces registered nothing more than disdainful annoyance and oily condescension; they offered no assistance: They continued to move slowly, woodenly toward the exit, like peacocks coolly shuffling toward Greene Street.

Bella was sandwiched between two glib couples who

showed neither a sense of urgency nor concern for a now-frightened little girl. I stretched, reached and tugged her by the front of her jacket; as I turned I inadvertently slammed my hip into a lean blond woman at her side. The woman stumbled, a wineglass falling from her hand. Her tallish escort barked at me, but to me it was only sound.

"Daddy—"

"Don't worry," I said. "We're moving."

Then I felt a hand on my back. I turned to find the lean woman's escort glaring at me.

"Sorry," I said to him, to the blonde at his side.

Suddenly, the tall man in the well-tailored suit reached out and shoved Bella. She tumbled backward, but did not fall. Shocked, she quickly steadied herself.

"There," the man said, as he looked back at me. "A taste of your own medi—"

I drove the flat of my right hand into his jaw, and he bit hard on his tongue. He groaned and gasped. The lean blonde in black looked on in horror as the man opened his mouth. Blood spread across his bottom lip.

"Anything else?" I asked as she dug into her purse for a handkerchief.

With that, I lifted Bella up and took off with her, banging toward the door, shoving through the crowd. I heard the protests, the whining shouts, the tepid complaints. But I pressed on, thinking of nothing but getting her outside, away from her thoughts of danger.

I stepped on the red runner and slid Bella onto the hardwood. We went out in the evening's cool air and cut off traffic as we crossed the cobblestone.

We reached the east side of the street just as a sinewy, long-haired man in a torn t-shirt and black jeans came up behind us. "Thanks, man, for clearing a path."

I turned to Bella and went to one knee. "Are you okay?"

"Now, yes."

"Scared?"

"I don't— At first, I couldn't see you. And that guy. He pushed me. An *adult*."

Around us, the crowd filled the street, and drivers, unable to continue north, began to sound their shrill horns. As she tried to cross the traffic, a young woman in a flannel shirt, a cowgirl hoopskirt and Western boots pounded impatiently on the hood of a black Jeep.

Behind me, Sadler Boyd shouted, "Did anyone remember to bring the champagne?"

And again there was laughter, and in a moment it was as if the party had simply moved out onto Greene Street.

I had stood and draped my arm on Bella's shoulder. "You okay?"

She forced a smile, then sighed. "Except for my dignity, I suppose so."

I felt a tap at my elbow. It was Edie.

"Terry, I think Judy—"

I turned and, at that instant, saw an orange flash. Then I heard a sound, not a roar but a compact, muffled explosion. A gasp from the crowd, and then smoke. A cry.

"Judy's inside!" Edie shouted.

Sudden silence, shock; and billows of smoke, racing out and upward. Then, the frenetic honking of car horns.

"Bella, you stay here. You stay with Edie." To Edie, I said, "Keep her close to you."

She moaned desperately. "Terry . . ."

And I ran back across the street, into the dark cloud as I took the steel steps with a leap.

The smoke was thick and made it impossible to see. And then, as I pushed forward, gagging, eyes stinging, the smoke vanished: The room was hazy. It had taken on an almost ethereal quality, looking only vaguely familiar, as if I had been there in a dream.

I shouted, "Judy!"

The only light was behind me, from the street. I moved slowly, with my hand on the brick divider that ran down the wavering center of the room. As I went farther, I could see the residue of damage: Several paintings were on the floor, the table in the corner that had served as a makeshift bar was overturned; broken glasses and champagne and wine bottles.

The white door in the back was off its hinges, and the surrounding frame was heavily damaged, and I proceeded carefully in its direction, crushing shards of glass. As I crossed under the cracked frame, I saw Judy on her back, apparently unconscious. Moving closer, I saw that blood flowed from the back of her head, and there were streaks of blood on her right calf. And then I noticed that where her left foot had been was now a mangled mass of flesh and exposed bone. Blood spurted with each beat of her heart.

I quickly took off my belt and used it as a tourniquet on her left calf. As I lifted her to address the wound on her head, a hand from behind me clasped my shoulder.

I turned, and there was a man in blue and with him two EMS workers, and they instructed me to go, brushing me aside as they went to work on Judy's leg and head.

I stood behind them as they scurried around her, and I moved aside as the rolling gurney was brought in.

Now a cop told me to move on, for the second time in three days, and I went through the dust and smoke, stepping over the fallen glass, propping up a pair of paintings that had dropped to the floor.

When I reached the street, I saw Bella, without Edie, and she ran toward me. It was then that I realized my hands were covered in Judy's blood. Surprisingly, Bella did not panic; she seemed to understand.

"Is she dead?"

"No," I said, "but she's hurt." I looked around. 'Where's Edie?"

"She ran," Bella replied. "She ran away."

BY THE TIME I emerged from the shower, Bella was in boxer shorts and an old t-shirt of mine, and was ready for bed. I threw on a pair of sweats and a long-sleeved henley, made a quick call to the hospital to ask about Judy and went down to the kitchen to fill Bella's favorite cup with cranberry juice.

I went back upstairs through the dull light, each footfall bringing an ancient creak from beneath the old carpeting. In her room, Bella was nestled in her bed, covers up to her neck, her head on her Winnie-the-Pooh pillowcase. She clutched an old, stuffed toy moose, and she smiled wearily. On her nightstand was *Franny and Zooey* and a dog-eared biography of Jimi Hendrix that Diddio had lent her.

"Are we going to have nightmares?" she asked as she sat up.

I handed her the cup. She took a sip and slid it next to the books.

"No," I answered. "We know Judy's going to be all right now."

Bella had shown no signs of fear; a little uneasy on the cab ride home, but now she seemed fine. The night, I suppose, had been filled with a chilling sort of excitement for her. I tried to get her to open up, but she kept insisting she was all right. "Little Mango can't beat this one," she said, as if what happened was nothing more than a new story to tell her friends. I don't know how she does it: She bounces back. She's indomitable. I don't need Elizabeth Harteveld to tell me that.

"You'll grind your teeth," she said.

"Maybe."

"You will, Dad. You should let Dr. Harteveld give you something."

I ran my hand across her smooth forehead.

"Are you sure you're okay?" I asked.

"I'm sure."

"You're too excited to sleep. You should read."

She nodded. "You know, you saved me, Dad."

I smiled. "I don't think so, Bella."

"No, you saved me. Really. I was in the corner you said Judy was in."

I leaned over to stroke her hair. "Good night, little angel."

She bounced on her side and retrieved Salinger's tale, and I headed toward the stairs, my steps echoing through the empty house.

TWO

THINKING I'D RUN AND maybe work the heavy bag after I dropped Bella off at school and before I went where I needed to be, I didn't take a shower, nor did I shave, and I looked very much like what I was when I went out to Harrison to pick up the *Times:* a man who had slept fitfully, if at all; a man whose morning grooming consisted of flicking cold water on his face after brushing his teeth.

The chill off the Hudson did little to invigorate me and I quickly came back inside. And there was Bella at the kitchen table. She hadn't showered either.

"Give," she said. "Please."

I cleared my throat. "Good morning, Dad."

"Yes. Good morning, Dad," she said quickly. "Now: Give. Please."

I handed her the *Times.* Bella had been reading newspapers since she was three years old. For her fifth birthday, she asked for a subscription. Marina blamed me for this, and I suppose she was right: I began to read the clever features I'd seen in the newspaper to Bella and Davy when they were in the cradle, too young to understand the words.

She asked, "Where will it be?"

"Metro section."

"I'm excited." She dug out the second section and flipped the broadsheet pages. After a moment, she groaned in disappointment. "Look at this. A little tiny box."

I looked over her shoulder. The headline read: EXPLOSION AT GALLERY. The matter-of-fact story was more or less correct, confirming what I had learned: Judy was in "serious but stable condition."

"Was there anything on the radio?"

I said, "I didn't have it on."

I went over and clicked on the box we kept on top of the refrigerator. As the NPR commentator droned on, Bella shrugged. "Well, now I know more than I'll ever need to about the farming habits of the Bantu-speaking Ovambo of Namibia," she said.

She got up and went toward the stairs. "One of us should shower," she offered.

"Your classmates will be pleased."

About 20 minutes later she returned, bounding happily down the stairs as I read the Arts section, something about a revival of Odets's *Awake and Sing*. I got a peck on the cheek as she went to the cabinet, removed a Pop-Tart and shoved it into the toaster. Her hair was damp.

"Anything yet?" she asked as she pointed to the radio. "About Judy, I mean."

"No."

"You need a press agent. I mean, if you're going to insist on doing this."

"Oh, I think not, Bella."

I saw it in a flash: coverage, and it confirms Addison's

unspoken fear: I do what it is I do now to embarrass him. Which is wrong, though on a few days not by much.

"You are the hero. People need to know."

I took a gulp from a bottle of water. "Look at this," I said as I pointed to the paper.

She grabbed the section as she sat across from me.

"You slept on the couch, didn't you?"

"I started a movie," I said. *"The Enemy Below* with Robert Mitchum, directed by Dick Powell. Next thing I knew it was 5:30."

The toaster popped and I served my daughter her breakfast of choice, along with a Kermit the Frog multivitamin. I noticed that a strap on her blue denim painter's pants was twisted and her black turtleneck was rolled up in back, but I said nothing. Earlier, Bella advised me that when it came to contemporary fashion, my judgment was in question and my help was anything but. "An irritant" was the exact phrase, I believe.

She looked up. "Your cabdriver that got killed," she said. "It's very sad."

The Sunday *Times* had a brief piece about Aubrey Brown. Today's story was the follow-up and the *New York Times* proved a proficient leg man. The cabby was a loner, the dispatcher Ellard Jackson said, and he had no family. He liked to hack. "Aubrey worked whenever he was healthy," he added. "The overnight shift, whenever he could make it."

The paper had a photo of the cab. The old Buick looked like a rolling coffin under the harsh streetlights.

Brown had emphysema, the *Times* said. He lived in a one-room rat-trap in East Harlem. In a passport-like photo provided by Jackson and his Dee-luxe Livery Cab Company, Brown was balding, with sagging skin and a world-weary slouch. His listless eyes looked straight ahead, through the camera, as if he was considering some far-off place, or thinking of absolutely nothing. It was a disturbing glare, and I'd had to blink, then look away. And as I did I saw him as I'd found him: head cracked, blood everywhere.

The coroner's office reported that Brown was killed by a combination of blows to the head. His nose was broken, and his skull was fractured from behind.

Police declined to comment, saying only that the investigation was ongoing.

(Also unspoken: Terry Orr has been invited to stay the fuck home.)

Brown's change box was emptied, and his wallet was gone.

The reporter had done a thorough job, going to Brown's apartment on 142nd Street and finding not much more than a hot plate, instant oatmeal, instant coffee, a radio and an old turntable. Brown owned one record: an old Thelonious Monk disk. The album contained the song "Ruby, My Dear."

Brown's wife Ruby died 40 years ago. They'd been married for eight months.

Brown's mother died in 1997, and for the first time, he had to live on his own.

"We're being real cautious right now," said Ellard Jackson. "But I got a job to do."

The *Times* turned up a niece. "I didn't know him too good," she said.

The niece, Shirley Tuper, lived around the corner from her uncle.

The reporter found a neighbor. "He did some odd jobs, I think. Maybe he was a short-order cook."

Friday was the best night of the week for a livery hack, the *Times* reported. A man like Aubrey Brown could take home $70, maybe 80; more, if there was a little rain.

Bella said, "It hasn't rained in three weeks."

"I know," I replied as I thought about how I'd spend at least part of the next few days.

I ENTERED THE Henderson & Son Funeral Service on 135th and Malcolm X Boulevard as the service was about to begin.

The closed coffin, not much more than a pine box, rested on a carpeted platform in front of the orderly room, before burgundy velvet curtains. Somber floral wreaths stood as sentries on either side of the box, behind the minister, who bowed his head and wrung his hands until he was assured of absolute silence. Slipping in back, I eased into a folding chair in the last row.

He lifted his head. He was a heavyset man in a gray, five-button suit, starched white shirt and gray bow tie. "Dear friends," he began, in a voice less authoritative than his frame suggested. "Friends of Aubrey Brown."

Between the minister and me were 11 rows of empty chairs. The first two rows were occupied. In front were three women in fine chiffon dresses, the kind favored by proper women of a certain age, upbringing and disposition. Their attractive hats, the kind rarely seen outside church services, were nestled in their immaculately done hair, and their white-gloved hands clasped leather-bound Bibles. Apparently, they were members of the same congregation as the minister, for he seemed to be preaching directly to them, and they anticipated his comments, nodding with knowing expressions, murmuring along, calling "Amen" with uncanny precision.

"Our good lord Jesus, he has called brother Brown home. And home with our sweet Jesus is a better place than brother Brown ever knew here."

Behind the three women sat two men in neat, informal attire and a woman in wrinkled slacks and a well-worn windbreaker that was several sizes too large. She slumped in her seat, her head hung at an odd angle. I made a silent wager with myself: Ellard Jackson, the dispatcher; one of his colleagues; and Shirley Tuper, the niece.

"And you know, brothers and sisters, that the gift of God is eternal life, through Jesus Christ, our Lord," he said flatly, with little enthusiasm.

"Amen," the three women responded.

"And that He died for all, that they which live should not henceforth live unto themselves, but unto Him which died for them, and rose again."

"That's right," added the one in pink, on the aisle.

The uninspired minister went on, seemingly preaching from cue cards, stacking passages from Scripture without explication, without direct reference to the life of the deceased. I made another quiet wager: This man never knew Aubrey Brown, and he and the three sisters were hired for this morning's event.

"He that believeth in the Son hath everlasting life."

"Tell it."

The two men looked at each other, barely containing their bemusement. They realized they were in a fixed game. They had expected to participate, and now they were as much mere spectators as I was.

"Oh, you know the Lord works in strange ways."

Now Shirley Tuper began to tilt, and her head, matted hair in disarray, landed on the shoulder of the man to her left. He pushed her off with a gentle nudge, and she snapped alert, recoiled, and nodded off again.

Meanwhile, the sermon continued to degenerate, as a string of rank clichés replaced the litany of Scriptural references.

"And, as you know, my brothers and sisters, life is short."

Out of the corner of my eye, I saw a figure quickly pass the back entrance; and then he returned, and stuck his head in the room: a teenager, about 14, 15 years old, his hair up top in tassel-like dreadlocks above shaved sides, skin the color of copper; in profile, his features seemed almost fragile, almost feminine. He wore a black down coat, too much for the mild October morning, baggy jeans, stylish black high-top basketball shoes; he kneaded a red stocking cap in his small hands. He shifted uncomfortably.

He turned and looked directly at me; now I could see the right side of his face. He had a mean scar that ran from the corner of his right eye and hooked to just below his lips, and he scowled at me with an intensity that was anything but fragile. Without a word, he spun and left.

I inched my way out into the corridor. At the end of the narrow hall, the door swung shut. I went to the door and looked out onto Malcolm X Boulevard, into the parade of people passing on the busy street, heading to the Peter Pan Diner on the corner, to the Lenox Cleaners next door, suits, skirts and shirts tucked under their arms, or toward Wilson's Optometry up the block. But I couldn't spot the boy: He'd either gone north and dashed into Harlem Hospital, or crossed the wide boulevard and torn down the entrance to the 2 and 3 subway lines. In less than 20 seconds, he had vanished.

"Can I help you?"

I turned to find a man about my age. Short, stocky, he wore a crisp blue suit with a vest, a conservative club tie and a white button-down shirt. His hair was cropped close to his head, perhaps to conceal an expanding bald spot, and his brown eyes, which matched the tone of his skin, were cold with suspicion behind glasses.

"I saw a boy, a teenager," I said. "He seems to have disappeared."

"I saw no one." He removed his glasses and wiped them carefully with a small chamois cloth. "And you say he was in here?"

"I was in the Brown service and he looked in." I ran my finger along the side of my face. "A nasty scar on his cheek."

He returned the cloth to his side pocket. By way of introduction, he said, "Lionel Henderson." He didn't offer his hand.

I withdrew my wallet and gave him a business card.

He frowned. "There's nothing for you here, Mr. Orr."

"Meaning?"

"Aubrey Brown. He has no family. There's no money for private investigators."

"I don't look for business in funeral parlors," I said.

"So you knew Mr. Brown."

"I found the body."

Henderson remained skeptical. "And then you attend the service?"

If he wanted to intimidate me, he was heading the wrong way. "I do what I want, Mr. Henderson. I go where I go."

"Apparently."

"I sense you've got a problem with that."

"Aubrey Brown deserves a little peace. I thought we'd have to accommodate a reporter or two, and we didn't want that either."

"A businessman who doesn't like publicity?" I thought of Bella's quip about a press agent. "No, I guess—"

"We don't need publicity, Mr. Orr. There's no shortage of business for us here. Old women and young men. Or a young woman on the pipe, like Shirley Tuper. A sad, steady flow."

As I considered his remarks, it occurred to me that Henderson was protecting Aubrey Brown, giving him a friend he may not have known he had. I decided to pull back: He was right to question why I was in his funeral parlor. He couldn't know of my agenda, nor would he, unless he asked around and his questions found their way to the Midtown Precinct.

"He was alone," I offered. "I had this image of him by himself at the end." That was true: Brown's tale could chisel a heart gone to stone.

Henderson nodded. "We take care of our own. But I appreciate your intentions." He stepped back and gestured toward the broad vestibule. "Let me tell you what I know about Aubrey Brown."

He opened the door and I followed him to his office, a small, neat suite with a mahogany desk, two hardwood chairs and a large oil portrait of a middle-aged man in a starched collar and wire-framed glasses who seemed to cast a wary eye on me.

"Is that your father?" I asked.

"My grandfather," he replied, as he switched on a desk lamp. "He founded this business in 1926. He's the original Henderson and my father is the original son. We never felt a need to change the name."

On the credenza behind his high-backed chair, Henderson had framed photos of his children and wife. Two of the three girls bore a strong resemblance to their father, while the boy, who was the oldest, looked very much like his mother.

I said, "Maybe you'll be calling it Henderson & Daughters."

He smiled and shook his head. "Mr. Orr, I did my undergraduate work at Columbia and intended to go to Columbia Law School. Then my grandfather died. I've told my father that he has to live until all four of my kids are well into their own practices."

A row of old khaki-colored file cabinets lined the papered wall to my left. I imagined contracts and standard forms, requisite carbons and photocopies, dates and names, countless links that together told the story of Harlem from the early teens of the last century to today, through the Harlem Renaissance, from the times of W. E. B. Du Bois and Marcus Garvey through the decline brought on by the Great Depression, through Adam Clayton Powell and Malcolm X and the dichotomy of today: the thriving businesses all along 125th Street viewed against the abandoned brownstones that dotted the side streets off Frederick Douglass Boulevard; the beauty of Central Park at 110th and entire blocks of burnt-out and ransacked buildings, now drug dens whose occupants entertained the white middle-class from the other side of the G.W. Bridge in their Volvos with car seats for their infants in back; and the majestic stone spire of the Ephesus Church and the sunlight on Manhattan Avenue and the smiles on the faces of Lionel Henderson's four children and the anger in the glare of the boy who had just disappeared.

"What about Aubrey Brown?" I asked.

"You needed to know his mother. Augusta Brown. In some ways, this is her day." He leaned on his elbows, which he placed on the blotter at the center of his desk. "Augusta Brown arranged this more than ten years ago, when she was closing in on ninety."

"She prepaid her son's funeral?"

"More than that," he replied. "Reverend Ramsay and those women? They're from the Good Shepherd. Augusta arranged that as well. She knew Aubrey would fade away after she died. She knew he'd be lost without her."

"Yes, but he didn't fade away," I said. "He was killed."

"That's how he died. But he was gone before that." He removed his glasses and put them on the desktop, near the black multi-line phone, a pair of scissors and a letter opener. "My father knew Aubrey when he was young, and he knew Ruby."

"His wife."

"According to my father, Aubrey was a quiet man, an industrious type, but when Ruby passed, that was it. He went back to living with Augusta, and he more or less shriveled up."

"Christ."

"He blamed himself, but Ruby caught a bad flu, and it turned to pneumonia and she died." He shrugged. "It happens, but you can't tell that to a man. It's important that they come to terms with it by themselves, in time."

"But Aubrey Brown never did."

"Not according to my father."

"And what about his job? Some men see some sort of romance in hacking all night."

"Not a man like Aubrey," he said quickly. "He would never think like that. He took whatever he could get. Not because he was pragmatic. He was sickly."

"Emphysema."

"He was generally weak. As I said, he shriveled up. But he had his mother. Until she died as well."

"And what about the men in there?" I gestured toward the wall behind Henderson, as if we could see into the room that held Brown's body. "Were they his friends?"

"They worked with him, but I wouldn't call them friends." He sat back. "I can recognize it when it's obligation that brings them in. But I don't judge those men too harshly. Just the opposite. Most nights, a livery cab on a gypsy run is the only one who'll come up here."

I saw Henderson look over my shoulder and, when I turned, I saw a thin, older man in a dark overcoat and fedora. He slipped his long fingers into white gloves.

"Mr. Henderson, we're ready for you."

"Thank you, Lee." Henderson stood. He said to me, "It's time to go up to the cemetery."

I thanked him for his time and insight. We shook hands.

"I should apologize for my suspicions," he said.

I waved him off. "You're right to protect your clients from people with business cards."

He came around the desk. "Are you going to look into Aubrey's death?"

I nodded. "Something there is about a lonely man..."

"Perhaps I can contribute. I can ask around."

"A robbery gone bad.-A lot of hacks get killed in this city and I understand that's the main reason." I shrugged. "Maybe the cops will catch a break."

"Maybe." He sounded disappointed. "Maybe not."

"No, probably not," I agreed, as he went for his black topcoat hung behind the door.

THREE

I REACHED LITTLE WEST 12th before noon, but not before Luther Addison, who was sitting in his big, black city-issued car, staring, it seemed, at the river, at the jagged cliffs on the Jersey side.

I tapped on the passenger's-side window. He reached over and popped open the door.

"We'll sit," he offered.

I shook my head. "Let's look around." I pushed the door until it shut.

Addison pulled himself out of the car. He was a light-skinned black man with freckles sprinkled across the bridge of his nose, his eyes a pale green. A big man, Luther Addison was broad-shouldered and fit, but with the beginnings of a belt overhang. He wore his customary black suit, white shirt and thin black tie; I guess I've seen him at least 100 times since he drew Marina and Davy's case, and I've never seen him without the black suit, white shirt and thin black tie. Early on, before it went the way it went, he took me to New Jersey to see Duncan against the Nets: black suit and tie, white shirt. I imagined it was some sort of symbol that he was always on duty, ever the vigilant cop. There are people who do things like that: Live with symbols instead of what's real.

He came around the back of the car and we shook hands. "What do you know?" he asked.

"Tsumeb can't handle agricultural goods. Only minerals, like vanadium, copper and zinc. No refrigeration. Be a good fuckin' idea to put a freezer in Namibia."

"Man walks from 135th and Lenox to Little West 12th and the river and all he can talk about is southern Africa."

He put his hand on the small of my back and nudged me toward Little West 12th.

"Hard to believe nobody saw it," I said as we crossed the cobblestone street. Before us, the Gansevoort Market was alive with workers in white smocks and thick blood-smeared gloves pushing sides of beef into refrigerated delivery trucks. Perhaps 50 men and a few women were on the stone docks, using fat black hoses to clear viscera. They wore hooks on their shoulders, and heavy rubber boots, and for all the grunting and shouting, they seemed engaged in their work, as trucks lined up to deliver meat throughout the tri-state area or haul the unusable parts of the carcasses through the Lincoln Tunnel to the New Jersey soap factories.

On a weekend night, though, this was a dark, menacing place, as the long, brawny warehouses shut down and amber streetlights cast a meager glow, providing a sordid spotlight for the male, female and transvestite hookers who worked the dark, brick-lined alleys and the crannies beneath the dilapidated piers.

I pointed east, away from the river's black water. "And you've got nightlife over there."

Funky restaurants and all-night dance clubs had

popped up near the old haunts like Hector's Place and Dizzy Izzy's, bringing taxis and limos and new cars into the area. Majestic old buildings had been converted to a series of 25,000-square-foot lofts for the upscale, and now there were florists and coffee bars, and movie stars queuing up outside a joint called Hogs & Heifers, the first in a franchise. It was as if the West Village was spreading east, or Chelsea sliding south. The meatpacking district—some were calling it the West Coast, perhaps dreaming that the Pacific, and not the Hudson, splashed against the barnacled stanchions and limestone—might very well become the new SoHo, the new TriBeCa, and that would be a far cry from a decade ago, when S&M clubs were two to a block, when more than 100 meat-related businesses operated in century-old warehouses.

"I haven't heard anyone say no one saw it," Addison replied. "We just haven't found him yet."

"Happened like that," I said, snapping my fingers. "Guy slams Brown's head against the steering wheel, breaking his nose. Picks up the Club, finishes the job. Ten seconds."

"We got four men in the neighborhood, day and night," he said sharply. "We'll turn up something."

We kept walking toward the spot where I came across Brown's body. A red Corvette heading south squealed as it came to a stop under a traffic light.

"You went uptown for a reason," he said.

"I went to the service."

"Why'd you do that? Wait—" He held up a hand. "You read the *Times*. You felt sorry for him."

He wasn't wrong, but there was a way to go before he'd be right. "You don't?"

"I don't feel for the victim. I feel for the survivors."

That, I had to admit, was true: Addison was a man of

boundless sympathy and understanding. Which was why I called him.

But I've learned that sympathy and understanding mean shit when the job hasn't been done.

We came upon the spot. Addison looked up as a truck backed away from a loading dock, its horn sounding odd, sour.

The wind off the Hudson was so mild it was meek. "How's Gabriella?" he asked.

"Great. Brilliant. A noodge."

He smiled. "You taking good care of her?"

"When she's not taking care of me."

"And what about you?"

"I get by."

"You look good," he said.

"Yeah, I'm all right." I looked north along West Street, at the stream of cars flowing from uptown. "We done dancing?"

Calmly, he asked, "More than sympathy sent you uptown, Terry. Isn't that right?"

"You tell me."

"You're going to work the case."

"And?"

He shook his head. "It can't be that way. My guys need no help."

"We'll see."

"The problem, Terry, is I haven't asked for help." He had locked his eyes on me. "Your turn."

"I got nothing," I said. "I'm going to do what I can to help Brown."

Addison's tried to warn me off before—he helped me get my P.I. license; apparently, he thought I was going to use it to make photocopies for Sharon and the other A.D.A.s or to snap photos of Johnny cheating on Mary— but he had to know that sooner or later I'd be in his territory. If he'd thought about it, he'd have realized there could be no other reason I'd consider going P.I., even if it wasn't clear to me at the start. He's smart enough to know that if I'm going to make good, I've got to learn how and learn it live.

A city bus wheezed toward us, then passed and caught the light at the corner. I pointed at it. "The red light. Maybe when the guy who whacked Brown could've been seen by somebody waiting for the green light. When the dome—"

"Terry." He turned back to me. "What is it? You identify with this guy? Brown's out there, lost because his wife is gone, drifting. Dangerous job, putting himself at risk."

"Luther, I've already got a shrink. All right?"

"Because you're not like him. Not as long as your daughter is with you."

I leaned against the fire hydrant.

"And you don't have to learn to work it, Terry. Weisz, we'll turn him out. I told you that."

I shook my head. "No, Luther, you won't. Your guys let him get away."

To the NYPD, Raymond Montgomery Weisz is now the man who never was. "Maybe we made the wrong guy" is how it was put to me, with a diffident shrug, by a sloe-eyed desk sergeant named Tannon. I took it for what it was: an admission that they couldn't find Weisz and they didn't want to keep looking.

Weisz. A red-haired madman, caked with dirt, his tattered, urine-soaked pants tied together with hemp, torn sneakers flopping on his feet. Had been in Bellevue 19 times in the past four years. They knew he was living below ground. They might've known he would one day toss a baby's stroller onto the tracks, and that the baby's mother would scramble into the mire to save her son.

Weisz was one of 14 people who watched as the subway roared through the 66th Street station.

Nine of them said Weisz was standing at the edge of the platform, lingering wild-eyed over Davy as Marina screamed and dove down after him.

I was looking at the slag on the green Jersey cliffs when I said, "He was here and your guys went at it easy."

They made the right guy. The man with an IQ of 180. Member of Mensa. Performed at Carnegie Hall at age 11. As a boy, he relaxed by feeding the wolves at the Bronx Zoo; *The New Yorker* found that charming. Later, after he snapped, they found him living at the zoo, subsisting on discarded food, bathing in the flamingo pond, crawling among the bushes, hiding in the trees.

I have 13 photos of Raymond Montgomery Weisz. One for each of the 13 people who refused to help the woman who frantically tried to save her son.

But that's all I've done: read files, studied microfiche until my vision blurred, collected photos, drafted his biography. My boldest move to date: standing on Park Avenue, outside of Weisz's mother's apartment. Not only didn't I see him, I never saw her.

No more standing around, thumb up my ass. At some point, theory gives way to action.

"I told you, Terry," he said tersely. "All you can do is fuck it up. You want to do right by Marina and your boy, stay home. Write yourself another book." He tugged at his belt, hitched up his black slacks. "You know, having an uncle as a cop doesn't make you a P.I. any more than that license does."

"My uncle was a stone drunk. He has nothing to do with nothing," I said. "I told you, plain and straight: It's about what it's about. Today, it's about Aubrey Brown."

"You like to rough it up, kid—you got the body for it—but hard-ass doesn't fit you."

"At least we know I won't walk away, Luther."

He started to snap off a reply, but he held back. After a moment's pause, he started back toward his big black car.

"I make time of death around midnight," I said, aiming at his broad back.

He paused, but did not stop.

I went west.

I TOOK THE elevator to the floor that held the critical-care unit and checked with the duty nurse, who told me that Judy was out of danger and had been moved upstairs to a regular ward.

Since it was only three flights up, I decided to take the stairs. When I turned to take the last set of steps, I found Sol Beck sitting on the landing. He seemed beyond forlorn, almost desperate.

"Hello," he said softly. "Terry."

"Are you all right?"

He said, "I'm OK."

He wore a black shirt and oversized khakis, and there were small splotches of dry paint on his well-worn sneakers.

"How's Judy?" I asked.

"She's sleeping."

"What do they say?"

He shrugged, then Beck hung his head and stared at the floor. He wasn't pouting, merely shy or lost in self-pity. He seemed frightened, his skin sallow on his gaunt face.

I asked, "Did you go back to the gallery?"

"This morning."

"Much damage to your work?"

"Broken frames. A lot of soot." He shook his head. "Not really."

I watched as he fell back into his own thoughts. I waited, but he was unable to shake off what was gnawing at him. I squeezed by and went onto the floor, toward the nurses' station.

Lin-Lin was at the far end of the antiseptic hall. I made my way toward her, past the station, past nurses with carts filled with charts in three-ring binders, pills, other medicines and accessories. A man worked the floor with a buffer, and a woman in a wheelchair beckoned for him to stop so she could roll by. She had a paperback novel in her lap, with its cover torn away. She was missing her right leg.

As I walked the long hall, men and women, curious yet somehow disassociated, peered from their beds, studying me, perhaps eager to see a new face, hopeful that the visitor was theirs. I peered sideways into the rooms as I went by, and I saw several canes, crutches and wheelchairs, and an artificial leg propped against a nightstand. Physical therapy was a morning thing, and the afternoon was for realizing just how much life had changed.

Lin-Lin greeted me. "She's sedated," she said.

She stepped aside and I entered the room. The shades had been pulled, and the only light was soft and low, from a fluorescent tube that hummed above Judy's bed.

In the dim glow, Judy seemed more an apparition than a physical being: Her skin was a ghostly white, and she looked like an old, old woman. Her head was awkwardly wrapped, and above her right eye was a deep purple-yellow bruise. Her jaw was slack and her body abnormally limp, as if she were unconscious rather than asleep. A thin, soft bedspread covered much of her, but the bottoms of her legs were exposed. One foot was covered with a pale blue sock; the other was gone, and the stump was heavily bandaged.

A clear solution dripped into a long tube that had been inserted into her arm. Bright flowers, artlessly arranged, filled the nightstand, hovering over the standard-issue telephone. I sat at the side of her bed and gently patted her hand. I noticed that the call-button had been hooked to the top sheet, in case she woke up. When she did come around, when she fought through the narcotic haze, she would understand, and I wondered how she would react. It was impossible to know, I realized quickly. No one could know how she would react; her true reaction would occur only when she was alone, when there was no reason to hold on, when all defenses, unnecessary in solitude, were banished. This I knew well.

I stared at her, and I began to drift and I saw Marina. Not as she had been, nor as I had ever seen her. I saw her as pale, incorporeal, without expression, bloodless, lying here in front of me, in Judy's bed, with my hand patting her tanned, tapered fingers.

But I hadn't seen her after she died. Her body had been badly mangled, I was told, and it would be difficult for me when I went to the coroner's to identify what remained.

I didn't go; I wasn't going no matter what condition she was in. So, Benedicto did. He flew in from Italy, and within 90 minutes of arriving in America for only the second time, he went to the coroner's office to identify his daughter's body.

And then he identified the body of his two-year-old grandson.

I didn't even go to the funeral.

Fuck that, I told Diddio.

I can't, baby, I told Bella. You go with Pop-Pop and Rafaela.

I stayed in the bedroom, opening the door only when Bella knocked.

I came out to put Benedicto and Rafaela, now his only child, in a cab to Kennedy.

And Bella and I walked for hours, along the Battery.

When we came home, we found that someone had put flowers and a candle on our front steps. By the next morning, flowers spilled onto Harrison. A photo of the makeshift altar appeared on the cover of *The Village Voice*.

"Excuse me."

I turned to find a young woman, stethoscope draped around her neck, clipboard in hand. So stereotypically controlled was she that I blinked, thinking I had imagined her as well.

I stood and slid the chair away from the bed.

She reached in to take Judy's pulse, stared at her wristwatch, then scribbled on a form.

"How is she, Doctor?"

She said as she wrote, "She's stable. Considering what she's gone through, I'd say she's doing well."

For some reason, the young physician felt I needed comforting, and she squeezed my shoulder and smiled kindly before she turned to leave.

I followed, and unable to find Marina again, I took a last look at Judy before joining Lin-Lin in the corridor.

"IS JUDY'S FAMILY on their way?" I asked her.

"I don't know," Lin-Lin replied. "But Edie said she spoke with her ex-husband and son."

"You talked to Edie?"

"This morning. She feels she is to blame. Perhaps she could have done more."

We stood for a moment in silence in the pale-green corridor, on pale-green linoleum squares. I looked down the long hall, past the hunched man with the buffing machine, past the woman in the steel chair who wheeled slowly toward thin rays of sunlight that squeaked through a window facing east.

"Terry, I must speak with you," Lin-Lin said solemnly.

We went to a small alcove near the elevators in which sat a single table covered with well-thumbed copies of an entertainment magazine. A vending machine offered fruit juices, and there was a telephone on the wall, hung low enough to be used by people in wheelchairs.

I joined her at the table. "We were told that you are a private investigator now. Is it true?"

"Yes."

"This is something extraordinary." She hesitated. "The bomb at the gallery."

"Yes..."

"Sol was hoping maybe it was something else. That maybe..." She let the thought fade away. "Whatever."

"Someone calls and says there's a bomb, and then there's an explosion, it's a bomb."

She ran her finger along the table. "It's difficult to be completely rational, Terry."

I leaned forward.

"We don't want to cooperate with the police. Sol doesn't want to."

"That's not a good idea," I said. "It'll bring trouble down on the both of you."

"We are certain that we know who placed the bomb in the gallery," she said directly. "Sol believes it was his father."

"Sol's father bombed his son's opening?"

She nodded. "We believe so, yes. I believe so."

"Why?"

She smiled. "How many answers can there be to that question, Terry?"

One, I thought, with a million reasons behind it. "I mean, what's the point?" The bomb was placed where it would do the least amount of damage. It was Judy's bad luck to go into the storage room.

"I don't know if he wanted to hurt Sol, destroy his paintings or ruin his opening. We can't say we know why he did it. But we believe he did."

"It's no small feat, to be that precise. It's easier to take down a building."

"He could do it," she nodded. "He was in the Army, in Korea. He was an expert."

"Where is he, the father?"

She dug into her white jacket and came up with a slip of paper.

I took the note. It said that Chaim Rosenzweig lived on Grove Street in the West Village. "Rosenzweig?"

"That is Sol's legal name."

I slipped the paper into my breast pocket. "I'll talk to him," I said. "But if I think he's involved, if he had something to do with what happened to Judy, I'll turn it over to the cops."

"I understand."

"You should've told them yourselves."

She disagreed. "It's better this way."

I stood, and she followed me as I went toward the elevator. "Maybe it'd be better if you tell your husband it had nothing to do with his old man."

"I cannot. He knows."

"Well, we'll see."

I pressed the button and the painted doors parted. "I'll call you," I said as I walked in.

Lin-Lin watched me as the doors began to close. She nodded and waved, waiting until I was out of sight.

MALLARD WAS PROPPED in his customary spot under the TV, which now offered NY1 without sound. He looked at me, nodded lethargically, then went back to his copy of yesterday's *Times-Picayune*. On the other side of the room, Diddio had the top of the jukebox open and was working under it, as if he were beneath the hood of a '64 Mustang.

"Dry," I said.

"Take," he replied. At 350 pounds, Leo Mallard expended as little effort as possible, unless he was extremely enthusiastic about the assignment.

I stood on the bar rail, reached over the counter and pulled out a bottle of sparkling water from the ice chest. I cracked the top off the quart bottle and drank half of it down in one long, satisfying pull.

The lazy overhead fan moved the smell of stale beer, cigar smoke and sawdust around the room. I sat on the red Naugahyde stool at the dead center of the bar. A blue neon sign provided by an uninspired salesman flickered unevenly in the front window, while in the back of the room an antiquated pinball machine let out a bleep and groan. Outside, a delivery truck skidded to a halt in front of Zolly's, a bagel shop on the other side of Hudson.

"Hey, there he is," Diddio said. "We were just talking about you."

I finished the cold sparkling water, put the green plastic bottle aside and reached into the ice for another.

"When did we see Elvis Costello at St. John's? I'm trying to remember the last time I had a driver's license," he said. "Remember, I interviewed him in your dorm room, 'cause mine was, you know, like disheveled?"

Diddio filtered everything through the world of contemporary music, though how contemporary is subject to interpretation. Though he's able to sustain a living writing about the current music scene, for his own pleasure Diddio listened almost exclusively to rock music from the late '60s and early '70s, in particular the Dead, the Band and the Allman Brothers. Despite working his beat in new-music clubs all over Manhattan, he was lost in rock's glorious past.

"Man, what kind of useless shit clogs you two up," muttered Mallard, as he flipped to another page.

Coincidentally, Diddio's taste for so-called classic rock and its rhythm-and-blues predecessors brought Mallard's Tilt-A-Whirl the kind of celebrity Leo never wanted. Diddio was constantly fiddling with the jukebox, bringing in compact disks from his own huge collection. The night a writer from *New York* magazine wandered in, the jukebox carried a varied, but somehow cohesive, selection and the following week, the magazine pronounced it the best jukebox in New York City.[1] Since then, the Tilt has been swamped with what Leo, generously, calls "Wall Street scum." Though it offered nothing but a dusty old pinball machine, a buck-a-game pool table, beer nuts, overpriced and watered-down drinks and Diddio's picks, the Tilt is packed with suits weekdays beginning a little after five. It quieted down about nine: Neighborhood people aren't too interested in the best jukebox in New York when the owner is trying to clear them out by turning on the lights, spraying Raid and complaining about "rats the size of raccoons." "One of these days, I got to get me a big rat, case somebody ask to see him," Mallard once said.

"What's going on, Leo?" I asked. On the screen above him, a shaky camera showed a reporter doing his stand-up in front of City Hall.

"Lunch," Mallard replied. His skin was closer to gray than olive, and he had raccoon-like rings around deep-set eyes. Wheezing, his white cotton shirt soaked with sweat, Mallard looked worse than usual today, and he labored as he stood to head out from behind the bar. "I'm making muffulettas," he said. "I got me some fresh mozzarella."

When Mallard returned with the three sandwiches, he instructed Diddio to lock the door and pull the musty

[1] See page 307

green shades. We sat at the corner of the bar. Ignoring Diddio's efforts, Mallard slapped on a cassette of Professor Longhair; New Orleans–style piano darted and danced as we ate ham, salami and mozzarella stacked on French bread with lettuce and a trickle of olive oil.

"You're all duded up today, Terry," Diddio observed, pointing at my outfit.

"Funeral. Up in Harlem. Cabdriver."

"That body you found when I was sitting for Gabby."

"I bet they was wailing all over themselves," Mallard said. "Blacks is worser than Italians at a funeral." He threw down a handful of napkins. "Hacking ain't a good way to make a living," he added. "Risky."

I nodded. I'd read that about 30 to 35 cabbies get killed every year in New York; 42, a couple of years ago.

Diddio seemed to be struggling with the oversized sandwich; a strand of lettuce had landed on the front of his black t-shirt. I looked behind his wire-rimmed glasses. Diddio was a world-class pothead, a connoisseur of weed. Today, now, he seemed fine.

Leo asked, "You gonna do something for this guy?"

"Why not?"

"Let me ask you this," Diddio said, as he touched his shoulder-length, midnight-black hair. "I mean, you know, were you like the only white guy up there?"

"In Harlem?" Until about 96th Street. "Yeah."

"Woof," Diddio said. "The only place I been to in Harlem is the Apollo. No, wait, I saw Craig Handy at the Lenox. And Andrew Hill at the Schomberg. It's a little too scary up there for me. Man, one block the wrong way and *bang.*" He smacked his fist into his open palm. Then, he added with a shrug, "Maybe it's me. Too much gangsta rap."

"Hey," Mallard cheered, "who's gonna fuck with the brooding man? Terry, you was brooding all the way uptown with that big frown and that temper you got. Six-four, 225 and stomping and brooding."

Diddio looked at Mallard and laughed. "Terry, don't get all defensive. We're only teasing you, man. I mean, like, don't bust up Leo's bar again, all right? If you're going to smack us with a pool cue, maybe you could do it outside."

This past summer, two guys who didn't make the shape-up at a construction site near the Holland Tunnel entered the Tilt in a belligerent mood, threw back their Beam-and-beers too quickly and started hassling Mallard, who at his weight, with his lack of mobility, can't really defend himself unless he produces the .38 Smith & Wesson he keeps taped under the bar. I was in a back booth, thwarted momentarily in my self-imposed tutorial by a particularly incomprehensible passage in a brief, when they went too far. I cracked one with a pool cue. The other I dropped with a right under the ribs and another to the point of his jaw. The second shot sent him into the jukebox, cracking the glass. I admit I've got a temper, and it's gotten me into more trouble than I can recall, but I was clear when I tore down those guys.

The cassette tape behind Mallard went silent, and Diddio sprang from his seat. "Leo, let me," he said and slid to the jukebox. A moment later, "Chest Fever" by the Band surrounded us.

"Diddio says you was at that gallery last night that blowed up," Mallard said. He reached into the ice and withdrew a Jax. Born and raised just outside of New Orleans, he was the most brand-loyal guy I knew, going so far as to have a week's worth of the *Times-Picayune* FedExed to him each Monday by his sister down in Lafourche. "You lucky you didn't get hurt."

I turned to Diddio. "How'd you hear about me being there?"

"Mango told me."

"Mango? Jimmy or Tommy?"

"Tommy the Cop. I saw him at the Delphi. He said you saved some woman. He pays attention to you, T."

"I didn't save her. She was hurt bad. Lost a foot."

Mallard said, "You can't trust nothing them Mangos say."

Diddio disagreed. "It's like the kid's game, Telephone. By the time the message reaches the end, it's all twisted up. That's how it is with Jimmy, anyway. His information is always secondhand, and he's crazier than Terry." He looked at me, alarmed. "Not crazy in a bad way, Terry." He rolled his index finger near his temple. "You know, the same kind of temper."

I nodded wearily. It was nearly impossible to be angry with Diddio, who was 34 going on 18, whom I'd known forever, which is how long ago freshman year at St. John's seemed.

"But Tommy's usually pretty reliable," he continued. "So I'd say Terry probably did save her in some way."

"My hero," Mallard crooned.

I stood and tossed a twenty on the bar. It was my turn to pay, and long ago I convinced Mallard he was going to have to take my money, friends or not.

"I'm gone," I said.

"What's she like, Terry, this woman you saved? She with somebody?" Diddio asked. Despite a sweet disposition, his minor celebrity and free tickets to every concert in town, Diddio could not hook up with a woman who'd stay with him for more than a few days, which was understandable. The ones he met wanted to live a fast life in rock, wanted to meet the kind of people he had access to, whereas Diddio wanted to come home to Florence Henderson, with an adjustment for his Lestat hours. He was always after his friends to set him up.

"D, she's 55 years old and in critical condition."

"Yeah? And?"

I said goodbye and undid the dead bolt. Music from Big Pink followed me onto Hudson.

I CAME HOME to find Mrs. Maoli out, and a pot of *minestra di riso e zucchini* burbling on the stove: The scent of basil followed me as I went to the back of the house and into my study.

I punched in Henderson's phone number and he answered the call on the second ring.

When I identified myself, he said, "I was thinking about you. I'd just about decided you wouldn't call."

"I had to clear something first," I replied. "Any—"

"I saw the boy you spoke of, the boy with the scar," he said, as his customary reserve slipped away. "He came to the cemetery. I saw him as we were leaving. He had been hiding, I guess."

On the wall above my computer, there was a drawing by Bella of, I think, turtles. Or cartoon dinosaurs. Davy, then about a year old, had scribbled on it. Marina framed it, calling it a collaboration.

Henderson paused. "They tell me his name is Montana, and that he used to go to Hurston Elementary. It may not mean much," he added. "But now you know."

I thanked him and cut the line.

I sat in the low light from the gooseneck lamp and made small geometric figures on the yellow paper. Suddenly—it is always suddenly—I was thinking about a boy with a scar on his face, an old man with scars on his back and shoulder, a little girl lost, a man trying to find hope.

Mei Carissima:

Bella's in bed; too much homework, she said. Translation: tedium. Only history interests her, and stories. She's reading two books a week. Books I read in high school, in college...

I've told you that already, haven't I? Sorry.

It's only 11:15. I've been to bed, and I'm back in the study with you, dear. Sadly, it was another nightmare that brought me to you. A nightmare caused by suppressing images as I bickered with Luther Addison, and by absently thumbing Bella's copy of "Heart of Darkness." And the rest of it all.

I was in Judy's gallery, clearly; then there was dust and smoke and seared bone, and I couldn't find Bella. Not again, my heart screamed; my God. Then: "Daddy? What's wrong? I'm fine, Daddy. Over here. Look!" I see my hands: blood in the lines on my palms, whirling red lights above blue-and-white patrol cars. A woman on the fire escape, her slip redolent of her scent. A baby's stroller shredded under rusted steel wheels. "Daddy!" Bella screams in terror.

I sit up in bed. I drop my head into my hands. Five, six minutes later, I lie back down and I indulge my misery, I feed it like a coal stove on a runaway locomotive. I resist it, I resist it weakly: "The horror! The horror!" Kurtz cried, breathed, Welles bellowed, Brando moaned. A cliché now; all truth reduced to trivia now, by misuse, by media, by truth itself, even a vibrating note of revolt, a step over the threshold of the invisible. (Am I awake? Asleep?) A rat sniffing bamboo; black snakes slither through a puddle of viscera. A baby flung onto the train tracks; his mother, frantic; the relentless white light of the oncoming subway train. I turn the corner, hopeful for the last time; patrol cars at our door. Bella screaming; a cop named Addison from the Midtown Precinct explaining. I leave our bed and command myself: Use what you know to block what you feel. Conrad wrote in English, his fourth language; I bought that copy long ago, used, for 25 cents at the Strand. Facts: a pitiable defense against recognition, desolation. I may have drifted off. I may have watched it unfold on the ceiling.

I came downstairs and I stood in my bare feet by your paintings, where you mounted them, tesora, on brick between the kitchen and the living room.

I cut the lamp above the gilded frame and I put my hand on the ridges left by your brush strokes.

You are so good, Marina. These paintings: "crystalline interpretations of natural settings, superb in composition, in use of light." "Colors burst from the canvas, yet manage to entice rather than overwhelm." That is what they've said. But who but you and I know what you let me see? Your love of your homeland, your passion for your father's house—the wellspring of your gift—this they may have guessed. The pure delight you felt when you worked:

This is what you shared with no one but me. And when I stare at these paintings, when I allow myself to feel, I am surrounded by the emotions you invested in the work, and, for the briefest of moments, the very briefest of moments, you are in the room with me and soon your scent and the warmth of your body will reach me as you take my hand.

My memories of you at work are among my most vivid; have I told you this before? Remember the day you finished "White Cliffs at Gargano"? Benedicto had given me a small bowl of figs, a bottle of a local red wine, and suggested I deliver them to you, his eldest daughter, and I drove to the green and golden field above the gulf where you were working. I approached you, but decided to hang back, because I could see you were concentrating, absorbing the scenery, interpreting it and creating it anew. I withdrew a book—a dog-eared paperback of Edmund Morris's biography of TR; I remember that clearly as well—and I read. Forty-five minutes passed before you realized I was no more than 100 feet away. And when you turned I saw on your face a remarkable look of absolute satisfaction, of unadulterated bliss; the result of the convergence of passion, intellect and achievement. I was stunned by the power of your expression; and then you smiled at me, gently, affectionately, inviting me to share the moment. And I did, and it was magnificent.

Now I go from here to there, quietly, lost in memories. Lost.

These things I do, as I go from there to here, they are more than diversions now. They are lessons, practical, stark. (Forgive me if I repeat myself. When I speak with you, I speak to me. You know that.) They prepare me; they will prepare me. There is this thing I must do that only I can do. I will not imagine what lies beyond that.

Bella, of course. But more? Something like liberation? Liberated. To face the abyss.

Sorry.

Sorry. I don't mean to put this on you. Scusa, carissima.

Let me tell you what happened today. That will be better for you, I think.

I saw Leo today. I remember when we ate at his old place, Big Chief's, when Bella was still in the stroller. When he hung purple beads around her neck.

I saw Diddio today. He mentioned my dorm room at St. John's. Where we made love, where, when I asked you for a photograph, you sketched in charcoal your face on the wall next to my bed.

I saw Addison today. He said he's going to bring in the Madman who took you from me.

The Madman who appeared, did what he did and vanished into the ether. The Madman who will reappear only when I am ready.

He did what he did.

Sometimes I think—and you know this; this I have told you before—he did not kill you and Davy. No, he killed me. You and Davy are alive in the world in which I once lived, where cool water laps the thin strand of sand far below white cliffs, where there is wine and bread, fragrant flowers, your smile as our baby coos.

I've been banished for my arrogance, self-satisfaction, venality, intemperance.

But I can't understand why Bella is here with me.

Why would any god punish her?

It is nearly an hour since I wrote those last lines, my dear. It's time to try to sleep. I'm off to the sofa, and the blue light of the TV.

A presto, Marina.
All my love,
T.

FOUR

I DROPPED BELLA OFF at school at the customary time, and walked over to West Street and back to stretch before I ran. My legs were sore—five miles in loafers will do that to your calves—so I was careful to work out the kinks. Starting slowly, I headed east to Worth, passing delivery vans up on the rounded stone curbs, and I crossed Broadway and ran through long shadows cast by the Federal Office Building, where new immigrants and aspiring citizens were milling about in a casual queue. I pressed on through a break in a crowd shuffling south toward the Woolworth Building, toward Wall Street. Passing the art deco Department of Health Building, with its bas relief façade, I pushed on to the Tombs, then headed south along Park Row. I cut through Paine Park, past yelping dogs behind the fence that enclosed their tattered walking path. Their owners sipped coffee from paper cups and scanned tabloid headlines. I thought of nothing as I ran; I thought of everything. Images appeared; thoughts followed, then emotion: out of the darkness, the haunting cycle, more dependable than time.

I crossed busy Broadway, easing a little bit now; at Hudson, I drifted south past Duane, where I dodged Stricks, dented delivery vans, gas fumes and a surly malamute, until I found the sidewalks along the crowded blacktop of Chambers. I was done now; I felt it: I was limber, heated, sweating good, my pulse at 138.

To cool down, I walked along the shady side of Greenwich, kicking off a twinge in my right knee, wiping my face on the sleeve of my t-shirt. As I walked in shadows, I recalled what I'd learned about the man I was about to visit, a lifetime summarized during three phone calls and 35 minutes online.

Rosenzweig, it turned out, had served in Korea. His C unit landed in mid-1950, saw heavy fire. Men were captured, tortured; many were killed, more were injured. Chaim Rosenzweig was one of the wounded: shrapnel, in the left shoulder and upper back. He was evacuated from Hungnam in December 1950. I knew about that episode: After the Chinese entered the conflict, the UN forces had to pull back, but their path was cut off. They were forced to fight their way out, through the vicious Korean winter, against fresh troops, to reach Hungnam, a port of escape.

Rosenzweig had been in Korea for less than six months. After leaving a VA Hospital in Livermore, California, he recovered in New York City while the wretched battles were fought at Pork Chop Hill, T-Bone and Heartbreak Ridge, when the Sabre F-86 finally overcame the Soviet MiGs, when Operation Killer chased back the Chinese. But he had been through hell, landing with Walton Walker and the Eighth Army, working behind enemy lines, with razorlike winds whipping from snowcapped mountains across the godless tundra.

I'd reached the corner of Harrison and I decided to

forgo the 15 minutes on the heavy bag I'd hung in the laundry room. After I'd showered, I'd go off to the West Village to see Chaim Rosenzweig.

HE NOW LIVED on Grove Street, a quiet, well-kept thoroughfare that ran between Bleecker and Bedford, a short walk from Sheridan Square. The tree-lined block was typical of this part of the West Village, where upscale couples, gay and straight, lived alongside seniors in rent-controlled apartments, where an old woman still took a whisk broom to the gray sidewalks as young men, strolling hand-in-hand, stopped to visit with her, to offer to do her food shopping. Rosenzweig had lived on this block, in this broad four-story brownstone, since 1982.

I left the taxi, went behind the thigh-high, cast-iron gate and under the dark steps to Rosenzweig's ground-floor apartment. A stack of newspapers wrapped tightly in cord was nestled next to a tall plastic can designated for recycling, and a black-and-white house cat licked its paws as it sat near an empty tin of salmon. Across the street, a stocky man in a blousy t-shirt and baggy slacks washed the sidewalk with water from a green hose. He was about Rosenzweig's age. He wore a Walkman and was humming aimlessly as he concentrated on his task.

I rang the bell several times and was ready to knock on the door when I heard a voice behind me.

"Hey, you. Hey."

I turned to find a short woman in a heavy cloth coat and slippers, her stockings crumpled around her ankles. Slumped and wrinkled, she had cloudy blue eyes, tight lips and looked like she'd spent a lifetime if not picking fights, at least doing little to avoid them. She seemed at least 75 years old, but could've been a tired 60. She had a gallon jug of red wine under her arm.

"Open this for me, willya?"

I reached over the low gate, took the bottle and snapped the frail cap without effort. When I returned the heavy bottle to her, she reacted with a blend of joy and relief.

"Thanks," she beamed. "Them jackasses make these damned things too hard to open."

"They forget who the customer is," I replied.

"Yeah, and I'm loyal to them. I don't know what I would've done if you wasn't here."

I nodded toward the man with the hose.

"McNaulty? A rat bastard."

The man seemed perfectly reasonable to me, but I kept my opinion to myself. Instead, pointing to the jug, I said, "That stuff'll kill you."

"I ain't got that kind of luck, mister," she said. "I'll be sober when I go."

She put the jug on the sidewalk and stood astride it, as if ready to defend her prize.

"You looking for Chick?"

"Chick?"

"Rosenzweig. Chick Rosenzweig," she said. "He's at the Greeks. All day at the Greeks."

She reacted quickly to my blank look.

"On Sixth, near the Waverly."

I lifted the latch and came from behind the gate.

"Tell him Gertie sent you. Tell him Gertie's got a new bottle."

I told her I would as I went off toward Sixth.

I ENTERED THE All-American Diner to find barren the row of sea-green spinning stools at the counter; two young women in pastel turtlenecks and jeans dawdled over coffee in a sunny booth in front. A bored man with an uneven mustache leaned on his elbow near the cash register, the kind that most resembled a manual typewriter and threw up an orange flag that said "No Sale" whenever it was opened, the kind of secretive machine the IRS hated. On the side of the beige register was a crucifix made of dried palm and a faded photo of a soccer team clipped from a magazine. A near-empty canister asked for donations to prevent cruelty to animals.

"Chaim Rosenzweig," I said.

The man sighed and pointed to the rear of the narrow restaurant. The scent of frying onions wafted overhead, brushing a stationary fan.

I walked to the back of the room, passing faded photos of the Acropolis, the Parthenon and marble busts of Socrates and Athena; more soccer, men with wild hair. In the kitchen, a lanky, teenage version of the man at the register hoisted a bag of frozen french fries onto his shoulder and carried them toward the grill and the hissing well of hot vegetable oil.

Two men sat at the booth in the back. They were of a kind: in their mid-60s with stubborn gray strands of hair that made it inaccurate to call them bald; round faces with Eastern European features pinched to the center; bifocals; dark sweater-vests over white shirts. The man to my right, with his back to the entrance, scanned the *Post* with a magnifying glass; the other man, back to the wall, read the *Daily News*.

"I'm looking for Chaim Rosenzweig," I said. Behind me, a splash and sizzle as frozen potatoes hit boiling oil.

The man with the *Post* gave up his friend in a heartbeat. "Him," he said, pointing.

I sat on the counter's last stool and told Rosenzweig my name. "I need to talk to you."

He stared at the newspaper, at a photo of a burning building and a headline charging arson.

"Chick," his friend said. "A guy."

"He hears me," I said.

"Are you a cop, mister?" the friend asked.

"No."

"A lawyer, maybe?"

I shook my head. "It's about his son."

Without taking his eyes off the newsprint, Rosenzweig said, "Sid, he thinks I tried to kill Solly." He flipped the page. "Sid, if I wanted to kill Solly where would Solly be?"

"Chick, you wouldn't want to kill Solly."

I interrupted. "Mr. Rosenzweig, let's get this done. Five, ten minutes."

Rosenzweig finally looked at me. "Sid, excuse us for five, ten minutes. Maybe you should call Marion, see if she needs something from CVS."

Sid stood. He nodded submissively at me as he grabbed his hat and left.

I remained on the stool.

Rosenzweig reached across the table and closed his friend's newspaper, back-page sports to the faded ceiling. "They think I put the bomb in the place? For what?"

"I don't know. For what?"

"To scare Solly?"

"That's an answer," I nodded.

"If I wanted to scare Solly, I'd walk up to him and say 'Boo.' He'd shit himself."

I said, "Your son is—"

"A *putz*. I don't have nothing to do with him. I wouldn't waste my time blowing up his phony pictures."

The teenager came up behind me and placed a glass of water and a knife and fork at my elbow.

I asked Rosenzweig, "You're a little hard on him, don't you think?"

"He's a nancy boy. Soft." Rosenzweig made a fist.

"He's got no fight in him. I carried him on my back. Now he's got Yoyo to do it."

"Yoyo?"

"I call her Yoyo. Like the Beatle guy's wife."

The empty-eyed teen returned. He scratched his head and stared at me. Then he asked, "Breakfast or lunch?"

I looked at my watch. It was 10:40. Too late for breakfast and too early for lunch. "Nothing," I said.

"Come on, big man," Rosenzweig chided. "You can't take up a stool when they got this kind of crowd."

I looked down the row. Now, Rosenzweig and I were the only two customers.

"Point taken," I said. I ordered an iced tea.

"I thought you tough guys drank bourbon."

"It's been a while since I've been one of the guys."

He smiled wryly. "Now I know more about you than you do about me."

"They airlifted you out of Hungnam and you went where? Yokohama? Osaka? You got out before Pusan."

He frowned in suspicion.

"What was it General Walker said? 'Stand or die'?"

"That's right," he said. "'Stand or die.'"

"I believe you may not be able to do much with that left arm, Mr. Rosenzweig."

"I get by," he said, as he looked away, wilting.

"You're a bit of a wiseass, Mr. Rosenzweig, and a bully. Maybe that's your right. Maybe you earned it. But I've got a friend in the hospital, and I'm going to find out who hurt her. So maybe you'll pay me the respect you won't give Sid. Or Sol. Or Lin-Lin."

He stared at the newspapers.

"All right?"

He looked at me. "My son's got no guts. And if he's ashamed of me, he can go to hell. I wouldn't bother trying to scare him."

hold it up as a model of superior achievement in the minority community. This I found ironic, since the principal reason for the success of Hurston Elementary was that it was one of the few schools in Harlem not run by the uninspired, self-protecting civil servants at the New York City Board of Education. A private school that annually had three times as many applications as it had available openings in its kindergarten class, Hurston Elementary was in fact a model, but one of how a school can succeed with an independent vision, a dedicated staff, committed parents who were involved in shaping the curriculum and extracurricular activities, and the support of private enterprise. According to the Letter from the Principal, Everett Langhorne, that was on the school's student-run web site, Chase, Sprint, Cisco Systems, Black Enterprise and PepsiCo were among the companies that had funded activities at Hurston.

I called ahead to make an appointment to visit the school, which was located on 125th, off Amsterdam, not very far from Columbia University. I had asked to see Langhorne—his very impressive letter, direct, eloquent even, and entirely focused on the achievements of students past and present, had me interested in him—but instead was granted an 11 A.M. conference with the vice principal. I showered, shaved, threw on a clean polo shirt, jeans and a pair of loafers, put thoughts of Sol Beck, Lin-Lin Chin and Chick Rosenzweig in my back pocket, and flagged a cab to take me to Harlem.

The school building, on the north side of the wide street across from the General Grant apartments, was a converted neighborhood bank, the kind that once housed smiling tellers, eager loan officers, a roving manager with a gold watch and fob extending from his dark vest, and waist-high tables with clogged ballpoint pens linked to

"Maybe he just needs a father."

"He had a father. Solly's the one who changed everything. He left. And for what? She don't want a husband. She wants a meal ticket."

The teenager had slipped the iced tea near the paper napkin behind me. I took a sip. It was flavored with cinnamon and it was awful. To clear away the taste, I withdrew the lemon and bit on the moist pulp.

"Where were you on Monday?"

"I was here. I was with Sid. They get people in here, believe it or not. People saw me."

"And Monday night?"

"I watch TV from eight to midnight." He paused. "I saw McNaulty when I put out the garbage."

"Maybe Gertie can vouch for you."

He seemed surprised. Then he said softly, "She can."

I nodded. "That's all I wanted." As I stood, I added, "I didn't mean any disrespect. I know what you gave in Korea."

"People your age don't know shit about Korea." With his left hand, he reached for the sugar dispenser and lifted it, but not very high. "See," he said. "I'm fine."

I nodded.

He added, "Korea don't have nothing to do with it."

I threw two bills on the counter and left.

OUTSIDE, SID WAS leaning against a parking meter. He was an old man, hunched, tired yet oddly hopeful. Younger men and women strolling through the midmorning sun passed him without a second glance.

He came toward me, waddling as much as walking, holding on to a small plastic bag from the drugstore. "He don't hate Solly," Sid said.

"No?"

"He thinks Solly hates him."

"Why would he hate his father?"

"Chick's not easy. He was very tough on Solly. He wanted different, you know, maybe like him. Somebody, you know... Not a painter."

"I see." The McDonald's on the other side of Sixth was crowded, and the fast-paced pickup basketball games were under way at the Cage up the block. I didn't see anyone I knew.

Sid added, "Maybe if he didn't go change his name."

"You don't hate your blood over a name, Sid."

"The name is blood for a Jew from Poland who comes here all the way, six years old, with his mother and sisters. Fighting then in the war. A hero, he is. Rosenzweig is his name, not Beck. Is it too much for his son to be proud of him?"

I shook my head.

"Maybe Chick should've done better. But maybe Solly could've been better?"

"You have kids, Sid?"

"Three. All girls. And five grandchildren. All boys. Go figure. You?"

I said yes.

"It's not easy. It's never easy."

"Yeah, but you forgive them, Sid. That's part of the job."

He nodded in agreement, then said, "But Chick don't forgive too good."

We shook hands and I headed north, toward midtown, past the leather-goods store, under the Waverly marquee, past the Rollerblading, fuchsia-haired woman and her endless legs.

* * *

SOL BECK AND Lin-Lin Chin lived on the first two floors of a brownstone closer to Varick than Sixth, on King, a block south of the perpetual queue outside the Film Forum. Their place was no more than a short, brisk walk from where Chaim Rosenzweig lived, from Gertie and the All-American Diner or from Judy's gallery. I wondered briefly if they all took roundabout paths to other parts of the Village, deliberately avoiding one another, peering left, right, stealth-like, in some pathetic comedy, Spy vs. Spy. Or did they expect to see one another and were prepared for a vitriolic confrontation, ready to sling incriminations like condemning stones, to recite through clenched teeth irrational bits of family legend as if they were fact? You; no, you: with spittle, bile. "As far as I'm concerned," one would scream, finally, "you're already dead." Or perhaps they imagined a reconciliation, a tearful embrace, concessions, forgiveness; a new beginning, an inspiring sunrise, fade in Alfred Newman strings, roll credits.

I turned right on King and, halfway to Varick, went to the door and rang the bell; an irony, albeit a small one: Beck and his father both lived in apartments that began under the stairs. Lin-Lin answered. She wore a long black t-shirt over black jeans. Her hair shone in the stark light from the naked bulb above her. An orange cat curled around her ankle.

"Terry."

"Your father-in-law's got a cat."

"You have seen him already?"

I nodded.

She lifted the cat. "Come in. Please."

She stepped aside and I entered. The hall was made narrow by the stairs that led to the second floor, where, I imagined, Beck's studio sat alongside a bedroom and drawing room, the latter mandatory in this type of building when it was constructed as a private home nearly a century ago. An eat-in kitchen, once part of the servants' quarters, was to my right, and a three-speed bicycle hung on the wall beyond the entrance to the kitchen. A long denim jacket had been tossed on the newel post. The mail, including magazines, sat on a painted radiator below an ornate mirror, next to a spidery potted plant.

I noticed at the end of the corridor a tarp that covered things that were thigh-high and square. It was a familiar sight.

I pointed at the tarp. "Pull those from Judy's?"

She looked toward the paintings under the tarp. "No, those aren't from the exhibition. Edie has those."

"I see."

I waited for her to continue, to tell me what paintings were under the tarp. But she didn't.

"You want your husband to hear this?" I asked finally.

As she let the cat drop to the floor, she said, "I don't think I would like to disturb him. He's working now. You understand, I am sure."

We followed the scurrying cat to the kitchen. More robust potted plants covered the front window, and an eclectic collection of spices—red pepper flakes, dried thyme, star anise, rosemary—were stacked unevenly on the ledge. The sink was an old-fashioned kind: a double, porcelain, without a drain board; and the U-shaped pipes underneath were visible, though copper couplings had been added. As I slid into the wooden seat at the round table, I noticed another sitting room beyond the kitchen, beyond a curtain of plastic golden beads. It too held an assortment of paintings under a tarp.

"I was going to have tea. Will you join me?"

I shook my head.

"Sol enjoys green tea now. I bring it to him when he's working."

Green tea tastes like liquid dirt to me.

"You live in TriBeCa, I understand," she said. "I think Sol would like to move to something bigger. But there is a very lovely light upstairs from the middle of the morning. The studio faces south."

As did Marina's, I thought.

"In TriBeCa, it is not inexpensive," she added. "You must have great success."

Approaching a heavy stove as old as the sink, Lin-Lin grabbed a box of stick matches, struck one and held it under a cast-iron pot. A whoosh; blue flame. I visualized the delicate tea leaves clinging to the surface of the water in the pot.

She replaced the matchbox on the shelf above the stove and joined me at the table, peeking discreetly at my small stack of international newspapers. "Tell me about Sol's father."

I leaned my elbows on the table. "He's a bitter old man and he feels his son somehow betrayed him."

"Yes, this is what we know."

"But he's not the one who placed the bomb in the gallery."

She tilted her head. "You know this already?"

" 'Know' is a tricky word," I said. "I can tell you what I think."

As I sat back, she leaned in, folding her thin arms in front of her on the bare wood. "Please."

"You and Sol might be basing your opinion on a faulty premise," I began. "In the military, demolition experts don't spend much time constructing bombs. Nor do they know much about defusing them. They use dynamite, shape charges, make gel gas, which is kind of like napalm in a barrel."

Lin-Lin frowned, not so much in displeasure as in concentration.

I continued. "These types of explosives aren't very precise. They aren't meant to create small, contained explosions, like the one at Judy's. These gel-gas things are about as subtle as a bomb dropped from a plane. Carnage is the usual result."

"A contained explosion. What is that, exactly?"

"Whoever planted the bomb in Judy's wanted to do a minimum of damage, that's obvious."

"But Judy was almost killed."

I nodded. "Because she was in the storage area when it went off. No one could've expected that. Especially after the call."

She reflected for a moment. "I think the bomb was very dangerous."

"It was intended to kick up a lot of dust, blow out a couple of windows," I said. "Judy was very unlucky."

The teakettle began to whistle. Lin-Lin excused herself and went to the jet. She cut the flame, but didn't lift the kettle. She returned to the table without making Beck's tea.

As she sat, I said, "Then there's the problem of your father-in-law's disability."

"Problem?"

"You know he was wounded in Korea."

"Yes," she replied, "but he is fine. I have seen him many times."

"I don't think he can lift his left arm above his shoulder. I don't think he can handle much weight."

"How much does a bomb weigh?"

"I don't know what was used, but I assume it was placed among the ceiling pipes, so no one would stumble on it accidentally. He'd have to secure it up there, and I don't think he's got the strength for that."

"Someone put it there for him, I'm sure."

Sid? Gertie? "I don't think so."

She seemed to sigh. "If not him, then who?"

"You'll have to ask the police about that."

"Do you think the bomb was meant to hurt Judy or destroy her gallery?" she asked.

"I think someone tried to disrupt the opening."

"So you think someone was trying to hurt Sol?"

I shrugged. "What else could it be?"

She paused to think, then suddenly stood. "I'm not sure you are right, Terry." She smiled.

I stood as well. Behind her, the teakettle stopped hissing. "Rosenzweig feels that there are enough people to account for him on Monday. He ate in a diner on Sixth, and he's got a friend who spends the evenings with him."

"I think he had a helper," she said. "I think he did it."

"Lin-Lin, you need to consider what his motive would be."

She began to move toward the corridor, toward the door. I followed.

"He hates Sol," she said. "That is certain."

"I'm not sure hatred is what it is. Sol somehow upset the order of things, and it gnaws at Rosenzweig, but it happened a while ago. There's no reason to take action now."

"Oh, I disagree. Now is Sol's time to succeed. I think his father would hate for him to have success on his own."

"You may be right," I replied. I'd given my opinion. She rejected it. I wasn't going to argue with her.

When she reached for the door, the orange cat appeared. But she didn't appear to want to escape. She seemed to want to observe, and she studied me with wide, passionless eyes.

"Is there a fee for your services?" Lin-Lin asked. She bent to scoop up the cat.

"No," I said. "It's for Judy."

I said goodbye as she opened the door.

* * *

I HEADED EAST to Sixth. I figured I'd walk home, and
after lunch, pick up Bella at school, help with her homework or join in on whatever distraction she'd cooked up
to help her dodge her school assignments. Perhaps I
could arrive in time to convince Mrs. Maoli that a feast
isn't necessary every night of the week. She used to listen
to Marina. Maybe one day she'd listen to me. Sure.

I paused for a moment at the corner of King and Sixth,
and absently looked toward uptown before proceeding
south. There, on the east side of Sixth, backpack slung on
his shoulder, was Sol Beck. He was walking slowly, dragging, but he didn't seem any more troubled or distracted
than before. In his hand was a plastic bag of supplies
from Pearl Paints: long brushes and sketch pads too bulky
to fit in the backpack. Head down, he wore an odd sort of
baseball cap, an old, baggy blazer, white shirt, black
jeans, sneakers.

Working upstairs, my ass. "He's working now. You understand, I am sure."

Sure, Lin-Lin. Thanks.

FIVE

THE ZORA NEALE HURSTON Elementary School had won a variety of honors over the years, mostly for academic excellence, several for community service; its graduates populated Fortune 500 companies, white-shoe law firms, major media outlets, faculties at Ivy League schools, scientific research institutions and medical centers throughout the country. Seven alumni were federal judges; two were high-ranking officials in the Pentagon, another was the lieutenant governor of South Carolina, and her husband, also a Hurston graduate, had written a popular, if controversial, book that cited the works of Claude McKay, Jean Toomer and Langston Hughes to defend the value of teaching Western literature to minority students. Many others had succeeded in the arts; for example, 19 graduates held positions with orchestras throughout the country, and one had written *North Star,* the opera on the life of Frederick Douglass. Thus, it was a favorite stop for politicians, black and white, who liked to small, beaded chains. Here, long ago, a customer could get a free toaster by opening a checking account, and an old woman on a meager pension could come in to verify what was written in flowery Palmer penmanship in her passport-sized savings book and be greeted by name, offered a seat and a sip of cool water in a Dixie cup. The building still felt welcoming, yet its spotless redbrick and white columns gave it a stately air, not unlike the aura of the private schools on the Upper East Side. Above me, the school flag—a black field, rimmed north and south in discreet green, yellow and red, with the words Zora Neale Hurston in bold goldenrod type—flew on a brass pole next to the Stars and Stripes.

I entered the building and in the vestibule was greeted immediately by another banner—"Education/Articulation"—and a muscular security guard. His head was clean-shaven and his skin, stretched taut over his sturdy frame, matched the coffee-black color of his intense eyes. He was my height and wore a Beretta nine-millimeter along with a police-style uniform of pale-blue shirt, navy polyester slacks and steel-toed boots. Politely but firmly, he asked me to identify myself—he said precisely that: "Please identify yourself, sir"—and accepted my card, looking at it quickly, as if he could not dare risk taking his eye off me.

"I have an appointment with Denise Williams," I said.

He had a small, square microphone pinned to his open-collared shirt and, stepping back, he whispered into it.

I heard the crackle, but not the words, of the reply. He instructed me to step inside the building and I stood near his office. Not much more than a large closet, it contained a mahogany table, an old-style wood swivel chair and three small TV monitors; it looked like the cameras were trained on the front and back entrances and the small parking lot in the rear. He reached in, withdrew a wand-like metal detector and ran it around me. When the thing didn't buzz, he returned it to the table.

"Your escort will be here in a moment," he said.

And in seconds a boy appeared. About the same age as Bella, and about her height, he was neatly attired in a white cotton dress shirt, black slacks and dark, rubber-soled shoes. He seemed very serious, well disciplined, and he greeted the imposing guard with a mannerly tilt of his head before turning his attention to me.

"Mr. Orr, I am Delroy Henry." He thrust his hand at me and gave me a firm, businesslike handshake. As he spoke, he held my gaze, suggesting a confidence I was not ac-customed to in someone his age. "I will escort you to Mrs. Williams's office."

And off we went, down the immaculate corridor. Classes were in session on either side of the hall and doors were shut, but a glance through the windows re-vealed rooms filled with about a dozen or so students not unlike smaller, younger versions of Delroy Henry, in both their youthful interpretation of business apparel as well as their sobriety.

"First through fifth grades are on this floor," Delroy of-fered, "and the administrative offices. Sixth through eighth upstairs."

From what I could see, all the students were of African descent, as were the teachers, who seemed a serious, en-thusiastic lot, at least from my cursory appraisal as I walked with young Mr. Henry.

"I can answer any questions you may have," he said.

Between the classrooms were cork boards covered with photos clipped from magazines, handmade illustra-tions and maps, students' poems and essays and handi-craft celebrating Americans, blacks and whites, Asian and Hispanic, of significant achievement. The emphasis was on educators, scientists and artists: I recognized most white faces on the boards—Horace Mann, Jonas Salk, John Singer Sargent, Robert Frost, Robert Kennedy—as well as some of the black ones: Mary McLeod Bethune, who I knew had influenced New Deal policies; George Washington Carver, Toni Morrison, Wynton Marsalis and Rita Dove. But many others were strangers to me until I read the summaries of their achievements beneath the photographs: the scientist Charles R. Drew, who devised a storage system for blood plasma; Phillis Wheatley, poet and slave; John Sengstacke, a newspaper publisher. The summaries had been written by the students, and had the kind of charm only kids' work can, wherein all facts are treated with equal gravity and proclamations are made with unbridled enthusiasm. One student had declared breathlessly: "When I grow up I am going to be like Countee Cullen," and had added six exclamation points to the pledge. But the work was thorough; I was about to tell Henry I'd learned as much about African-Americans during our brief walk than during my eight years in elementary school and four years of high school. But I decided against that.

"These are all very good," I said.

"Thank you."

"Did you do any of them?"

"All students participate in all projects," he replied.

We passed a water fountain. It emitted a low buzz, a warm hum.

I asked, "Do you like Countee Cullen?"

"Yes, but he is not my favorite. I agree with our teacher Mr. Allen, who says he is too derivative of Keats."

"I see."

"Do you know Countee Cullen, Mr. Orr?"

The question seemed to have a bite to it, as if Delroy Henry expected me to say no. But I knew Cullen's work;

I'd read "Copper Sun" and his novel *One Way to Heaven*.
Walter Riley, a teammate and fellow history major at St.
John's, insisted I study the Harlem Renaissance if I was
going to concentrate on turn-of-the-century New York.

I replied, "All Romantic poets are derivative of Keats."

We made a left turn at the end of the corridor and arrived at the principal's office. Henry rapped on the
beveled-glass-and-wood door, which was opened by a
stout, matronly woman in a cream blouse and dark skirt.
Behind her was a small anteroom between the offices of
Everett Langhorne and Denise Williams. I noticed a
thick, wooden fence with a swinging door, a remnant
from the building's banking days. I imagined that this
suite once belonged to the bank's president, its manager
and their attentive assistant.

"Miss Oliver," Henry said, "this is Mr. Orr."

"Thank you, Mr. Henry," she replied. "You may be
seated now."

He squeezed by her to enter the reception area.

She nodded politely. "Right this way, Mr. Orr," she
added and held back the door for me to pass.

DENISE WILLIAMS REMAINED at her desk as Miss
Oliver closed the door behind me. With a flip of her thin
hand, she suggested I sit.

The small office was sparsely but neatly furnished: an
old, attractive sofa to my left, a small table to my right on
which rested scores of color-coded folders, a row of
three-ring binders and a computer printer that was linked
to the CPU under Williams's desk. Her monitor and keyboard were to her left; apparently she was using the computer as I arrived, culling information from reports that
had the official drabness and stern uniformity of government documents. As I looked at the papers, she reached

over and hurriedly rearranged the stack near the keyboard, flipping over the top sheet. I thought nothing of it, and instead imagined that a vice principal must spend a great part of her day filling out an endless supply of such forms.

I noticed that the bright screen saver scrolled the phrase "Education/Articulation," followed by a quote from Zora Neale Hurston. As I began to read the Hurston quote, Williams reached down and snapped off the computer.

"I wasn't finished," I said. The spindly arms of spider plants covered the ledge of the window behind her.

"You have questions about a boy that used to attend our school, Mr. Orr?" she asked tartly. "We're very busy."

I'd suddenly begun to feel as if I were a student here, accused of some unnamed infraction, who had been summoned to the vice principal's office. "Is it something I said?"

"Have you been treated rudely, Mr. Orr?" she asked, peering sternly over her glasses.

" 'Rudely' isn't it, no. It's more like too efficiently."

"Excuse us for being efficient."

"I don't know if this needs to be difficult, Ms. Williams."

"So now we're difficult. Efficient and difficult."

" 'Curt,' I think, is another word."

"The word you're looking for is 'uppity,'" she said.

And I felt the electric charge, the red rage, and my eyes tightened. But I said nothing. I stood, held up my hand, opened the door and walked out through the swinging gate, passing Miss Oliver, who didn't look up from her electric typewriter, and Delroy Henry, who, startled, withdrew as I blew by.

I went quickly, silently down the corridor. Seething, I moved purposefully, trying to contain my raw anger. I avoided looking into the classrooms, where diligent students were at work. I didn't want to disturb them. It wasn't for me to let them know their vice principal was a practiced race-baiter, a rank racist.

"One moment," the well-built guard said firmly. He positioned himself between me and the exit, the wash of light on 125th.

I moved toward him, stepping in to let him know I'd accept a challenge. Now we were face-to-face; I could feel the heat of his breath, and see the thin red veins in his eyes.

I said, "Unless you're ready to pull that nine, I suggest you let me slide."

"I have to detain you," he said firmly as he tapped the small microphone and speaker near his collar.

"Step aside, friend."

He narrowed his eyes. "I can have a squad car here in two minutes, Mr. Orr."

"Do what you want," I said. "I'm gone."

As I moved around him, he grabbed for my left arm and caught my sleeve. I snapped free and, regrouping, squared myself for the fight. He was a big man and fit. I'd have to strike first: It would have to be the midsection.

I heard a voice behind me, feminine, urgent. But I didn't turn.

"Mr. Orr, no, wait." It was Denise Williams, and she understood that there was about to be a brawl in her school, and unless the guard dropped me quick, it was going to be nasty.

She may even have realized that it was she who had pushed it to this point.

"Mr. Reynolds. In your office," she commanded.

I watched him. He was confident. He was breathing fire through his nose, and his fists were clenched tightly at his sides.

"Mabry," Williams whispered, "*please*. The students."

And at that quiet, desperate plea, Mabry Reynolds stepped back with a military snap. He held me in his gaze until Williams came between us.

I told myself to relax. But my heart continued to leap against my chest, and I could feel the fever at the back of my neck.

Williams placed her hand on Reynolds's arm and instructed him to step outside. He looked down at her, nodded and did so, neither eagerly nor reluctantly. His confrontation over, he simply adjusted his belt with its Beretta nine, and went. But he didn't go far, remaining at the front door, his broad back toward us. I noticed he was leaning against the glass, keeping the door ajar with his heft, as if he wanted to hear me approaching, or listen to what I was about to say.

"Mr. Orr, if we could return—"

"Are you—"

"Mr. Orr—"

"I came to you in good faith."

"Granted; I may have misunderstood," she said lamely.

"You knew what you were doing."

"Can we continue this in my office, please?"

"Why? You've thought of a new way to call me a racist?"

"I didn't—"

"You did." I added sourly, "You must be a big disappointment to Dr. Langhorne."

"*Touché,* Mr. Orr," she replied. "Now, can we go back to my office?"

I took a breath and tried to think of Aubrey Brown, his frail body slumped in the front seat of the battered Buick, his skull smashed, his eyes empty; and the angelic-looking boy with the savage scar, peeking tentatively into the funeral home, scowling at me. And then I saw a baby in the oily water between subway tracks.

"All right," I said.

And we went along the corridor, Williams's heels clicking on the pristine floor, as we ignored tales of pride and accomplishment.

SHE SETTLED BEHIND her desk. "I suppose I was a little put off by the idea that you assumed we would help you investigate one of our former students," she said, as she began to recover.

Or maybe it was the nagging stack of the government forms, or something a tardy student had said, or the way the sun rose that morning: to the east, very early in the day. She still didn't like me. Only a vague sense of obligation told her to bring me back; or perhaps she was afraid I'd tell a tale that would embarrass her or the school. But I could feel that she wanted to dismiss me as quickly as possible, though not as abruptly as before.

But I didn't care what she wanted. I wanted to know about the boy Henderson said was called Montana, the boy with the scar.

"I'm still not sure we should be doing that," she added.

"I'm looking into a murder," I said. "This young man may have nothing to do with it. He just keeps turning up, like he's following the body."

"I see."

I explained, telling her about Aubrey Brown and his lonely life; Montana's visits to Henderson's place and the cemetery, and about the police and what they did not find. As I spoke, I noticed that my right leg had stopped shaking. Involuntary tremors: the aftereffect of aggression unreleased. After a game in high school and college, if my playing time hadn't been enough, if I hadn't gotten to mix it up the way I liked, I'd tremble until I got to the shower and, sometimes, after that.

When I finished, she nodded and said, "His name is Andre Turner Junior, and he was a student here until about four years ago."

"So Montana—"

"He wasn't known as Montana here."

"All right," I said. "You're saying Turner dropped out in, what, the fifth grade?"

"In a manner of speaking."

I shook my head in confusion.

She replied, "I'm thinking of the best way to tell you about Andre."

His story, she said, would explain why he was no longer at Hurston Elementary and why he was now beyond their arc of influence. I thought of him: his dreadlocks and shaved temples, baggy jeans, the red stocking cap. He was a Hurston boy no more; trendy pop culture had its talons in him now. He might still be reading Alice Walker and Countee Cullen, but now his peers and the media told him how to behave.

Williams said Turner had been brighter than most boys his age. His parents, both of whom had successful careers downtown, insisted he excel in academics and were adamant about his attending private school.

"He met the entrance criteria and was accepted," she added.

"What are they, exactly? The criteria."

She lifted her hands from her green blotter and counted on her fingers. "His parents had a commitment to academic excellence; he demonstrated the fundamental intellectual capabilities we require, scoring well on the qualifying exams; he found financial support—"

"Financial support? Tuition is that high?" She'd said Turner's parents had successful careers; he was an executive with Fox, she a partner in an advertising agency. I wondered why they'd have to seek outside funding for their son.

"Actually, tuition is one dollar per year per student. We require that parents participate in our underwriting program by securing donations to our general fund. They are our fund-raisers, essentially."

"An interesting system," I said.

She nodded. But she didn't care whether I thought it was interesting or not. "It is imperative that we have the support of commerce and industry as well as the community."

I noticed that she had mentioned several times the role of parents in the school. I asked her about that.

"It's the core of Dr. Langhorne's philosophy: Family background has a greater impact than the school experience on many of the objectives we are trying to achieve. Dr. Langhorne has promoted this ideal since the mid-'60s."

"He sounds like a special man."

"Dr. Langhorne is a special man," she replied proudly but pointedly, as if working alongside a visionary had permitted her to absorb his brilliance.

She returned to Andre Turner Jr. He had adjusted well, she said, and had been doing his work, more or less, neither distinguishing himself nor falling behind. In the second grade, he began to drift, as she put it, and was occasionally disruptive.

"The second grade can present a challenge to someone who might be immature," she said. "It is the time when academics truly take precedence over socialization. But with Andre it was more than that. He became lethargic, introverted. He simply stopped achieving. His teacher, Mr. Amaral, tried to reach him, but..." She shook her head.

At Hurston Elementary, she reported, parents met with their children's teachers once a month. "Mr. Amaral and I discussed this with the Turners and they said they would work with their son."

"Did they?"

"He managed to do enough to be promoted to the third grade in the spring, but Mr. Amaral deserves credit for that, entirely. He worked with Andre. Here, at his own home on Fort Washington Avenue. Weekends at the library."

"Dedicated," I offered.

"We are here for the students," she announced.

I managed to keep quiet.

Williams continued. At the first parents' meeting of the new school year, Andre's mother was absent, she said, for the first time. "We discovered that his parents had separated over the summer and Andre was downtown with his father. Shortly thereafter, Mrs. Turner went to family court to secure her right to return to her life at home with her son."

"I assume she won."

"Yes, and Mr. Turner was instructed to surrender Andre, which he did."

She was telling me more than she needed to and she wasn't hesitating. I began to suspect that she wasn't revealing any confidences, that Andre Turner Jr.'s story was a matter of public record. This tale wasn't about to have a happy ending.

"But he returned."

"Not immediately, but yes, and he was arrested for assaulting his wife. And then came the allegations. That he had been abusing Andre."

"Abusing? Sexually?"

"Yes," she replied directly. "Mr. Turner was arrested again and the story was well publicized. It was said he was granted a leave of absence from Fox. But in fact, he was fired."

"And?" I asked.

"And a year later Andre Turner killed his wife."

I flinched. "Christ. How?"

"Stabbed her to death. At her apartment."

"And Andre saw this?"

She nodded sadly.

I ran my finger along the side of my face. "The scar—"

"Exactly. He tried to save his mother."

"Christ."

"It was terribly disruptive for all of us."

At least that for Andre Jr., who must've been about 10 years old at the time. The enraged father, the terrified mother, the glistening knife, screaming, swearing; the blood, the slash across his face, pain, burning pain, his mother's death; the death of his protector, his future. "The horror," said Kurtz. If he only knew.

"Where is the father now?"

"In prison. I don't know where."

"So the boy left Hurston."

"In fact, Andre returned to us when he recovered. We have a fund for such cases, but they rarely work out. Without the involvement of the parents, without that partnership, despite our efforts, mine and, in Andre's case, Mr. Amaral's, it is very, very difficult for the student. After a while, we had to transfer Andre to public school. It was best for all, given the situation."

She reached and tapped a button on her telephone. She instructed Miss Oliver to send in Delroy Henry.

The student entered and gently closed the door. He waited for instruction. When Williams told him to sit, he did so. He folded his hands in his lap.

Williams said, "Mr. Henry knew Andre. Mr. Henry?"

"Yes, ma'am."

"Please tell Mr. Orr what we spoke about earlier."

Henry shifted in the chair to face me. "Andre started out in my brother's class."

"Here or in public school?" I asked.

Williams answered, "Here. Mr. Henry's brother now attends Xavier. On scholarship."

"And where is Andre now?" I asked.

"Mr. Henry?"

The boy, who had seemed so self-possessed when I first met him, now seemed uncomfortable, almost nervous. "He's on the street."

"He has no family?"

"No, sir. He used to live with his aunt, but she ain't seen him."

"Mr. Henry," Williams scolded.

He bowed his head. "Sorry, ma'am."

"Do you ever see him?" I asked.

"I see him now and then. But he never comes around."

"Do you have any idea where he's living?"

"No," the boy replied.

I decided to try another way. "Do you know if he's been in any trouble? I mean, has he been arrested?"

"No," Henry said, shaking his head. "I don't think so."

Williams interrupted. "Mr. Henry, you can tell Mr. Orr what you told me this morning."

I said, "Is there some question of confidentiality?"

The boy looked at me.

"I won't give you up," I said. "I'm not a cop."

He looked at his vice principal, then at me. "People say Andre is a prostitute."

"Do you know where he works?"

"I don't know where," Henry replied, "but he's on the street. He's out there."

"Is someone keeping him? You know what I mean?"

"Mr. Henry could not know such a thing," Williams

said, barely concealing her disgust. But it didn't matter: She was irrelevant now.

"He's out there," Henry repeated, with a gesture.

I paused. He was telling the truth, and I appreciated how discomforting it might be for a young teenager to have to talk about this in front of his vice principal, *this* vice principal. But I decided to press a bit, on the chance that he could bring me even closer.

"Is there any way I could see him?" I asked.

"Not that I know about," Henry said.

"I saw him Tuesday at 135th and Malcolm X. Would I see him there again?"

"I don't know. I don't think so. He doesn't come around." He suddenly smiled. "You can't hang at 135 and X for too long without someone asking you what up."

"Indeed," Williams echoed.

"Yeah," I said, "I'm too tall."

"Now, Mr. Orr—"

I waved my hand as I stood. "I understand." I said to Henry, "Can you tell me why they call him Montana? Is he in a gang or something?"

"Naw," Henry replied. "It's from the movie about the gangster. *Scarface*. His name was Tony Montana. They call him Montana because of the scar on his face."

"That's cold."

Henry shook his head. "He gave himself that name. He likes that scar. He likes the whole thing with his father and his mother getting killed. It's like Hollywood. He used to say it made him hard."

"Did it?"

"Naw. He's a boy. That's why he's a 'ho' now."

"Mr. Henry!" Williams shouted. "I am going to need to speak to you, young man."

I thanked them both, shook hands with Henry and, as she glared at the sheepish teenager, Williams. As I left the office, I could hear her lecturing him, hectoring him, even through the closed door.

I nodded goodbye to Miss Oliver, who responded silently but sympathetically and then returned to her typewriter.

I left the small suite, turned right and went along the corridor, passing carefully printed words on construction paper, excerpts from Hurston's *Their Eyes Were Watching God* and *Seraph on the Suwannee,* and tributes to Anthony Davis, Fiorello LaGuardia, Garth Fagan and Johnnetta Cole. From behind a closed door, I heard echoes of ringing words of praise; to my left, through the window in the door, I saw a young girl, seven years old at most, beaming, bowing politely in front of her classmates.

Good for you, I thought. You did it.

The guard was waiting for me, arms crossed, outside his cubby of an office.

He said nothing. He stared at me, and he didn't blink.

I was going to say something, but didn't. I left.

AND SO I had this, I thought as I paused in the gray light on 125th: Brown is killed in an area used by hookers to service low-budget clients; Montana, who's somehow compelled to follow Brown's body to the grave, is a male prostitute. Too neat, I told myself. I headed to Malcolm X.

To kill time, I picked up a copy of the *Sporting News* at a small cigar shop, and thought about making my way to lunch at Sylvia's, the cliché move for a white man in Harlem. I started walking south, going past brownstones on the shady side toward the Park. I'd enter, I thought, near the Harlem Meer and waggle by the Conservatory Gardens to the exit at 97th, where it'd be easier to grab a cab.

I was thinking about the chances that a few early ducks

would be at the Pool—Bella did a paper on the White-Fronted Duck, which seemed an unimaginative name to me, then and now—when an unexpected idea popped. I pulled out the cell and dialed.

She told me to come now. She had a lunch date at 1 P.M. With Kofi Annan, Secretary General of the United Nations.

SIX

SHARON KNIGHT HAD AN office no bigger, no better equipped, than what a middle manager on the way down might have at a small brick-and-mortar. But there was no mistaking her authority, regardless of her austere, bureaucratic surroundings. It was deeply ingrained, deeply personal: Here was a woman who knew herself and was completely at ease with the knowledge. Only people impressed with bluster and sophistry could misunderstand.

This natural aura, this sense of command, was the root of her success. As a prosecutor, Sharon was a winner: passionate, resolute, direct and with a record any D.A. in the country would be proud of. And she was media savvy. Thus, she was well respected by the city's white, liberal establishment and by the African-American business-political axis that yielded considerable influence on the Democratic Party's left and center. A Giuliani aide once tried to deride her by calling her "a poor man's Janet Reno." Al Sharpton struck back with "your boss hasn't succeeded in making every sister poor." Refusing to play the race card, Sharon instead praised fellow Harvard alumna Reno, focusing on her stint as state attorney in Dade County, and pointedly offered to meet the aide to present her accomplishments. Ever since, the *Times* has floated her name as a candidate for every office, city and state.

"I'm a prosecutor, Terry," she once told me. "Wanted to be one since I learned there was such a thing." She jabbed her finger hard on her desk. At about 240 pounds, with close-cropped hair and alluring brown eyes a shade darker than her unblemished skin, Sharon Knight knew how to hold all the light in a room.

I said, "You ought to make them think you're doing them a favor by staying here."

She winked at me.

Now, sitting in the same seat in her office at Hogan Place, I told her about my trips uptown to Harlem.

"I know Everett Langhorne," she said.

"Seems like a good man."

She let my comment hang in the air. Instead of answering, she leaned on her elbows and said, "Let me anticipate your question: Can I get the police to cooperate with you?"

"Hell, no," I replied. "When a livery driver gets killed? I'll get along better without them."

She suppressed a smile.

"What I want to know is if you'd be comfortable getting me some information on someone."

"And this has something to do with the murder of brother Brown?"

"'Brother Brown'?"

"It's an expression, Terry," she said dryly.

"I know. I just haven't heard it since the '80s."

"I'm dating myself, in other words."

I said, "None of us is getting younger, Sharon."

"No, but this conversation might be speeding up the aging process." She drummed her fingernails on the hardwood desk.

I told her about the explosion, about Judy, Beck and Lin-Lin.

"You're working two cases at once."

"This one's a favor. The gallery owner was Marina's agent."

"I see," she said, her voice softened by an undercurrent of sympathy. She looked at her thin, silver wristwatch and stood.

"Two at once, Terry. A bit ambitious, wouldn't you say?"

I left the hard chair. "I'm just going where I'm going, Sharon. I might've thought about it, but every time somebody tells me to stop, I run the red. You know?"

"Your devil's your angel." She tamped down the long, wide skirt and ample jacket of her dark blue suit and absently tapped at the black pearl that lay beneath the open collar of her blouse. "We could all use a bit of your perseverance, I suppose. Your dedication. To whatever it is."

I reached for the black coat that hung on the back of her office door and held it for her.

She turned, began to button the coat and nodded toward a small pad on her desk. "Give me the name. I'll see what I can do."

I grabbed a felt-tipped pen from a cup and scribbled the short name on the sheet. When I handed the paper to her, she didn't look at it. She folded it and reached for the doorknob.

"Where to?" I asked, as she opened the door.

"The Ambassador Grill."

"Nice."

"Better than a sandwich at the desk," she said, as she

stepped into the corridor and began to move toward a secretary's cubicle. Someone in the distance had a radio; someone nearby had heated leftover Chinese in a microwave.

"Thanks, Sharon," I said. My time was up.

She turned. "You need a lift, Terry?"

I told her no.

She nodded, then said, "Be careful. A deep breath every now and then."

I said OK.

I STOPPED AT the Delphi for lunch. I saw no one I knew, which suited me fine, and I ordered a turkey club. By the time the blue-eyed waitress slid it onto the counter in front of me, I was surprised to see it. Daydreaming, I'd forgotten what I'd ordered. I'd started out thinking about Montana and how his father had failed him, shifted to Beck and Rosenzweig, thought about Bella and went somewhere else; once again, I'd floated to Marina's side. A walk along the Rio Guadalquivir after a visit to the Museo Artes; *tapas* and too much *reserva rioja* in an open-air square behind the cathedral in Santa Cruz: in Seville, for an exhibition of her work, and time to grow together.

I finished the sandwich, dabbed away the mayonnaise and put $10 under the water glass. Sated, feeling not at all guilty about the extra bacon, I made my way into the shadows on West Broadway and decided to go south, to go to Greenwich via Thomas, for no other reason than to do it a different way. I reached Hudson as a wave of cars, vans and taxis roared by, and I thought I saw someone I recognized in a passing cab. She was a young woman, dark-haired with a round face, and I placed her instantly and thought, coincidence. Ninety minutes ago, I'm in her boss's office... And then I remembered her name. Julie Giada, another of Morganthau's army of prosecutors. I had good feelings about Julie, but couldn't remember why. More than likely, it was because she was on Sharon's team.

I came to my place along the west side of Greenwich, which was typically quiet on a chilly mid-afternoon, though not so quiet that I could nudge myself back to Seville. When I turned the corner onto Harrison, I saw it right away and I knew it was no coincidence that I'd seen Julie. Sticking out of my mailbox was a large manila envelope, curled just so to fit under the locked box.

I opened the envelope to find a photocopy of a computer printout: name, address, charge, disposition, sentence. Precisely what I needed.

I put the paper back into the envelope and tucked it under my arm. Ninety minutes. Christ. And as I punched in the security code to the lock on the front door, I knew what that meant, beyond confirming what I'd suspected. It meant Sharon Knight was going to stand by me. And that would mean something the next time Luther Addison tried to get me to go home.

BELLA CAME INTO the living room and handed me the handset of the cordless phone. She beamed. I knew it was Diddio on the other end.

I put the tattered copy of Conrad on the coffee table.

With enthusiasm, Diddio announced that the '70s group Yes was playing that night at the Beacon. "It'll be a pisser. Art rock by geriatrics." He sang, badly, in a cracking falsetto, "'Cause it's time, it's time in time with your time and its news is captuuuuured... for the queen to use!' Heh-heh. Let's go. We'll bring Gabby. OK?"

"You tell her already?" I looked over at Bella, who continued to glow.

He hesitated. "Can I lie?"

She's got homework, I thought, and she needs sleep, and we're seeing Harteveld tomorrow.

Finally, I said, "I may bail."

Bella clapped her hands. She jumped in place. I think she squealed.

FOUR HOURS LATER, we walked in stubborn silence through the darkness toward the TriBeCa Grill to flag a cab, and took one from two briefcase-toting men with ties at half-mast. Our dour driver nodded at my suggestion that he take Tenth until it became Amsterdam to avoid the bottleneck on West.

"You're angry," I said. "You want to let D see you pout, that's all right with me."

The taxi swept past a weed-covered lot south of the Javits Center.

"You started it. You're in one of those moods of yours," Bella insisted, her arms folded as she sat as far from me as possible in the broad seat. "So I'll keep to myself."

She wore a black beret, her faded denim jacket over a black, long-sleeved t-shirt, patched jeans and her green-and-red bowling shoes. I caught a glimpse of one of the frail patches on her jeans, and realized it was clipped from her baby blanket: I recognized the small, cheerful, innocent bear with outstretched arms. Diddio helped her patch her jeans, and he'd sewed the yin-yang on the beret. I'd been in the other room.

"And I don't pout," she continued. "I don't like it that you made me rewrite my essay because you were mad at something. Or was it because Dennis asked me to go?"

I shook my head. "That essay was beneath you, Bella, and you know it. Thomas Paine deserves better. *The American Crisis* is a masterwork. You rushed so you could go to the concert."

"I don't like history as much as you, Dad," she said. "And you should've waited dinner for me."

"Maybe." I ate the *carciofi alla romana* while Bella rewrote. "It's not easy motivating you. Besides, you ate."

"Leftovers."

She was impossible to argue with; the times that try men's souls, indeed. I kept the braised artichokes warm, and I served them, in their sauce of lemon, white wine, garlic and fresh parsley and mint, over linguine. She ate while I showered.

"Don't be mad at me," I said. "Be mad at you."

We rode in silence, heading toward the land of Singer, Civiletti's Verdi and Zabar's sable. We entered the mid-40s, coming to a halt across from a Hess station where scores of taxis queued for cheap gas.

She continued to stare out the window. When the traffic light went green, we pressed on and approached an empty horse-drawn carriage, its weary engine slowly clopping toward its stable. I noticed that Bella brightened for a moment at the sight of it, before she remembered she was angry. She immediately resumed her frown, and continued to stare at the tenements, the corner bars, the rusted gates on drab storefronts.

I looked east and saw the lights of the Broadway theaters; the eight o'clock curtains had been raised, and the streets were empty.

"You won't show up tomorrow," she said finally. She'd found her rejoinder.

"I'll be there," I replied. "Don't nag."

But she was right to push; I knew she was right. I'd

blown off other meetings with the unbearably smug Elizabeth Harteveld, with her judgmental glares over gold bifocals, her forced equanimity, her faux compassion, nod, nod: "How awful for you." Harteveld manipulates, distorts, misinterprets. With a wave of her glittering Cross pen, from her green leather club chair, she dispenses opinions about things she cannot possibly know, and they are based on the faulty notion that people belong to one or another category, that there are a certain number of types, and behaviors are predictable and, thus, easily altered, or at least alterable. With me, she prattles. I learn nothing. I tend to myself.

But I concede this: Bella returns to me as if unburdened. There is an unmistakable lightness to her, and she brims with a kind of radiant optimism. She bounces. I think it's unnatural, because Bella has lived through what I have and there is no source of brightness there, I can assure Elizabeth Harteveld. But I don't think it's all bad and I am grateful that Bella responds. Perhaps it's nothing more than having the chance to talk with a woman the same age as her mother would be; or maybe Harteveld can enlighten a clever twelve-year-old. Maybe she can deceive her into optimism. But it's good for Bella to feel better, and it is a pleasure to see her smile.

But—and I should remind Elizabeth Harteveld, M.D., Ph.D., of this—the glow will vanish, and Bella will be faced with the hard truth: It is all different now. It is unalterably different, and there is no sense in believing it will ever be as good or that we will ever be as good. And as Bella realizes this she will cry and, as the tears roll down her face, she will go to bed in our empty house, and there will be no poetic lullabies whispered tenderly by her mother and she won't wake up to her baby brother's jabbering down the hall, and she won't pad into my study in her pajamas, Moose under her arm, and be lifted onto my lap to read what I've written in the cool, quiet hours as the rest of our family slept.

I resent Harteveld for letting Bella believe that this colorless facsimile of life is life as it was before. But I say nothing. I do what I am supposed to, I do as instructed. I am a willing participant in the deception of a sweet, intelligent twelve-year-old.

"Terry, I cannot seem to get a sense of you," she once commented.

"That's because there is no me," I told her. "Just a giant hole where I used to be. In the hole—some facts, a bit of attitude; a plan, maybe."

She leaned closer to me. "A sense of responsibility?"

Tenth had become Amsterdam at 57th, and Amsterdam crossed Broadway, and then there was the Beacon and the crowd milling under the old-fashioned marquee, filing into the former turn-of-the-century movie palace. From a van sponsored by a classic-rock station, a man handed out bumper stickers, pins and, to the very lucky, a painter's cap. As I slid a $10 bill through the small cup in the taxi's stained Plexiglas, Bella noticed Diddio amid the people in front of the liquor store next door to the entrance.

"Are you going to keep scowling, Bella?" I offered her my hand as she slid toward me to exit the taxi. She ignored it. "I think you should. I want Diddio to see you as I do."

"Nice try, Dad," she replied, and went into the night air toward Diddio. I watched her go. She liked him, wanted to take him in, like a straggly stray cat. "He has sad eyes," she once said.

"Hey, Gabby." Diddio greeted her with a hug. "Cool beret," he said. "You got all the other girls beat." I got a handshake and an unsteady gaze.

He put his hands on Bella's shoulders and steered her

into the slow shuffle toward the ticket takers inside the door.

He turned to me. "How's your friend? The one in the explosion."

"She's getting better and she's still too old for you," I groused.

"Too old? Mmm, I wonder how old that'd have to be. Like, eighty-nine?"

I leaned in to whisper. "You're stoned, aren't you?"

"Ssssh," he said, nodding toward Bella. "I just took the edge off. I got three shows tonight."

Bella grabbed Diddio's sleeve and gave it a harsh tug. "Remember me?" she smiled, oozing saccharin.

"I'll talk to you later," he said to me. "I've got to spend some time with my Gabby." He gently flattened the collar of her denim jacket. "Tell me a story, Gabba-Gabba-Hey."

As Bella basked in Diddio's attention, I looked around while we waited in the logjam under the marquee. Most of the crowd was at least a decade older than I am: men and women in ill-fitting jeans, ancient t-shirts and an odd assortment of short coats and baseball caps; bald spots and ponytails, and a few suits, with collars unbuttoned and ties hanging low. But not much hippie garb, as at the Allman Brothers shows here that Diddio dragged me to, at which young women not much older than Bella wore long, flowered skirts and danced in the aisles to the delight of tattooed teenaged boys from Brooklyn who wore Stars and Bars bandannas over shoulder-length hair. The conversation around us was oddly cerebral and technical, as if Yes fans were plucked from the mid-level executive ranks at Silicon Alley computer companies. The nostalgia was sweet, heightened: "I saw them at the Garden. Nineteen seventy-three. Topographic Oceans, man. Incredible." A breathless woman behind us said, "I seen Steve Howe with Asia. I never thought—I *never ever* thought—I'd get to see him with Yes." Her companion, equally enthused, replied, "And with the classic lineup. Wakeman, White. *Man*. Now it's a supergroup, like Blind Faith." A grump in front of us said, "I'd rather see Bruford than White." His wobbly associate, who had a pint of Yukon Jack tucked in the back of his jeans, said "It's *Yes*, man. Who gives a shit? Bruford, White. White, Bruford."

"Bruford," Diddio whispered to me. "Very muscular drummer. I can tolerate White, though. He played with Lennon and Harrison."

I thought of Rosenzweig. "Yoyo." The old prick knew what he was saying.

We inched forward, bumping into the people in front of us as we were bumped from behind. We were in the vestibule now, and when I inadvertently stepped off the worn industrial carpeting, my running shoes stuck to the terrazzo tiles. I said, "I don't know how you can do this every night."

"I think it's very cool," Bella said quickly, defending the stray cat.

"I'm chronicling the culture," Diddio said proudly.

As we passed into the cavernous lobby, with its high ceiling, ornate woodwork, faux gold leaf and crowded concession stands, the bottleneck in front of us started to widen as people went toward their seats. I noticed Bella had stopped to watch as a security guard located the Yukon Jack on the man in front of us. There was a tussle—the befuddled man groped for the bottle as it crossed in front of him, lost in the guard's tight grip. "Hey, man. That's mine," he managed, then added, with a drunkard's sincerity, "I brought it from home."

I reached out and put my hand on Bella's shoulder.

"Stay close," I cautioned.

The large, bearded guard easily held back the smaller man, who reached in vain for the half-empty pint.

"You sell drinks here, man, so what are you against? What do you think, I'm gonna throw the bottle? Shit, I wou—I wouldn't do that."

"You can pick it up after the show," the guard said sharply. He wore a vest, and his bare arms were thick and muscular. "Now, get moving."

The drunk would have none of that. "Ah, fuck you, you fuckin' Nazi."

"Bella—" I wrapped my arms around her.

The wobbling man swung and missed. The guard quickly squared himself, stepped in and brought a short right to the man's stomach. The drunk instantly dropped in a heap, then rolled into a fetal position, releasing a guttural moan.

The guard stepped back. He turned to the man's skinny friend, who stared at him with a combination of awe and fear. As the guard moved toward the boy, I stepped in.

"He doesn't want any of that."

"What are you, his fuckin' father?"

As he turned toward me, I said, "You made your point, big man. You don't need to take the next step."

He sneered. "That's my call," he said. But he didn't move.

Finally, the big man turned back to the other guy. "Drag your friend to his seat, or drag him outside. Get him out of my lobby."

"Yes, sir," the boy replied, compliant as a new buck private. Behind him, Yes t-shirts sold for $40.

We moved on, as the crowd gawked at the bright-red man on the floor, knees at his chin.

As we approached the sweeping stairs of the old theater, I asked, "You OK, Bella?" I brushed her hair with my fingertips.

She nodded hesitantly. She seemed more concerned than shaken. "He didn't have to hit him."

I said nothing. He had to hit him, but only him and only once. After that, it was sadism.

"Some times they overreact," Diddio said as we started upstairs. "I saw a teenage kid get his nose busted outside the Bottom Line. Blood everywhere. They thought he was crashing, but he had a ticket. A real mess." He added, "Lou Reed. Good show. Robert Quine. Fernando Saunders."

Bella had one hand around the dented copper rail, the other in mine.

I HAD ATTENDED enough shows with Diddio to know we'd leave before the first encore, and was grateful for the practice since Bella had nodded off during a ham-handed organ solo by the keyboard player, who had a greater infinity for bravado than Brahms. Before she fell to the temptation of sleep, her head on my chest, her beret tugged over her eyes, she enjoyed the spectacle, especially the mirror ball and the lava lamp–like blobs on the screen behind the drummer's enormous kit. The group played with bombast, and when the crowd sang along, Bella joined in; Diddio pointed out the other critics who preferred to sit downstairs, and she felt special, especially when I told her I hadn't seen anyone under 18 in the theater.

"What'd you think of the bass player?" Diddio asked me as we walked down the stairs, at eye level now with a violet cloud of lingering cigarette smoke.

"Tall."

"I mean, as a musician."

"I don't know a damn thing about it," I replied. My ears were ringing.

"He's the one I'm profiling for *Bass Guitar* magazine."

"Very cool," Bella said. She stifled a yawn.

As we crossed the lobby, a muffled version of the pounding music surrounding us, I noticed near the t-shirt stand the mountain-sized guard who'd flattened the drunk. Behind him, on a marble shelf, sat several bottles of cheap wine and the half-empty pint of Yukon Jack. With his bland expression—only the slightest hint of a frown—he seemed placid, supremely confident, as if he was completely content to do nothing other than stand watch over an enormous, almost-empty lobby. I imagined he had at least a hefty Swiss Army knife at the end of the thick chain that looped like a giant's fob from his belt into his vest.

"Terry, hold on a second," Diddio said. "Come over here, Gabba-Hey."

Diddio took Bella to the concession stand. I started to protest—I didn't want him spending money he didn't have—but I said nothing. Instead, I went outside, away from the smoke, the faint odor of human sweat, the garbled, booming sound, and into the fresh air and the relative quiet of the night.

And there was Sol Beck, pacing under the lights of the marquee, behind the blue wooden sawhorses set up by the police.

Hands thrust deep in the pockets of his black jeans, he was hunched, and he shook his head repeatedly. The up-turned collar of his black jacket covered the bottom of his ears. He was here to meet me, clearly, and yet when I said his name, he turned but didn't seem to recognize me.

He was ashen and agitated.

"It's Terry," I said.

He blinked, then seemed to snap to. "Terry," he repeated.

"What is it?"

He said flatly, softly, "Lin-Lin."

"What happened?"

"Someb— She's in the hospital. Somebody attacked her."

"Christ. Is she all right?"

"A concussion." He ran his thumb under his eye socket. "A broken bone, maybe." He touched his face above his top lip. "Her teeth."

He seemed to reel as he spoke, and he didn't seem to want to make eye contact, peering instead at my chest, my shoulder, the glass doors behind me, the soiled cement beneath us, his own black shoes.

But then he looked squarely into my eyes. "She said you would know who did it."

I shook my head. "I don't, Sol."

"Terry. She said it."

Now wasn't the time to tell him that his wife was wrong.

"Sol, come with me." I reached for him. "Let me take you where we can talk."

I went onto Broadway and flagged a cab. As it pulled into the wide space in front of the Beacon, Bella and Diddio came out. I silently explained—pointing with my thumb; extending my hands, palms out, easy, easy; gesturing with my head; bringing an index finger to my lips—as I let Beck enter the cab.

She kissed Diddio on the cheek. She thanked him for the Yes patch he'd bought her.

I called to her. As she approached, I bent over and whispered, "You recognize him?"

She nodded.

"I'll explain later. But everything's OK. Don't be worried."

She was tired, and she surrendered to my counsel. "OK, Dad."

I held open the door for her to slide in next to Beck, and nodded quickly to Diddio as I jumped in and slammed the door behind me just as the cab pulled out. Bella turned to watch Diddio grow small under the marquee, under the sullen sky.

The driver made a U-turn at 75th and we headed back downtown.

HE'D GOTTEN MY number from Judy, who'd suggested that I also might be found at the Tilt. After leaving the hospital—the same one in which Judy was recuperating—Beck had hurried to the bar. Mallard told him about the concert at the Beacon. Beck took the 1-train uptown and waited outside the theater, pacing, agitated, struggling to understand the rash of misfortune, the bleak cloud that seemed tethered overhead. I could have told him that there's nothing to understand, because there is no logic, and that fate is nothing but indifferent and thus enormously cruel. But in his case, the source of his misery was not merely fate, and it was knowable to some extent.

"YOU'RE GOING TO have to give it to me again," I said, as I returned to the kitchen table. Bella had called me, and I'd left Beck alone for a moment and gone upstairs. A good-night kiss was required, and I tugged Moose under her covers. "It isn't very dull, is it, Bella? Our life."

She gave me a weary smile. Exhausted, she was already more than half asleep. "'Night, Dad," she murmured as she snuggled in, turning her back to me.

Beck had his hands wrapped around a glass of Valpolicella I'd poured for him. I slid back into my seat and took a sip from a green-plastic bottle of water.

I wanted him to replay the tale. "You found her outside your building?"

He nodded as he stared at the rich red wine, fingering the stem of the glass. "I heard the doorbell but I thought she'd answer it. I forgot. I forgot she went out."

"Where'd she go?"

"We needed something." He frowned. "For dinner. We hadn't eaten."

"What time?"

"Around eight, eight-thirty."

"Was the bag there when you found her?"

"Yes," he said. "Well, no. It was up the block."

"Closer to Varick or Sixth?"

"Varick. There's a deli on Varick."

"Your side of the street?"

He nodded.

If she was coming from Sixth, a busy thoroughfare, people might've seen the attack. But Varick carried little foot traffic after dark. And there was the obscuring scaffolding set up for the repair work on the corner warehouse, and two wide driveways for Stricks near the end of the block. The construction crew and the warehouse employees entered and left the building via Varick. If they were still on duty at eight, which was unlikely, they probably didn't head to Sixth: The 1-train stopped right outside the warehouse.

I said, "It's a perfect place for a mugging. Unless somebody's out moving their car, and no one's doing that at eight o'clock."

He took another sip of the Italian red and returned the glass to the table. "They didn't take her money," he said finally.

"You're sure?"

"At the hospital, they gave me the change and the receipt. They were in her pocket."

"You have the receipt with you?"

He pulled it from his jeans pocket. "I didn't go back home."

I took the small, crumpled piece of paper. Lin-Lin had spent $8.21 on a variety of items. Her change was $1.79. The time of the transaction was 20:11, or 11 minutes after eight, and the date was today's. Those types of cash registers are either incredibly inaccurate, putting 35 days in a month or 27 hours in a day, if the receipt is at all legible, or they are fairly close to correct. Unless Lin-Lin chatted up the proprietor after the transaction, she was accosted just before 8:15.

"She took most of the change in quarters," Beck mentioned. "For the laundry."

Earlier, he had told me the extent of her injuries: a concussion, damage to the malar bone, stitches in her upper lip, two cracked teeth, a lot of bleeding, purple swelling. Apparently, according to the intern on duty in the emergency room, she'd been struck once on the left side of her face by an object. "Probably a baseball bat," Beck said, recounting what the intern had told him. The cop who questioned Beck agreed. He told him, "She's lucky they didn't leave her dead."

I asked, "What about her hand, her arm? Any damage?"

"No. Why?"

"She didn't see them coming. She didn't defend herself."

Now he took a long drink of the wine.

"Did you eat?"

He replied morosely, "I only had twenty-nine cents, after I bought the token."

I stood and went to the refrigerator, brought out an apple to the counter, quartered it, and put it on a plate with a chunk of Pecorino cheese. The bread from Zito's was in the freezer, so I dug out a pile of Carr's crackers. I put the small meal in front of Beck, with a paper napkin and a cheese knife.

I refilled the wineglass as I sat, as Beck lifted an apple slice and absently took a bite. I leaned back and waited for him to eat more. He cut a corner of the cheese, swallowed that and nibbled on a cracker. Then he looked at me. "Lin-Lin said you know who did this."

"I don't."

"But . . . She seemed certain."

"You ought to eat," I said, trying to postpone the inevitable.

He let out a sigh and he looked as if he would collapse under the weight of what was careening around his mind.

It was after midnight now, the rest of the house was dark and silent, and I could hear the ticking of the clock in the face of the old stove.

"Sol, Lin-Lin thinks your father put the bomb in Judy's gallery. I suppose she thinks he attacked her."

Beck grimaced in confusion and tilted his head. He blinked before looking at me.

"She told you this?"

I nodded, and told him about the conversation at the hospital, omitting the part where she said Beck had suspected him as well. "I told her I didn't think he did it."

"No? Why?"

I said, "Sol, do you think your father would try to disrupt your opening?"

"My father believes he doesn't have a son," Beck said, peering into the blackness.

I nodded again. "All right. So . . . ?"

Beck toyed with an apple slice. Finally, he said, "He

hates Lin-Lin." Then he added, "She would do anything for me, so . . . You know how it is."

I didn't reply.

"You talked to him?"

"Yes," I said.

"He's . . . very difficult."

"Sol, there's a huge gap between being an irascible old man and a bomber who may have assaulted your wife. Your father is bitter, but this vindictive? I can't believe that."

Beck shrugged.

"And I don't think he knows how to make a bomb like the one that exploded at Judy's, unless you can show me he learned to do it after he was discharged."

He said nothing.

"And you know he can't really do much with his left arm. So, no, I don't think he planted the bomb or attacked Lin-Lin."

"Maybe you made him angry." He said it without conviction, as if it had popped into his mind and then out of his mouth.

"Yeah, but what: He comes out tonight and assaults your wife? Come on, Sol. Your father spends his evenings at home with a friend, drinking jug wine, staring at the TV."

He nodded. "I know Sid."

"Actually, I think he's got a girlfriend."

"I'm not surprised," Beck replied. "He did when my mother was alive."

I kept still. I knew he would tell it.

And he did, softly, haltingly, but with surprising strength and conviction; and if not linearly, then with much detail, as if he had spent long, agonizing hours organizing his jagged memories, reliving painful moments to know which were worse than the others, what had led to what else, how he had gone from a bright, hopeful boy to an apprehensive and abstracted young man, perpetually in doubt, incapable of self-direction. I would have wagered that he didn't speak as many words in a month as he did when he told his tale. Maybe it was the wine on an empty stomach—or simply an outpouring in the aftermath of the adrenal rush from the evening's frightening excitement. Whatever the reason for his opening up to me, it was clear he knew what had made him the man he was today.

Rosenzweig, according to his only child, had not returned from the war with a sense of heroic accomplishment—or if he had, it did not ennoble him. He was arrogant, petty, intolerant, dictatorial, railing at every perceived injustice; a bully, especially with his wife and, eventually, their young son.

His rants served to confirm the low opinion that Beck and his mother had of themselves, an opinion introduced by Rosenzweig.

"We knew it was our fault that he didn't succeed."

"Succeed at what?"

"At things. At life," Beck said, shrugging. "If my mother had been as supportive as that one, or clever as that one...She was quiet by nature; shy, really. The things he said..." He paused, searching. "They affected her." He reached for the wineglass and took another long, deliberate drink.

"And you?"

"And me, I was nothing. A stain. I was never going to be a man."

He returned the empty glass to the table, and I prodded him for pleasant memories, recollections of special occasions.

"You mean, like vacations? A nice trip to the Poconos, maybe? Atlantic City?"

"Sure."

"In the summer, my mother and I took the subway to Coney Island." With a cheerless snicker, he added, "My mother got an iron for her birthday."

"A tool."

Beck said, "He knew what he was doing."

He could afford more, Beck added. Rosenzweig made a decent living, first handling odd jobs, then joining the International Brotherhood of Electrical Workers, where he was hired on for a number of large-scale projects in lower Manhattan in the '60s and '70s, including the construction of the World Trade Center. There was money for nights at Monahan's, the local gin mill: Schaefer on tap, Bushmill's on the side, Sinatra on the jukebox, Phil Rizzuto and the Yankees on TV; a modest indulgence, in some contexts, but not to Beck. And Rosenzweig liked the ponies, a more costly pastime: Aqueduct, Roosevelt, Monmouth Park; the neighborhood bookie, a trip over to OTB.

"Meanwhile, he had an angel at home."

"Your mom."

"That's right."

Then he went on, describing the heart-numbing routine of his youth. His lean face betrayed the pain of his memories: He grimaced, squinted, pursed his lips, sealed his eyes as they became red and moist. Across from me, a man was a boy again, flinching in fear, scowling in anger.

In time, the father turned on the son.

Beck's mother stood by her child, defending him always, however meekly, which led to Rosenzweig calling him "a *schmo,* a mama's boy, a little *faygeleh.*"

Beck said now, "That got to me. I don't know why. I should've been used to his insults." The son considered that maybe it was so: He was a loner, quiet. And growing into his teens, he didn't share with the other boys their obsession with the girls from St. Theresa's in their hiked plaid skirts and blouses that seemed ready to burst at the chest; dimples gone from their knees, their necks suddenly inviting, if not to him. Confused, perhaps granting some authority to his father's invective, he withdrew from his mother's affections, preferring instead his solitary pursuits, particularly drawing, charcoal on coarse paper, simple wax crayons on notepads. His mother, alone now, withdrew from everything.

"She'd stand on the fire escape, staring at the Hudson, at Jersey, at the rest of America like she wished she could fly away and be free."

"You lived on Worth then?" I asked.

"Yes. How—"

"'D. Rich Co.,'" I replied, citing the one work I'd studied at his opening. "Is that woman in the painting your mother?"

"In spirit," he said, "but she was small, too fragile."

"So, what happened next? Your father lost his work? His injury began to act up?"

"He was fired," Beck said. His face was red from storytelling, from too much wine. "It had to happen someday."

Chick Rosenzweig had managed the rare feat of getting canned from a cushy union job in New York City. According to Beck, he was on a crew wiring an office building down near Wall Street when he kicked over a bucket of cold rivets that'd been left behind. They dropped 35 floors like deadly rain and landed on a new, black Cadillac that belonged to an upstairs guy from the Teamsters who was checking on his drivers. "I knew he was drunk when he told us he wasn't," Beck added.

Today, a guy like Rosenzweig might wind up in a rehab center, and his outlook might change and maybe his family would survive. But, back then, they probably picked him up and threw him off the site, flinging his lunchbox at him as he hit the pavement. Given that he damaged a Teamster's new Caddy, he's lucky they didn't break his elbows.

"The union got him some sort of severance," Beck said, "but he went through that. We couldn't afford the rent and had to move from Worth: My mother was humiliated, I guess; no, she was, for certain. All her friends lived there. She used to sit on the stoop and listen to the neighbors *kvetching*.

"That's how he ended up in the basement on Grove Street," he continued. "He got a job as the janitor in that building and the one next door. He did some odd jobs too, until his shoulder started acting up. Home all day, he was even more unbearable."

"And your mother?" I asked. Then I stopped, deciding to come at it another way. "Anyone would crack under that kind of abuse."

"People don't crack, Terry," Beck said. "They lose their spirit, their— You're a writer; what's the word? Their *essence*. They fade away, like my mother faded away. Can you give yourself cancer? Can you will it to come and take you?"

"I don't know, Sol."

"I do. The answer is yes."

"You left when she died?"

"No, I was out of there long before that, in school in Rhode Island. I came back to help her die. You know, the bastard found reason to criticize me over that, too."

Meanwhile, Beck said, Rosenzweig just walked away from his dying wife, hiding in Monahan's, drinking his beer, chasing women, betting his VA check on slow horses.

"You took your mother's name."

"It drove him nuts. My one act of defiance."

He chuckled. Then he shook his head and drained the

wineglass. "My father thought he was the smartest man in the world," he said, "and he was too stupid to hold on to the one thing that matters."

And with that Sol Beck ended his tale, and he instantly withdrew, falling into himself. Something had shaken him, something he hadn't considered before. In the sudden silence, I knew exactly what he was thinking. I'd been listening; there was only one place his thoughts could go.

"Terry, I don't know what I'd do if I lost Lin-Lin," he said. "I don't have anybody else. No one."

He wiped his eyes. He looked at his damp thumb and forefinger.

I suggested he call the hospital. To give him privacy, I walked him back to my study, snapped on the desk lamp and showed him to the phone. I slid the envelope from Sharon Knight into a drawer and pulled the top sheet off the legal pad on the desk, crumpling the doodles. Then I retreated to the living room and dropped onto the sofa. As I reached for the table lamp, I remembered I hadn't yet changed the broken bulb. I sat in darkness, my head against the back cushion.

A minute later, I heard Beck drop the handset onto the receiver. He cut the light and came to me.

"She's better. Stable," he said.

I rose and tapped him on the arm. "That's good news, Sol."

"She might come home Saturday."

He followed me into the kitchen. I looked at the clock. It was past two.

"Maybe it's better if you stay here," I offered.

He shook his head. "I want to go home."

"It's not going to be easy to get a cab." I dug into my pocket. "Go over by the Sporting Club on Hudson, or up by the TriBeCa Grill." I handed him the $40 I had on me.

I led him to the front door. Greenwich Street was quiet in the long, soft shadows cast by the streetlights. In another two hours, delivery trucks would be grinding along the battered cobblestone, and after that, yet another day.

He said, "Thanks, Terry."

As he went down the front steps, I said, "Sol, your father didn't plant that bomb."

He didn't reply.

"You ought to think about who did. Maybe that'll tell us who attacked your wife tonight."

He nodded and walked off down the dark, silent street.

SEVEN

I WORKED ON THE heavy bag, banging away hard and fast until my wrists were as sore as my knuckles under the Everlast bag gloves. Afterward, as I soaked my hands in ice in the kitchen sink, I finished the Conrad. I showered, and then just puttered around for the rest of a wet Friday morning. Finally I got dressed and went out the door. The rain, which had been more of a mist, let up. I threw my baseball cap back inside and redid the security code.

An hour later, I set up on the corner of 125th and Amsterdam and waited. A crosstown wind barreled along the wide street, and I buried my hands in my leather jacket. The only white man in view, I imagined I was as conspicuous as I could be, yet the old women who passed by, pushing their empty shopping baskets toward the market, and the young mothers who chased their laughing children toward the park at the brick projects all ignored me.

As I watched one child in a heavy, oversized coat waddle ahead of his mother, I thought of Bella. She awoke bright-eyed and full of enthusiasm. She sang in the shower. She'd been to a genuine rock show, and her friends would envy her. So there.

"I went to the Beacon with Diddio," she hummed, as she finished the crunchy yogurt-and–Grape Nuts combination she liked. "Everybody wishes they knew Diddio like I do."

In the past year or so, we'd seen Patti Smith window-shopping at American Leather, Billy Corgan sharing lobster tartine with Jonathan Demme at Sanzin, and, of course, Ron Wood at Judy's. Several rock stars had shot their videos near here: Cock Michaels, up the block on Vestry; Eagle-Eye Cherry at the Independence School; and Ben Harper in the funky alley off Hubert known as Collister Street. (I suppose that's who they were; Bella said so.) But, since Bella knew him, liked him, and knew he cared for her, in her mind Diddio was as big as the acts he covered.

"And I'm going to tell Little Mango all about Beck and his wife. He won't know about that." She wiped her mouth on the dishrag and tossed it toward the sink. It landed on the floor. "Whoops. Sorry."

"I'll get it. Go, get your backpack. And wear a hat. It's raining."

She returned with her heavy pack, wearing her bean-bag, Yes patch pinned to its floppy front above the narrow brim. She caught me staring at the uneven patch. "I'll sew it later." She stopped. "*After* we get back from Dr. Harteveld's."

I slipped into a hooded sweatshirt. "Is that today?"

"Dad—"

"I'm only kidding. Yes, today. Three o'clock. Sixty-second and First. And, Bella, be discreet with Mango, okay? Stick to the facts."

As she wriggled into her denim jacket, she said, "I need money for the cab."

I handed her the folded $10 bill I stored in my wallet. We both knew the drill: Always immediately reimburse Mrs. Maoli when she puts out money for us.

"Now I'm broke," I said as we went outside.

"There's $140 in the trunk of my Barbie car. You can borrow it." She walked on, crossing Harrison. As I caught up, she added, "At prime, I mean. I expect to find, let's see, $154 when I get home tonight."

"Is that with the vig?"

We stepped into the gray light on Greenwich, and passed a bald man in a brown suit struggling to tie his Welsh corgi's red leash to a parking-meter post. Up ahead, the uniformed driver of a boxy bread truck delivered a plastic pallet filled with English muffins to Gristede's, and two Koreans hustled fresh vegetables into a restaurant on the east side of the street. Uptown, on Sixth, Fifth or Madison, at this time of the morning they were packed shoulder-to-shoulder; down here, fewer than six people could be seen on a broad city block of weather-beaten asphalt and cement.

"You need money to make money," Bella said. "My $140 isn't so bad, since I started with the $50 I won in the American-Italian Society essay competition."

"Yes, 'Travels of Donatello.' For an eight-year-old, that was quality work."

"As opposed to my essay on Paine? Thanks, Dad. Really."

"Your essay on Paine is very good now."

"'Now,'" she muttered under her breath.

I CAME BACK to the present when I saw him. He headed east and I crossed 125th to catch up.

When he was about to reach the Popeye's near the corner, I called his name. He turned and seemed surprised to see me.

I pulled my hands from my pockets and held up open palms. He wasn't wearing the Beretta, but he still had the nightstick on his belt.

Reynolds's clean-shaven head shone in the dull light.

"She tell you why I came?" I asked.

The security guard said no.

"I'm working," I said as I drew closer. "Aubrey Brown. The cabdriver who was killed."

It didn't register, but I could see he was curious. He hadn't entirely let down his guard, but he was ready to listen.

I stopped near him and I told him about Brown. "You had a student with a scar."

"Montana," Reynolds said.

I nodded.

"What about him?"

A blue-and-white patrol car rolled by, heading coolly toward Hamilton Heights. Neither cop gave us much of a look.

"He's been following the body."

"Don't mean much," he said with a shrug.

A crisp breeze snuck up from behind. "You kill a stranger you don't go to the funeral."

He shifted, then said, "All right."

"But I doubt he knew Brown," I said. "If he was checking it out for somebody else, who would that be?" I asked.

He thought for a moment. "Big city."

"No doubt." A Postal Service truck passed us. I turned to see it stop in front of Hurston Elementary. "You don't have to spend your lunch hour on it," I added.

"I'll think about it."

"Fair enough." I handed him my card. He stuck it in the breast pocket of his blue shirt.

IN MID-OCTOBER, there is a certain clash of monochrome and brilliant color to Fifth Avenue high on the Upper East Side. Many of the once-green leaves of the robust trees that stretch over the avenue have turned from astonishing yellows and reds to a musty brown, but they're still thick enough to prevent the bleached mid-autumn sun from arriving unfiltered. Endless rows of sturdy apartment buildings on the east side of the avenue seem taciturn and miserly as they refuse to surrender the dying light. On the street, buses plod along, wheezing, straining almost, spewing gray fumes with little enthusiasm. On the west side, behind the stone wall, Central Park is quiet: Children are back in school; sunbathers have completed their summer-long ritual and stashed away their lawn chairs for the winter, leaving the vast expanses of grass empty and silent; the men and women who walk under the withering leaves seem old, tired, without destinations, and there is a shallow look to their eyes, as if they know what it means when something is gone.

I entered the Guggenheim a little before two o'clock. As I started the long walk up Frank Lloyd Wright's spiral, I remembered how Bella had once decided to see if Davy's stroller would roll all the way down to the lobby from up near the glass dome if she positioned it *just* right, if she let it go at the right moment. Something to do with gravity and motion: She figured Davy and his bottles and sundries, packed in a woven basket hung between the handles, would give the stroller the extra weight it needed to stay grounded as it raced down the corkscrew; the subtle slope from the concrete walls, she deduced, would keep the stroller from flying over the edge. "Hey, Dad. Watch this." Scurrying, I grabbed the stroller's curved handle. I told her, "You know, Bella, maybe it's not such a good idea to let your baby brother, you know, go zooming all the way down there. It's a little too far, don't you think?" Wright's "constant ramp," if unwound, would extend for several hundred yards.

She considered this. "OK," she said finally. "Put me in the stroller and let me try it."

Now, I made my way through the tranquil galleries, spending extra moments with several favorites: de Kooning and Pollock, feeling their sense of action; with the dichotomy of Beckman's "Paris Society"—that couple in the forefront on the right, so despondent, so disconnected—with Seurat's peasants; with Delaunay's and Chagall's modulating views of the Eiffel Tower; and I avoided Modigliani's reclining women: too sensuous, too real, too familiar, with their languid poses, inviting softness, tufts of dark hair, tranquil faces, overwhelming beauty. I spent a minute or so under Calder's "Red Lily Pads"; I'm certain the mobile caught Davy's infant eyes. He was sighing in delight, gurgling, his eyes darting in innocent curiosity; I'm sure he was studying it from his stroller as it wafted above him.

The stroller Weisz grabbed and flung onto the tracks, my son strapped to its soft seat. What did my Davy see then? In the last seconds of his young life, how much did he understand?

I placate myself, as I have placated Bella, with the thought that he was too young to understand any part of it.

I shook my head, took a breath and moved from Brancusi's exquisite sculptures to what I call industrial mess. Assemblage is what the curators and critics call it, or, more accurately, Junk Art: a twisted collection of automobile parts, a battered typesetting machine; a platinum Star of David with a ball and rails like a child's puzzle, wood glued awkwardly to wires, terra cotta flung against a wall, puffy vinyl, chromium rods. To read the Guggenheim's catalogue is to confront an exercise in justification. Normally, I pass, particularly when so much challenging brilliance is nearby.

But I was drawn by the memory of one work, perhaps the best-known one-off to come out of the downtown scene of the early '80s. Vlad Smith's "Angel/Angle" was essentially a polished-aluminum box, about five feet on all sides, crudely welded, with a suggestive slit torn in its top, with rough shards of metal seemingly reaching for freedom. I'd heard the piece compared to everything from David Smith's welded sculptures to Georgia O'Keeffe's plates. Sexual cubism, Vlad Smith called it. And it was acquired by an enthusiastic collector (for a phenomenal sum, I suppose), then donated to the Guggenheim, which displayed it alongside Chamberlain and Beuys and, sadly, not very far from Brancusi and Noguchi.

But Smith, who went by the street name Bullethead, never came close to producing a work comparable to "Angel/Angle," which, it turned out, was the result of a minor accident. No visionary, but wise to the ways of the scene in the '80s, Smith had merely set out to blow up the cube and to sell the remnants. Smithereens, he was going to call the little pieces. When he set the explosive charge, he had no idea that he would create the cube's vaginalike aperture or the concurrent fingerlike shards that stretched from the abrupt opening. According to a piece I'd read in AbEx magazine, Smith had spent the next few years blowing up aluminum cubes, trying in vain to replicate "Angel/Angle," selling a few fragments here and there, converting the profits into powdered cocaine and ramming it up his nose. Of all the frauds that were exposed as the '80s faded into history, Bullethead might've been the biggest. If memory served, a particularly scalding brand of arrogance and obnoxiousness made him perhaps the most satisfying flop of the decade.

As I looked at the piece, alone in the white-walled gallery, I wondered where Bullethead was today. And, if he was still downtown, I wondered if he ever learned how to use explosives. I chuckled as I imagined him demonstrating his artistic skills to a gaggle of fawning devotees, who, hoping to bid early on the next "Angel/Angle," crouched behind heavy Plexiglas shields as he "created" his next masterpiece. And I imagined their silence as the aluminum box either did not burst in such a way as to create a sensual or suggestive shape; or it exploded into— Christ—Smithereens.

A short woman about my age in blue overalls, a raspberry t-shirt, scuffed Birkenstocks and raspberry socks tiptoed in reverentially and joined me at the sculpture. She stood on her toes to better examine the opening. After several seconds of teetering and nodding, she turned to me.

"It's something, isn't it?" she said in admiration.

"Well, it is something," I replied flatly.

"You can never tell when genius will strike," she said.

"No," I said, "and someday it might."

She smiled, as if I'd agreed with her. "I can't get enough of it," she said. "It says everything about the power of liberation."

She was still smiling, still studying the cube, when I left the room.

I ARRIVED AT Harteveld's building about 25 minutes after the hour, girded myself as best as I could, and took the elevator down to her basement office. When I entered the cramped waiting room, Bella was entertaining John, Harteveld's assistant and office manager, who was at his station behind a white, waist-high counter. I couldn't be sure what they had been talking about since as soon as I stepped into the room, John, who had been smiling broadly, gestured with his head; Bella turned and they were both immediately silent. Rail-thin, effeminate John, whom I'd never seen outside his crisp lab coat, looked at me and nodded curtly. I was certain he didn't approve of me, and if the relationship between psychiatrist and assistant was anything like boss and secretary, it was because Harteveld told him she didn't approve of me or how I was raising my daughter. I was certain of that.

"Mr. Orr, good afternoon," John muttered dourly. "I'll tell Dr. Harteveld you're finally here."

He frowned as he picked up the handset.

As Bella came toward me, I noticed on the table, near a collection of outdated magazines, one of her marble notebooks, the latest chapter of "My Personal Archive." In addition to her notes, clippings and drawings on the explosion at Judy's, it likely contained her thoughts on Diddio and the Yes concert and the ride uptown with Sol, and maybe there was something in there about me and how I'd been sharp with her over her Paine essay or how I still walk her to school. Or how I won't let her get a tattoo—"Francine's mother said *she* can get one"—and how I don't want to see Harteveld and "get better again, like before." How I will never write again.

"You're late," she said. "You're always late."

"I'm not late. I thought you'd still be in with Dr. Harteveld."

"I don't have an appointment today. *You* have an appointment today."

"I guess I didn't understand," I replied meekly, as I reached into my back pocket and withdrew a postcard I picked up at the Guggenheim. "Peace offering."

She looked at it. "Braque," she said, reading the legend on back. "'Violin and Palette.'" She turned it over and glanced at the detail. "Very fourth-dimension."

"Put it in your journal," I said gesturing with my hand.

As if to prevent me from grabbing it, she reached for the book and clutched it tightly.

I was going to remind her that many times she had left the notebook out in plain sight and that I'd never even sneaked a glimpse. Instead, I asked, "Where's Mrs. Maoli?"

"She's in the ladies' room. She wants to go home."

"All right," I said, "send her home. I'll go see Dr. Harteveld." I started toward the desk, toward John, then stopped. "Did you repay her for the cab?"

She looked at me sternly, with wide eyes. Apparently, I am a stupid man.

"You may go in," John added.

I went down the white corridor.

ELIZABETH HARTEVELD HAD the requisite couch, a green leather one, and matching green leather club chairs that sat not quite facing each other in front of her large rosewood desk. She didn't require her patients to lie on the sofa. Instead, she usually came from behind the desk and took her place in one uncomfortable green chair while the patient sat in the other.

She shook my hand at the door and let me pass. As I stepped on her red-and-cream Persian rug on the parquet floor, I saw that nothing had changed in the office since my last visit nearly a month ago: A small microphone sat near the potted plant on the end table between the couch and her desk. I once wondered aloud how the plants managed to look so healthful in a room without windows.

Harteveld smiled, but didn't reply. I assumed she simply replaced them when they started to yellow and sag. When something is merely of a kind, it is easily replaced.

Her diplomas, riddled with calligraphy and Latin, were hung on the wall facing her patients. She had a computer monitor on the credenza behind the desk, but it was turned off. Soft, formless music came from somewhere. Shutting the door, she went to her desk to retrieve a pale-blue file. She invited me to sit. As I did, the music stopped.

"Does the chair trigger the recorder?" I asked.

"No. There's a foot pedal under my desk, actually," she said. "The music stops when the recorder is turned on."

"I see." She was more forthcoming than usual.

She adjusted her lab coat as she sat, and she slid on her gold-framed bifocals. With her Cross pen, she began jotting a few notes onto a sheet of paper inside the file folder.

I studied her as she wrote. I guessed she was about 10 years older than I was. Her dark-brown hair was swept back from her long face and held in a small, practical bun by a gold clip. I had to admit that she was an attractive woman, lean and fit, with well-defined features: a thin nose, dark eyes, a pleasant mouth. She didn't wear a wedding ring, but I knew she was married: Once she slipped and told Bella something about her two sons, ages 17 and 20. Bella told me she asked Harteveld if her sons liked having a psychiatrist for a mother and she replied that her husband was one as well. Bella said, "Everybody must be pretty careful about what they say at breakfast."

With me, Harteveld did not reveal as much. On the assumption that her practice was sound and lucrative, I once asked her why she kept a small office in a basement of an apartment building off First Avenue. Her response:

"Does it matter to you where we are now, Mr. Orr?"

Today, as she closed the blue file, she began with the basics: "How have you been, Mr. Orr?"

"I'm fine, Doctor. How are you?"

"I believe we said that you would call me Elizabeth." She smiled her professional smile.

"Only if you called me Terry."

She nodded agreeably. "It has been a while, Terry."

"Yes, but I remember the rules."

"I understand you had a little excitement this week."

I knew what she meant. "I wouldn't call seeing Yes exciting, but I suppose art is subjective."

She smiled again. "Tell me about returning to the Henley Harper Gallery."

"I didn't know it was going to explode."

"Of course not. I'm just curious as to why you decided to visit the place where your wife's work was presented."

"I didn't decide. Bella did. And Marina's work was never shown at that gallery. Judy had a place on West Broadway back then." That was before West Broadway in SoHo began to resemble an upscale strip mall in Paramus.

"Bella said—"

"No, no, no, Doctor," I cautioned. "Remember the rules."

Now only I called my daughter Bella. Marina had preferred the full, formal Gabriella, the name she'd chosen. But when Davy, then a little more than a year old, tried to pronounce his sister's name, it came out "Bella." Which was perfect; Marina turned and told me Davy had just called his sister "beautiful" in Italian.

"My apologies," Harteveld offered. "*Gabriella* said she enjoyed herself until the disturbance. Would you mind telling me what happened?"

"Somebody said there was a bomb and there was a bomb."

"Did you feel you were in danger?"

I shrugged. "It's almost always a prank."

"And did you feel Gabriella was in danger?" she asked.

"I got her out of there in record time."

"But you hit someone. Someone who you thought threatened her."

"Someone who hit her. Do you know a father who wouldn't defend his daughter when that happens?" I asked, rhetorically. "If you do, get him in this chair."

"I understand," she said calmly. "So you perceived that she was in danger but that you weren't?"

I thought for a moment. "Yes."

She made a note in the folder. "I think we've agreed that you enjoy a sense of danger."

"I don't remember agreeing to that."

"You've said that one of the things that interests you about being a private detective is that there is a sense of danger."

"No, I didn't."

I've never told Harteveld why I'd become a P.I. The reason ought to be clear to anyone, especially a psychiatrist. But if I confirm what she ought to know, she will never help me understand the madman Weisz.

I hope no one thinks I come here for any other reason than that.

"I said," I told her, "that I thought it might get the adrenaline going. And for the record, I'm not a private detective. I don't detect: magnifying glass, litmus paper, no. I investigate, and mostly by reading briefs and digging out files at the County Clerk's office. And I do it for myself, though I don't mind helping the D.A. with a little legwork, if I can. But if you think reading through a bunch of Blumberg forms is dangerous..." I let it go.

"The adrenaline. Yes, as when you were playing basketball."

"Yep."

"Do you think you will be able to replicate that feeling as a private de—investigator?"

"You're fishing. The work is interesting sometimes. Maybe even rewarding, when I'm reading a brief and I suddenly understand what's really going on. But an adrenaline rush? No."

"I understand you are investigating the bombing at the gallery, Terry," she pressed. "Does that give you the rush you like?"

"No," I said.

"And what about the murder investigation? Is it safe to say that it gives you a physical sensation that you miss?"

Christ, what else did Bella tell her? "No."

"Will you elaborate, please?"

I shook my head. "I'm looking into the bombing because my wife's friend was injured. The murder is about curiosity, nothing more."

She looked into the blue folder. "May I try something with you, Terry?"

"Why not?" I shifted in the soft chair.

"Are you still resistant to the idea that you pursue these activities to seek a form of absolution as a reaction to the murder of your wife and son?"

"Ah, Bella's Batman theory. Again."

"You must concede that it's possible you want to atone for not being able to protect your family."

"What I do now cannot undo that."

"No, I understand, Terry—"

"Sixteen years in Catholic schools taught me all I need to know about the inadequacies of the sin/penance/absolution myth. Elizabeth."

She permitted herself a small smile. "Yes, of course, but surely it is more than that. Anyone in your situation—"

"Ah!" I exclaimed, snapping my fingers at her. "My 'situation.' It is not a *situation,* Elizabeth. It is not temporary."

"Of course not. What I'm suggesting, though, is that perhaps if there is a better understanding of your behavior..."

"My 'behavior.'"

"...you might address your circumstances, shall we say, in a more productive manner."

"Maybe. Maybe not."

She waited.

"Your turn," I said finally.

"Is there a more productive way, a more linear way, do you think?"

I uncrossed my legs. "I don't know. I'm just living. That's all. Just living."

"You have these thoughts of what you could have done—"

"I wasn't there," I said sharply. "I was somewhere else. Remember? Remember?"

"Yes, Terry, and what began as a typical day suddenly, inexplicably..."

I should have been there. I could've stopped Weisz, or I could've gotten Davy back on the platform before the train barreled through. Marina would never have had to jump down after him, groping, stumbling as she frantically reacted. I know I should have been there. Christ, I know.

"And I do agree, Terry, it is not temporary. But how you...how you proceed toward recovery— Terry, are you all right?"

I felt a constricting tightness across my chest and my head suddenly felt as if it might burst.

"Terry?"

I bent at the waist and put my head in my hands. "I'm fine."

"Are you certain?"

"I'm—I know me," I said as I stared at her.

"It's difficult, I know. But this, I think, is something worth discussing. This concept of atonement—"

"Look, I've told you why I'm doing what I'm doing." I sat back.

"Yes, I know you have. But might I suggest that thinking of what you do as a prelude to revenge—"

"I've never said that," I snapped.

"The real issue for you, I think, isn't revenge, but vindication. And this is quite legitimate. It is how we give meaning to our lives after profound, personal trauma."

"Elizabeth, why the hell do you always insist there's something more to it? Christ. 'Atonement.' 'Vindication.' It's bullshit!"

"You are shouting, Terry."

"Yes. I am."

"You are annoyed," she said. "Are you annoyed with me or—"

"Elizabeth, that question answers itself whenever it's posed."

She slid her gold pen into her top pocket, paused, then stood, adjusting her starched lab coat. She asked, "Would you like something to drink?"

A time-out. Which meant she was annoyed with me as well. Good; emotion from the icy inquisitor. "A drink would be nice," I muttered.

"You prefer sparkling water." She pushed a button on the black telephone and requested the water. John entered a moment later with a large bottle of Pellegrino, which is what Harteveld always served to me. I wondered if she chose a water from Italy for a reason.

As John left, she filled the two glasses. I lifted mine and, as she sat across from me, I said dryly, "Cheers." No longer cornered, I'd begun to catch my breath.

She smiled and did not lift her glass of bubbling water.

I took a long drink as she slid on her glasses to review her notes. Since she was ignoring me, I stood and walked to the deep-green brocade curtain covering the long white wall that faced her desk. There were many things that I couldn't stand about this room, and one of them was this pointless curtain. Well, not pointless: Its point was to conceal by suggesting something else. To suggest that something rare or extraordinary might lie behind it, something distinct; a view, perhaps, or the mysterious: a secret passageway, a two-way mirror, a wall safe. But because I'd peeked behind the curtain, I knew what lay behind it: nothing. A long, simple, white wall, and nothing more, from ceiling to parquet. When I see the curtain—a very attractive curtain, to be fair; well-kept, hung just so—I ask myself, Why? What does it conceal? That the white wall is bare; is that worth concealing? The existence of the curtain, in fact, reveals rather than conceals. It reveals that it is concealing nothing more than a blank wall. I refuse to give it meaning. It's a curtain in front of empty space.

Christ, I hate this place. It couldn't be smaller, stuffier, more repressing. This fuckin' curtain. The low ceiling. Supernatural plants. The Persian rug. This woman, prodding, probing, accusing, trapping. Here, where complex thoughts and actions are reduced to a line in an index of behaviors. People reduced to archetypes. People compelled to confront thoughts they were wise to have hidden.

And that lab coat. What an affectation.

"Terry? Shall we continue?"

I turned.

"You seem lost in thought."

"Yeah, I was thinking of something." I gestured toward the curtain "A view: light shimmering on the East River; a lone, lazy sailboat. And in the distance, the broad spires of the Brooklyn Bridge and, as if in a work by Monet, the Verrazano, an apparition, mist."

"Poetic," she nodded.

"I saw that from an office on the 53rd floor, at 49th and Park. A woman hired me to look after her father. Turned out she wanted me to testify that he was incapable of overseeing the foundation he ran. She wanted his job."

She removed her bifocals and let them dangle on the gold chain.

I added, "Some people just can't be straight with you, can they?"

She frowned with interest. "I'd like to see you run with that, Terry."

"No, I don't think so."

"You feel you are being deceived."

"Not by the world at large," I replied. "But every once in a while..."

She waited, but when I said nothing more, she abruptly changed the subject. A familiar tactic. "Terry, what would you say if I suggested that your new vocation is merely a hobby?"

"I wouldn't be offended. Maybe it is, maybe not. If you do something without regard for the money, maybe that's what it is: a hobby." I added, "By the way, you've used the word 'hobby' when you talk about me with Bella. Not nice. Counterproductive."

She crossed her legs and asked, "Do you feel it necessary to continue to focus so intensely on your hobby, Terry?"

I returned to the chair across from her and slid the water glass onto an end table, near the microphone. "How intensely, Doctor? Let's be direct."

"I don't understand."

"You're implying I neglect Bella. You're suggesting that I'm focusing so intensely on my hobby that I'm ignoring my daughter."

"Am I? Are you?"

"No," I said bitterly, shaking my head. "That's ridiculous."

"I know you love her, Terry. That is beyond dispute."

"Well, thanks for that," I mumbled.

"But is there some ambivalence?"

"None."

"Define her role in your life."

"She's my daughter. Simple."

"Would you agree that she is dependent on you?"

"Yes. That's the problem."

She reapplied her bifocals and circled something in the blue file. "Continue, please," she said.

"'Problem' is the wrong word. 'Challenge' is better, more accurate. The challenge is to help her become independent."

"Terry, a comment, not a criticism: She is twelve years old. She cannot be independent at twelve."

"I agree. I'm preparing her for independence."

"That's admirable. But it is inappropriate. She is thoroughly dependent on you."

"That's unfortunate," I said.

"Why?"

Because she is better than me, I thought. My influence can't help her.

"Terry?"

"Well, for one, a parent can die suddenly."

"Actually, it is unusual when a parent dies suddenly, Terry."

"Not for Bella."

"The idea that the surviving parent may die is terrifying to a child."

I nodded.

"As it is for your daughter."

"Nothing's going to happen to me."

"You are seeking danger, Terry," she said, "and it's my belief that you will continue to seek it."

I repeated, "Nothing's going to happen to me."

She leaned forward. "It is more likely that something will now than it was before. You must agree with that. There certainly wasn't much danger when you were writing."

"All right. I'll give you that. When I was sitting at my desk I was safe. Now, to hone a craft, to help some people I don't mind, I go to a basement on Centre Street and pore over docket sheets and books of court minutes. Very dangerous."

She reached for her water glass and took a small sip.

"Terry, do you know who Mordecai Foxx is?"

"Is this a trick?" I asked. "I know Bella's teachers. She'd tell you I know them too well."

That smile again; practiced, insincere. "Are you still calling the school every day?"

I paused, remembering that I'd once admitted to calling the principal's office at the Montessori School daily to make sure Bella was safe. "No. I stopped."

"Mordecai Foxx? The name means nothing to you."

"No."

She looked at her notes. "According to Gabriella, Foxx was a private detective who was employed by Samuel Jones Tilden in his crusade against Boss Tweed and Tammany Hall."

"Really?"

She nodded. "Your daughter has been spending her

days in the school library researching Foxx. She told her teachers she was helping you with a new book. The librarian, Mrs.—"

"Gottschalk," I said.

"—has been helping her. Apparently, your daughter is a dogged researcher, Terry."

"Apparently." Secretive, too.

"Were you? Are you? I assume so."

"History is research," I said blandly.

"Will you encourage her, Terry?"

"To continue?" I thought for a moment. "I'll tell her that I appreciate it, but that I'm not going to write about Foxx or about anybody. I'm not a writer. Not now."

"She wants to help you."

"That I understand." But it can't be the way it was. There is something I must do.

"She believes that you need her."

I said, "That's also unfortunate."

"'Unfortunate.' Why?"

"A child shouldn't bear such a burden."

"I see."

"If I fail, she will feel she's failed. That's obvious."

She drew a line under something in the blue file. "You say 'fail.' Fail at what, precisely?"

I wagged a finger at her. "It's unreasonable to ask someone to predict their own failure." I took a long drink of the Pellegrino. "Parents shouldn't disappoint. Let's leave it at that."

She said nothing.

"But, I'll add this," I said. "Not that I give a shit what anybody thinks, Doctor. But I am reliable. I'll be there."

"Terry, is that enough? To be there?"

I frowned as I leaned forward. "That's pretty fundamental. A good starting point."

"Or the minimum," she said quickly. "You deny yourself your greatest pleasure—writing. You put yourself in physical danger. I suggest you are punishing yourself. You are trying to reduce your life to mere existence."

I waved my hand in disgust as I sat back.

"But there is a contradiction. You have your friends, Terry. And your interests: basketball, art, books, fitness—"

I interrupted, "Look, I came to talk about Bella, not me."

"Is there a contradiction between your work as an investigator and your responsibility as a father?"

"Elizabeth, the subject is Bella."

She nodded. "She's a precious little girl. She needs your attention. You must realize her reality can't be summarized."

"Yes, it can," I replied. "Her mother and brother were killed. Now she lives with her father, who will not be led into believing things are the same as before. That's her reality."

"I might suggest, Terry, that you are projecting. Certainly, what you've described is your perspective."

"All right, but what happened to me happened to her."

"Not exactly. You have chosen a way to live that may not be compatible with the choices that she will make," she said. "You have chosen to limit your options. And this is why I return to the concept of vindication. If you assess accurately *why* you do what you do, it may give meaning to your actions. And this meaning may benefit not only you, but also Gabriella."

As I began to reply, she sneaked a glance at her wristwatch and began to write quickly in the folder, her thin pen scratching rapidly against the bond paper.

I leaned over again and said, "Terry, our time is almost up."

"As a matter of fact, it is," she said as she looked up,

"but I'm very interested in where you're going. I'd like to discuss the issue of the contradiction—"

"No, I think that's enough for today," I said. "Thank you for making me realize that I don't know what my daughter is doing all day at school. Thank you for suggesting I'm ambivalent."

Harteveld replied, "She is thinking of you and your needs. And I agree: That's an unnecessary burden for a twelve-year-old."

"Well, we agree. Good."

Adding a few final notes to her sheets, she calmly shut the folder and returned her pen to her white coat. I stood, knowing she was about to. Next, the walk to the door, a handshake, the compassionate nod.

And she did stand, but she hesitated. "Terry, Gabriella has asked me to ask you something for her."

"What?"

"She wants to try out for the school basketball team."

"So? She can, if she wants to. I can't believe she went to you with this."

Harteveld said, "She was afraid you wouldn't let her."

"I'll have to ask her why not."

"She said you told her that you didn't want her to be like you."

I thought for a moment. Yes, I probably did say that. I'm sure I did. "I don't remember saying that. But if I did, it was certainly in another context. I'd like her to play ball."

"Terry, she would rather be like you than anyone else. Try to remember that."

"I wouldn't—" I stopped. No, I'll keep that one to myself.

"She's a very clever but very dependent twelve-year-old."

"All right. I got it."

She turned and opened the door.

"Please make an appointment with John, Terry," she said as she shook my hand. "There's much to discuss, I think."

No compassionate nod. Instead, a concerned frown. It seemed almost sincere.

EIGHT

WE REACHED SECOND AVENUE, having had no luck on First as we waited in the fading light near the rattling Queensboro Bridge and under the creaking steel wheels of the Roosevelt Island tram. On Second, I left Bella at the curb, near the newspaper honor boxes and the "room-mate-wanted" flyers taped to the traffic-light stanchion, and went halfway to the center of the avenue, my hand in the air, index finger extended, anger and resentment buried until I got to the place where I could deal with Harteveld and her ludicrous theories.

Waves of yellow cabs blew by as if I were Wells's invisible man. Finally, a cabbie who'd dropped off a fare on the west side of the street made a frantic move to pick us up, veering his hack across the avenue, cutting off honking cars, faceless minivans and swerving delivery trucks. He smiled mischievously as he jerked to a stop in front of me, revealing a gold tooth and a Nixonesque five o'clock shadow.

I held back the door as Bella jumped in, slid next to her and gave the driver the name of the hospital where Judy and Lin-Lin were recovering.

I looked over to Bella. "Tomorrow morning, we'll go to the B-ball courts on Houston. Let's see if you've got a game." I let Mordecai Foxx slide, at least for now.

The cab sped under a yellow light on 51st and pressed its wild pace, only to catch the red a short block later. As we waited, listening to the driver sing to himself in Spanish, I watched as a messenger, a black man, thirtyish with a yellow pencil between his teeth and a highway-cone-orange ski cap on his head, bounced up onto the sidewalk, slapped his battered bike against a thin, leafless tree and secured it with a heavy-duty chain and a Yale lock. Without removing his Walkman, he adjusted his bicycle shorts, pulled a manila envelope from his tattered pouch and dashed into one of those small-run print shops, where photocopies cost 25 cents apiece and business cards are likely to come back with your name misspelled.

I felt a tap on my elbow. "Did you give Dr. Harteveld a hard time?" Bella asked.

"About what?" I snorted. "Basketball? No."

We pulled away easily, without a shriek, and fell in behind a slow-moving limo. I understood the Spanish swear words the driver was muttering.

"Not about basketball," she said. "About things. You know. Did you?"

"No, Bella, I didn't give her a hard time."

The orange-capped messenger, back on his bike, whipped past us, darting recklessly between cars. Preoccupied pedestrians scurried and scowled.

Bella pressed. "Did you cooperate, then? Or did you play games?"

Elizabeth Harteveld got in her digs, I thought. But she sees nothing. Her world is clean, bloodless, full of theories and accusations, spotless lab coats and prescription pharmaceuticals.

She believes a man can forget that his wife and child have been murdered. She believes a man will allow the murderer to roam free.

"Dad?"

"Bella, what's to say? I don't find her as useful as you do. I go, but I don't get much out of it."

" 'Cause you put nothing into it."

"Don't be so clever right now, all right? Let's start the weekend in peace."

We went around the limo, caught up to the messenger, but then were boxed in as a battered 4x4 began angling toward the curb from the center lane. Orange cap zipped by, slaloming, adjusting his earphones, chewing his pencil, ignoring the traffic signs, ignoring the big old Oldsmobile that seemed intent on crushing him, ignoring the young policeman on the corner who eyed him with a faint glimmer of admiration for a man who was moving hard to get something done.

That's what I ought to do, I thought. Move hard and get something done.

WE WALKED QUICKLY along the antiseptic hall, where open doors served to frame the misery inside: fragile men and women in thin, open-backed gowns staring vacantly at the early news or absently flipping the pages of supermarket tabloids; wilting flowers, half-eaten Jell-O, a handmade greeting card from a preschool grandson, crumpled tissues on the floor; wheelchairs, walkers, crutches, an artificial limb. Uneasy, a bit fearful, Bella now held my hand as I shifted her backpack on my shoulder.

"This is awful," she muttered, as she tugged on the

front of her jacket. "I wouldn't want to go to this hospital."

"No, me neither," I replied, silently swearing at the out-of-order elevators that were closer to Judy's room.

"Does anybody ever get better?"

And then, from the far end of the narrow hall, we heard the faint strains of bright music, orchestral, full of color as it echoed in the corridor; and then, louder, richer, as we moved toward it. An audible sign of life, Bella and I silently agreed; a sudden burst of sunlight, full of brilliance and warmth, in the immaculate, morose dungeon.

We rushed suddenly, hastening toward the glow.

We found Judy sitting up, the top of her bed raised, a multicolored, crocheted throw covering the lower half. She was haggard, pale, drowsing a bit; and she seemed many years older than she had just four days ago when we ran into her on Greenwich Street. But she seemed to brighten when she turned and saw us. When she held out her arms, Bella stepped in front of me, removed her hat and took the hug.

"Oh, Gabriella, sweetheart. You shouldn't have come to see me. Look at me; are you looking at me? Step back, dear. Oh, goodness, I'm looking at you. You are beautiful."

Someone had done modest redecorating in the otherwise drab room. A poster was taped to the wall: Harold E. Frazier's "Caribbean Dance Hall," the remarkable eruption of colors, the loose limbs and gleeful expressions of the licentious dancers; the little boy in the corner, watching in amazement, in nervous admiration. Judy represented Harry, who was a good man. Seventy-six years old, the grandson of a slave and half-blind now, he still wrote to me, in care of the gallery, asking after Gabriella, praising Marina's heart and kindness.

Saint-Saëns's "Havanaise" wafted from a small cassette player on a table near a low-slung chair.

"Marina's baby," Judy moaned sentimentally, and she started to cry. When she pointed to the tissues on the nightstand, Bella dug near the woven basket of yellow and rust asters and passed her the box.

Judy called to me, and I slid Bella's bag onto the tiled floor. I stepped in and hugged her. I spotted a few small nicks on her cheek, a bruise on her neck, and saw that the back of her head had been shaved and bandaged.

"Thank you, dear," she whispered. She kissed my ear. "I know what you did."

I said nothing, and held on to her, my arms around her soft flannel robe, which bore the faint scent of her light, floral perfume.

She kissed me again and pushed me gently. "Next time you decide to come see me," she scolded, "call ahead. I can put on a little makeup. Be a little presentable. Am I presentable, Gabriella? Don't. *Don't* answer that. Children lack that filter, don't they? She's likely to tell me."

"You look great," Bella announced.

"So, Terry, Terry Orr, what do you want?"

I shook my head. "We wanted to drop in and—"

"Terry. Terry." She wagged her finger at me. "Visitors—and I know; the world's been in here to cheer me up—they bring flowers, candy, magazines; Sadler Boyd brought a photographer. Bastard. Excuse me, Gabriella, dear." She tapped the side of her head. "Brain intact, Terry Orr, if a bit frazzled. Thanks to you. Gabriella, be a dear and hand me my lipstick and compact, will you?" She pointed to the nightstand. Bella complied.

"Oh, mother of God. Here, here. Take it away, the mirror, the paint; Lord. Yeah, well, that they didn't tell me: You lose a foot, you lose your looks."

Bella laughed as she returned the items to the drawer.

Judy said, "Ask questions. Ask, Terry." As I hesitated, she shifted on her elbows.

"Terry, what? Query me; grill me. I could use the excitement."

I turned to my daughter. "Bella, how would you feel about getting Judy some water?"

"The pitcher's full."

"It's probably warm."

"There's frost on the plastic. Look," she said, pointing.

I dug in my pocket and came up with a dollar bill. "Go buy something."

She frowned. "How long do you want me to stay away?"

"Ten minutes."

"Fine," she groaned.

"Thank you."

Judy winked. "Call me later, Gabriella, I'll tell you *every*thing."

Bella smiled, put her hat back on and went out into the hall. I reached and slid the soft chair next to Judy's bed.

"Do you know who did it?" she asked as I sat.

"That's why I came to see you," I began.

"Terry." She met my eyes. There was no playfulness in her now. "Tell me now."

I said, "The voice on the phone—"

"Nondescript. A man. I don't remember an accent. There may have been. Eastern European? Maybe."

"And he said what?"

"'There's a bomb in your gallery. Get everybody out.' And he repeated it."

"Did he give a time? You know, like there's two minutes, five minutes . . ."

"What I said is exactly what he said." She pursed her

lips, and she frowned. "Then he hung up. I was sure he was telling the truth."

"Why?"

"He just sounded like he meant it. He was clear. Adamant."

"OK," I said as I leaned back. "Nothing there."

"You sound like those detectives who were here."

"I don't mean to," I said. "I've got a few ideas, that's all."

"Are you doing this for me, Terry?"

I hesitated.

"Because I want you to," she said. "I want it to be personal."

"It is," I said finally.

"You're hiding something. Tell me, Terry. Do you think whatever you say will be worse than hearing my foot is gone?"

"No," I replied.

"Someone hired you, didn't they?"

"Yes, but that's irrelevant now."

"Edie?" she asked.

"It was Lin-Lin Chin."

"Lin-Lin?" Judy said. "Really?" She sat back and shook her head. "Well, I'll be fucked. Oops; oh, well. But, I don't believe it. Really, I don't. It's impossible."

"Why, Judy? Why impossible?"

"Because Lin-Lin loathes me."

"*Loathes* you?"

"Maybe that's too strong, maybe. She wants me to let Sol go. She wants to represent him herself."

I thought for a moment. "Does Beck have the same deal with you that Marina had?"

She nodded.

Marina's contract with Judy, more or less a standard

personal-service deal, permitted either side to walk away on a handshake, granted all commissions were paid and all work was returned. Beck should be able to drop Judy whenever he wanted to.

I said, "What does Beck say?"

She shrugged. "Sol is frail. Sol is a boy, sometimes. But Sol is stubborn. And he understands the level of his talent. He needs someone with experience to sell him."

I shifted in the chair. "You don't think much of his stuff," I led.

"It's salable. I don't pretend to be a critic." She added quickly, "And don't think that applies to everyone I represent: Marina was gifted, Terry. Sol Beck is essentially a mimic. Hopper, Wyeth, Eakins, Sloan, the Ashcans. I'm not knocking it. He understands the craft, but..."

"Can he grow?"

"I've heard he's done other work, but I haven't seen it. I agreed to mount the show, to try to move the stuff, and I did. If he wants Lin-Lin to represent him, good luck."

I paused for a moment. The paintings under the tarps at Beck's on King Street. Middle-period Beck. I wondered what they looked like. How free could Beck be? How far from his influences could he move?

"Terry, what are you thinking? Tell me. Don't keep secrets, Terry Orr."

"Judy, nobody meant to hurt you. You understand that, don't you?"

"I find it hard to take a lot of comfort in that, Terry."

"You were supposed to leave like everybody else."

"I've been telling myself, 'If only I hadn't gone into the back...'"

"I'm sure the explosion was meant to disrupt the opening." And there were only two possible reasons for that: to abruptly end the show, or for publicity. But when Judy was injured, it all changed.

The publicity angle intrigued me, but it didn't work for Beck as I saw him: a seemingly ordinary guy whose early, craft-dependent work was so derivative as to be easily forgotten. Had the work been at least trendy or innovative, had Beck a reputation, a persona, that could have been romanticized by a menacing event like a bombing, it might've worked. But pretentious critics and skin-deep commentators who would've loved that angle were likely to have walked away from it as soon as they saw Beck's work, which was neither fashionable nor new.

"Terry, tell me why Lin-Lin hired you."

I let out a breath. "It doesn't make much sense. She told me she thought Beck's father did it. Because he hates Sol."

"Really?"

I shook my head. "That's what she said. But it's not possible. His father can't do the kind of work that the explosion required." I pointed to my shoulder. "Besides, I don't think his hate runs in that direction."

Judy paused. "Did you see Sol's painting called 'Father's Day'?"

I told her I hadn't.

"There's a old man sitting in an outdoor café on Bleecker Street. He's all alone, very bitter, small, diminished. You don't doubt that no one wants to be anywhere near this guy. He drove everyone away."

"That's Beck's view of his father."

"We had the painting at the show."

"Really? Where?"

"Let me think," she said. "In front, on the south wall."

"Not near the back room?"

"Where the explosion happened? No. Why?"

I said, "Just a thought." But I let it go: If he'd wanted to destroy "Father's Day," Rosenzweig would've had to see the exhibition before setting the explosion. I told myself to stay focused: The bomber wanted to terminate the show by damaging the gallery without destroying any of the work, and maybe get a little free coverage at the same time. The universe of people who would want that was very, very limited.

"Judy, I've got to be direct, all right?"

"Of course." She reached out and patted my hand.

"Tell me about Edie. Has she been here?"

"You mean do I think Edie could've done this?"

"I'm just brainstorming, Judy."

"Is it trite for me to say she's like a daughter to me?"

"No." I smiled. "But it's not very useful."

She nodded. "Edie's ambitious, Terry, and she'll have her own gallery someday."

"Judy, has she been here?"

"Yes. Yes. Today. And she calls. She calls." She flung up her hand: a dismissive gesture.

"All right, Judy," I muttered.

"So where does it all leave us?" she asked.

I slid the chair away from the bed and I stood. I went to the nightstand and poured cold water into a clear plastic cup. I handed Judy the cup and a plastic straw. She took a satisfying sip.

She returned the cup to me. "They give me a lot of pills, Terry. But I think I'm pretty sure what's going on. I'm not really a ball of fluff, you know."

"Yeah, I know that, Judy."

"I'm going to beat this thing." She brushed her hair from her forehead and she pinched her cheeks. "I'm alive, Terry. You know, they rolled me down the hall this morning. Very bad idea. Very bad. I had this awful vision: me, ninety-seven years old; you know, like I never left here. A one-legged skeleton in a medieval wheelchair." She feigned a shiver. "Brrrr. Not Judy. No, not me. Not I. Oh no."

"No, Judy, not you."

"I'm determined to get out of here as soon as I can."

I nodded.

"But, Terry, go out and get me a little peace. Understand? Let me know that it was an accident."

"That you were hurt? I'm already sure it was, Judy."

"Well, be certain." Firm, almost forceful, she directed me: "Get the prick who did it. Then we'll know."

I nodded.

"Now, move back that chair. Turn up the music, and let's lighten up before that beautiful girl of yours returns."

I did as she asked and sat for several moments near the tape player; now Massenet was playing, seductively, powerfully. I found myself calmed by the tender violin solo and delicate piano and string section, and when I looked at Judy, I saw that she had drifted off to sleep, jaw slack, head nestled against the undersized pillow. I let the music continue, but I stood to turn off the fluorescent light above her, and I went to wait in the hall. I watched a weary nurse at the far end push along a cart filled with charts, lotions, ointments, and pills and other pharmaceuticals; I listened to Massenet.

I dug into my daughter's crowded backpack, found a piece of paper and a pen and scribbled a "Be Right Back" note that I slid under the cassette player.

I WAITED A minute or two more, then went off to the nurses' station to find Lin-Lin Chin.

HER ROOMMATE HAD been beaten as well. She had both arms in casts, and there was a thick bandage over her eye and fluid flowing into her from a clear plastic sack on a silver pole. It was hard to make out this dark woman's features, with only the pale light from the hall reaching her, but she seemed to express pain even as she slept.

A thick curtain divided the room, and I passed it to find Lin-Lin, in the gray glow from the window, in the morbid spotlight: I could see the sickly yellow-green swelling on her face, the purple knot above her left eye, the red-and-blue marbling under her raised cheek. The stitches just above her eyebrow were exposed, and a tiny piece of the black string hung precariously near the frail hair; precariously, because it looked as if someone could simply reach in, tug it and reopen a gaping wound.

She had her hands folded on the top blanket. The serving tray had been swung over her and on it there were a cup and straw and a Polaroid photo of her cat.

Lin-Lin was staring absently at the dusky sky and the hovering buildings that crowded the downtown hospital.

I crossed in front of the dust-laden window and sat near her, placing my elbows on the bed and my head in my hands. She turned away; she was facing the curtain and the battered woman on the other side.

I whispered, "I assume you have a new assignment for me."

She didn't reply.

"Or is it the same one?"

"Go away, Terry."

"Are you thinking of telling me it was a coincidence, Lin-Lin?"

"I was mugged."

"A very inefficient mugger, wouldn't you say? Hitting a woman without a pocketbook who's carrying a small bag of groceries, almost certainly coming from the corner store."

She turned to me. "Muggers aren't very clever, Terry."

"Lin-Lin, are you in pain?"

"No. Not really," she said stoically.

I lifted my finger and held it above her cheek. "So, if I was to tap your cheek, right there, right where that little knot peaks . . ."

She stared into my eyes, then slowly lifted her hand to cover the side of her face. I pulled back my index finger, then pointed it at her.

"It's you who isn't clever," I explained. "The bomb was a bad idea."

She replied, "Yes, it should have never happened."

"Lin-Lin, if you were just a little bit smarter, you would've known you can't chase off Judy by trying to hurt her. And anybody who reads the papers could've told you that whatever publicity you got would go as fast as it came."

"I don't know—"

" '—what you're talking about.' Good, Lin-Lin. Now we got that thing out of the way."

She rolled her eyes slowly, then shut them. I saw swollen purple veins on one eyelid and red scratches near the bridge of her nose. She seemed tiny in bed, alone and broken; but then I thought of Judy, trying to help Beck, working the room on his behalf, taking the phone call, chasing out the elite onto Greene Street. The explosion, jagged glass, smoke, dust; Judy on the floor, blood flowing, shooting from the bottom of her leg.

"Lin-Lin, play me straight. Lin-Lin."

"I'm so tired," she moaned.

"What were you thinking?"

She said nothing. She kept her eyes shut.

I went on. "An explosion. And then I'd tell Judy that it was Beck's father. She'd drop your husband and you'd handle him. You'd be handling him as he rode on the publicity from the bombing. Was that it?"

"Terry . . . I want to sleep now."

"And you'd need another gallery to mount the show. Then what? Sell the new paintings by Sol Beck, notorious artist? Those paintings under the tarp at your place on King Street? You're an agent, Lin-Lin?"

"Terry—"

"What you are is a thief, a petty thief. Shoplifting. Four years ago. It put you in the system and you were out $1,000. So that's you, Lin-Lin: You see something, you take it. The rules don't apply."

I added, "Does Sol know he's married to a thief?"

She looked at me and I could see the bitter stubbornness in her eyes, despite the dark, angular shadows cast across the bed.

"Sol knows that only I can help him. This is his reality, Terry."

I shook my head. "Here's the reality: Judy is injured in the explosion. Rosenzweig is incapable of planting the bomb. Christ, Lin-Lin, how inept did you think I'd be? Did you think I couldn't find out about a man who's collecting a pension from the VA?"

"You do not think clearly," she said flatly. "You do not calculate." She tried to swallow. Her throat was dry; the cup and straw were on the rolling serving tray. It was the same type of cup and straw that Judy was using one flight below.

She coughed. "Sol is coming back."

"We'd better hurry, then," I replied.

"I can tell you nothing."

"You can tell me about Bullethead."

"Bullet—" She frowned and a thin, sour smile crossed her bruised lips. "You calculate, but you do not think clearly. Inexperience."

"Remember what you asked me to do? Find out who did this to Judy. And I did. It was you, Lin-Lin. So you've got to do one thing for me, so I can close this up: Tell me who you hired to plant the bomb."

"I didn't hire anyone," she whispered.

"You know Bullethead, don't you?"

"I did not hire him," she repeated.

"You owe money to this man you hired." I shifted, moving closer again. "You owe money to the man who beat you."

"I didn't see him."

"He's coming back. He'll be back."

"No."

"Why? Did you pay him?"

"Terry, leave me, please." She coughed and that caused her to grimace.

"I'm going to find this guy, Lin-Lin. Are you going to help me?"

"I can't. I choose not to."

"Will Edie help me?"

She squeezed her eyes shut. I saw the bloody pinpricks near the black lashes.

"Look at me," I said, "Lin-Lin."

She did.

"He'll come after Sol next."

I thought about pushing the cup of water closer to her, so she could reach it and let the cool liquid soothe her arid throat.

But I didn't. Instead, I just left.

WE DEBATED MUNDANE matters on the short ride from the hospital and decided, finally, on sandwiches. The cabbie dropped us across from the Tilt, at Zolly's Bagels. Rare roast beef for Bella, smoked turkey for me, and a pint of German potato salad, with thin slivers of bacon, for us to share. With a little friendly coaxing from Zolly's wife Sheila, Bella ordered a garlic pickle and a can of Yoo-hoo. I shivered at the thought.

We stepped outside into dusk, into the suddenly chilly late-evening air. I pointed to the Tilt. "You want to say hello to Leo?"

"It smells in there," she said, wrinkling her nose.

"Yeah, Leo doesn't want people getting too comfortable."

"It smells like Leo," she replied, shaking her head.

We went south toward the house, staying on the east side of the street, away from Leo and his jukebox, passing brick and fireproof steel doors and cast-iron railings, crossing the rounded cobblestones, slowing to take in the ginger-and-pepper scent wafting from the Thai takeout shop before heading west toward the murky Hudson, toward Greenwich Street, toward home.

Suddenly, Bella stopped and pointed to our house. I followed the line of her gaze and saw him: a menacing-looking man standing on our front steps.

"I know him," I told her, and I could see she was relieved.

Mabry Reynolds came down the steps. The muscular security guard still wore his police-style blue shirt and navy polyester slacks, but had traded in his steel-toed boots for a pair of black running shoes. A heavy blue coat added bulk to his thick frame.

We crossed Harrison and I told Bella to go inside, and she went up the steps, acknowledging Reynolds with a nod and a smile.

"I'll take the groceries," Bella said.

Reynolds turned to me, reached, took the paper bag. He walked it to Bella, extending his leg across the four steps to hand it to her.

"Thank you," she said.

Reynolds nodded.

As Bella closed the door, Reynolds came back to me.

"What'd you hear?" I asked.

"Not much," he said. "Brown was an old guy. People are saying he shouldn't have been driving." He ran his hand over his bald head. "Nobody said 'serves him right,' but it's rough out there."

The cold wind off the Hudson kicked up and smacked my pant-legs against the backs of my calves. I began to shuffle and sway. "Anything on Montana?"

He said no.

"Nothing?"

"Nobody is talking about him, no."

"Yeah, well . . ."

He reached into a rear pocket and withdrew a small envelope. "Principal Langhorne sent this."

I took the envelope.

"What's it about?" I asked. My name was typed on the front.

He shrugged.

"Something about Montana?"

"I don't know," he said, and he moved past me, into the shadows, toward a beat-up Dodge Scamp parked in front of the hydrant on the north side of the street. I followed him.

Awkwardly, I offered, "You need anything? Drink of water, maybe? Use the phone."

He shook his head as he opened the driver's-side door.

On the backseat, there were pink and lavender plastic ponies and Chunky Board books. Reynolds had a daughter of his own.

We stood for several seconds in the bracing wind blowing east.

Finally, I asked, "How am I going to get closer to Montana?"

"No idea," he said slowly.

"There's something off about Williams, isn't there?"

He shrugged. "Vice principal to Dr. Langhorne won't have much to do."

"And the teacher, Amaral. His story is what?"

He bit his bottom lip, he nodded to himself. "Bad divorce. Wife kicked him out, then she took their boy to her folks in Georgia."

"Good teacher?"

"Must be, if Dr. Langhorne keeps him around."

I said, "Dr. Langhorne knows everything."

Reynolds smiled.

"Tell me something he doesn't know," I said.

"You mean about Williams and Amaral?"

A ferry crossing the choppy river let go with a blast of its guttural horn. "Sure," I said, "Williams and Amaral."

He shook his head and frowned disagreeably. "Can't be true. Not no more."

"Why not?"

"Amaral isn't inclined, if you know what I mean."

I said, "Which is why his wife left."

"Probably."

"Has he been working?"

"Every day," he replied.

He slid into the car, closed the door. The engine was stubborn, but it kicked over and Reynolds left.

I went up the stairs and into the house.

"WHAT?" BELLA ASKED. "You look confused."

She'd already begun to prepare the sandwiches. The vinegary potato salad sat in a bowl, as if it were a centerpiece. Two place mats had been set out.

I sat at the kitchen table and hunched into my coat. "I asked one question, I got about nine hundred answers."

"Must have been an outstanding question," she mused.

"I guess."

"And what's that?" She pointed to the small envelope on the table.

"The damnedest thing," I replied. "A letter from the principal of the school I went to."

"Why did you go to a school?"

"Not for you," I said as I tore open the envelope. "Unless you want to commute to 125th Street."

I read the letter:

> *"Dear Mr. Orr:*
>
> *I understand your greeting this morning was less than gracious. I offer my apologies on behalf of myself, my staff, our faculty and our student body. All are welcome here, sir, and ought to be met with the dignity we expect to receive ourselves.*
>
> *Yours truly,*
> *Everett Langhorne, Ph.D."*

At the bottom were Langhorne's initials, followed by the initials of his secretary. I nodded. Someone had tipped him off. Miss Oliver, or maybe Reynolds.

"Let me see," Bella said.

"Don't get any mustard on it," I said.

THE MOVIE WAS *They Were Expendable,* starring Robert Montgomery. Bella was up in my bedroom, watching her programs, snacking. After a Yoo-hoo and a garlic pickle, she was eating a bowl of cheese popcorn to accompany a show about serial killing and the occult, with a dash of romance tossed in when the blood wasn't cascading.

I stretched out on the sofa and nodded off. I woke up with Bella shaking me by the shoulder.

"Ten o'clock already?" I asked.

She was in a t-shirt, and barefoot. "B-ball tomorrow."

I sat up. "I'll be there. Bring your best."

"My best what?"

"It's just an expression," I said as I stood.

"That's good. I want to learn all the expressions."

We headed toward the stairs. "All my expressions are from the '80s. We'll go to the courts on West Fourth to pick up new ones."

She was ahead of me. "Cool."

She reached the top of the stairs and more or less bounced down the short hall and jumped into bed. As I caught up, she grabbed the Salinger from the nightstand. "I'm going to read for a while," she said.

I was going to say something: Bella, did you think about Mama today? Bella, don't be mad at me; I'm trying to understand your moods. Bella, about Harteveld . . . Did seeing Judy upset you? You know, I went to talk to Beck's wife. Don't let that letter from Langhorne fool you, Bella. This is still some fucked-up world.

But I said nothing. She seemed happy. Content, at least. We would play ball in the morning. That's how it should be. Then we'd have our typical Saturday-night date, alone, and that was all wrong.

We're trying to get by.

"Good night, Dad," she said.

"You're kicking me out?"

"This is a good book."

"OK. Good night, little angel."

I left the door ajar, and I went downstairs.

I passed the shimmering TV, the by-now-warm bottle of Badoit on the table, and went to my study.

Mei Carissima:

Is it possible that I will spend my life endlessly, repeatedly, trying to save you and Davy?

Or that I do what I do not to learn to take down Weisz, but to make amends for my negligence, my arrogance, my self-satisfaction?

And that I would abandon Bella to do that?

I would hurt Bella?

Stupid. Asinine. Ridiculous. Really stone stupid.

That line of thinking—which amounts to nothing more than an attempt to catalogue my misery, to file me under...I don't know, whatever—is burning a hole in my brain tonight. Unbelievable.

See, that's why I reject Harteveld.

You understand that, I know. You would not tolerate that level of hostility.

I can hear you defending me, your jawline quivering as you try to hold back the fire. And you would, to a de-

gree, control your temper. You would begin slowly, deliberately: "My dear Dr. Harteveld. Perhaps it is a problem of language. Or perhaps I am not familiar with this American custom..."

Or would you suggest that I listen?

Would you suggest that I listen to someone who does not understand?

She uses the word "atonement," Marina. And "vindication." I should atone for what I've done. If I acknowledge that I'm seeking atonement through my actions, I will be vindicated.

This, instead of simply doing what must be done.

At least she mentioned revenge.

I wouldn't reject a suggestion that I seek revenge. Who wouldn't entertain such thoughts?

But be it for justice, for revenge, to make something wrong right again, for whatever reason, Weisz has to be taken down.

And if that's so—and it is so—how is it better to do so seeking vindication instead of revenge?

Bella.

OK. All right.

OK.

But, in the end, knowing little about Weisz and my true ambition, what Harteveld is doing is suggesting that I make my mission something noble, something that might in some way satisfy. So that when I succeed I will feel whole again.

And I will be whole again if I—I don't know. If I help children, help our friends?

No, I completely reject that. Completely.

That is tantamount to a suggestion that it matters not if Weisz is taken down.

Oh no, Marina, don't say that.

***

You were with me, dear, early this afternoon. I could feel you at my side. I felt the heat of your breath, the warmth of your hand on mine. I saw the light dance on your hair.

We were in London. I don't know why. Of course I do: I was walking toward you. First along a drab, non-descript block in midtown, cracks in the sidewalk, shallow puddles, and I thought of London. Remember? The light flooding the Courtauld Institute Galleries was perfect—the sun had pushed through the gray at the moment that we entered the top-floor room—and were alone with Van Gogh and the golden wheat and the tumult and solitude, and with Monet and his violet mountains and jagged, rocking seas at Antibes. By the time we were ready to leave it was raining again, and we were prisoners under a lifeless dome. We hid for a moment in a red phone booth, then ran to a pub off the Strand and had pints of Bass Ale before the Ploughman's Lunch arrived. Bass, you pointed out, was what the forlorn girl in Manet's "A Bar at the Folies-Bergère" had served. I kissed you: Your lips tasted of cream and barley and hope.

And I thought of you as I walked from Harlem along the stretch of Fifth Avenue, with its cobbled sidewalks and robust trees, where we fell in love; or where I fell in love with you: where we'd walk along hand-in-hand and I would listen as you went on about a single work we'd just seen and we'd stop on a bench under these robust trees and you, with the faintest trace of an Italian accent, would explain to me the relationship between art and the world—a stretch sometimes, too much rapture; even a neophyte such as I knew that. But did I mind? Not at all, because I knew, listening to you, trying to see things as you did, trying to share your passion, that I was about to change: Indirectly, but indisputably, you were changing me.

An afternoon with you, your ebullience, your effusiveness, thin, perfect hands waving madly all over the place, your black eyes and splendid face beaming as you bounced off the bench to make a fine point, taught me more about what life could be, ought to be than I'd ever known before, than I would have thought possible. I knew somehow that what you had was what I needed. With you, I would feel rather than be, understand rather than see; I would live rather than only exist.

I interrupted your fevered soliloquy on Bellini's Saint Francis in the Desert.

"I love you," I said. "I do."

You stopped and stood upright. "Oh," you said. (Do you remember this as clearly as I do?)

"That's it?" I said. "'Oh'?"

But I wasn't threatened, dear. I knew it was going to be fine.

"You say it in a strange way," you replied, "like you are making an announcement."

"If I was making an announcement, I would stand up on this bench and shout it. Maybe I ought to do that."

You came to me and you kissed me on my mouth. "I love you, Terry," you whispered. You kissed me again, and again, softly, tenderly, and you ran your fingers on my cheek. "That is how you say 'I love' the first time."

That was almost 13 years ago. The leaves were impossibly green, the sky was as blue as it can be, and all around us, on Fifth, in the park, on that bench, there was life and laughter and purpose.

And today, I sat on that bench. And, for more than an hour, I waited for you.

I could feel you, hear you.
You did not come.
Oh God, how I miss you.

> *A presto, Marina.*
> *All my love,*
> *T.*

NINE

I NUDGED BELLA AWAKE and, as she dug in the laundry room for the right clothes, went back to my study, where I'd stayed last night until almost 2 A.M. As the heat from the floor vent stroked my bare ankles, I switched on my PC and went online. In minutes, I was where I needed to be.

Amaral, Perry G., was a dues-paying member of the American Federation of Teachers. He had to be: Dues were automatically deducted. But there was no home address, no other data.

A mouse-click to a more conventional search, to an on-line phone directory. Amaral's phone number was listed.

He lived at 455 West 14th. That would be near Tenth Avenue.

Not far from Little West 12th, where Aubrey Brown was found, cold blood on his blank face.

And very far from Fort Washington Avenue.

Reynolds said Amaral's wife got the apartment before she took off to Atlanta.

I'd bet Williams knew where Amaral lived now.

As I snapped off the computer, I heard faint strains of Monk's "Ruby, My Dear" in my head.

"PUSH IT WITH your fingertips," I yelled.

But she shoved the ball toward the asphalt with her palm and it flew up and nearly caught her in the face.

She was at the other end of the court. "All right, just run it back. No, no, don't try to dribble. Just pick it up and run with it."

It was going to be a beautiful day: The early-morning sun was bright above the Houston Street courts; for now, thoughts of Harteveld and her allegations had been banished. Cars flooded Sixth, rolling off the Williamsburg, off the FDR. The shop owners on MacDougal were unfurling their awnings, spraying the sidewalks with water. At the other end of the long playground, two men in their 40s were playing a spirited game of handball. They grunted as they slammed the little black ball against the graffiti on the tall cement wall.

Bella was wearing one of my tattered old St. John's t-shirts and her school gym shorts, black high tops that I had to lace up for her and a purple beret, and about nine rubber bands on her wrist.

"Come here."

"I want to shoot the ball," she said.

I took the ball. "Let's loosen up."

"I'm loose." She jangled her arms, rolled her head. "See?"

"No, first, let's run a little drill I know that'll get us going." Frankly, I needed the work. I no longer had a routine. I took it when I could get it.

She followed me until we were under the basket. I

said, "Let's walk to the other end. I'll throw you the ball. You throw it back."

We began. So far, so good. I threw it, she caught it, she threw it back; then again. We reached the half-court line.

"Boring," she sang.

I bounced the ball and she caught it.

"Good. That's a bounce pass. Give it back."

She led me nicely and we stayed at it until we reached the other basket.

"OK. Now, let's do it running."

And we did and she wasn't half bad: She dropped a pass near the foul line but, reacting quickly, she slapped it back and I didn't have to break stride.

We turned. "Let's push it hard."

We went up and down, up and down, up and back. She started out laughing, but very quickly became serious, almost intense; and then she was out of breath. She put her palms on her knees and hunched over.

"Give me the ball," I instructed. I dribbled down the court, threw the ball hard against the wall and it came back to me as I turned. I caught it in stride, dribbled hard and passing the foul line, took off and dunked the ball, slamming the rim with my forearm. The ball hit the ground with force.

"I want to do that," Bella yelled.

I tapped the ball, caught it in one hand, then rolled it the length of the court to her. She stopped it with her foot, picked it up. With the ball between her hands, she stared up at the rim, calculating. She tucked the ball under her arm and started toward me.

I walked out to the top of the key and clapped my hands. She tossed the ball to me. I caught it, turned and shot. Nothing but net.

"Terry Orr. Number 44. For three!"

I turned.

"Hi, Mr. Mango," Bella said.

Jimmy Mango was standing near the sideline. His sky blue t-shirt was saturated with sweat: He had been one of the men playing handball at the other end. I hadn't recognized him beneath his straw cowboy hat and red bandanna. His tube socks reached his bony knees. His costume made him look like a classic rube.

"How'd you do?" I asked. Mango didn't play if money wasn't on the table.

"I buried him. What do you think? You think I get in a game I don't win?" He held out his palms and smiled broadly, wiseguy style.

"What'd you take him for?" I asked.

"Twenty. Why? You want it?"

Mango was about 5'5", 5'7" at best, fit, spindly; a grinder with a nasty streak. In B-ball, I'd beat him 21–2, 21–3, but I'd be bruised up and down my legs for a week. And he'd tell everybody he took it to me. As if I gave a shit.

He knew I could take him in a straight game. "Horse?" he suggested.

In Horse, you had to duplicate the shot your opponent made, no matter how ridiculous. A guy like Mango had trick shots coming out of his ass.

I countered, "Round the World." Six shots from predetermined spots on the court.

"You lay five-to-one," he said.

"On the twenty? Fine."

"And Gabby plays, even money."

That meant if I won but Mango came out ahead of Bella, he'd break even. The problem with short-end guys like Mango is they always figure the opponent doesn't know the odds as well as they do.

"Game," I said.

I pointed to the lane stripe, near the basket. I said to

Bella, "You got to make it from there, sweetheart."

"'Sweetheart,'" Mango repeated. "You lose your killer instinct, Four-four?"

"Let's play, Jimmy," I said. "Go ahead, Bella."

I MADE SIX shots without a miss, but Mango beat Bella, who, to her own amazement, hit the foul shot but couldn't reach the basket from the top of the key. It was a good experience for her: I could see she liked the competition and she was frustrated when she tanked the first chippie. She punched at the ball and, for some reason, discarded one of the rubber bands on her wrist.

I'd brought a towel and a big Badoit bottle full of tap water. I poured the lukewarm liquid over my head, Bella drank a third, as did Mango.

"Don't like to lose, huh?" I asked her.

Her face was red and damp, and I ran the old towel over her cheeks and eyebrows before sliding it around her neck. She replied, "I could do better than that."

I ran my hand through my wet hair, pushing it back off my forehead. "You did all right for the first time out."

She said thanks, but waved off the compliment.

As we went toward the gate, Bella dribbled the ball, using her fingertips.

Mango caught up to us. "So, a push, Four-four. You did good. You still got it." Smirking, he added, "Some of it."

"You beat a twelve-year-old, Mango. Don't be cocky."

"Hey, I was shooting left-handed."

Bella started to protest, but I interrupted. "Don't listen to him," I said. "He's a lefty."

Mango smiled. He was just short of a worm, crazy like a hyena, but I didn't mind him. He never bothered me. If he liked you, he might watch your back.

We were on Sixth and I started north, toward the courts

on West Fourth. I wanted Bella to see the schoolyard game, and the best one downtown went on all day long at the Cage, a short walk from where we were.

"Terry, let me buy you and Gabby some steak and eggs." He jabbed the air as he spoke, then he pointed to the All-American Diner, where Rosenzweig stationed himself.

I said no.

"You going to try to get in a game? Huh? Terry?"

"No."

The sidewalk was cracked and raised above the roots of an old tree. Bella lost the dribble for a moment, but she retrieved the ball before it rolled under the mailbox.

"Terry, we can turn this twenty into serious money," he said.

I shook my head.

"Gabby, did your father ever tell you how we used to clean up here?"

"No," Bella replied.

"Gabby, your father made me a couple hundred dollars one time. Shit, Terry, why don't people think you can play? Gabby, your father starts popping threes, then they come out on him, they think he ain't quick, so he goes down the lane and *boom!* In their *face*."

"Really, Dad?" She'd stopped dribbling and was carrying the ball.

"Then they start to bang him and you know your old man: He's like a firecracker. An M-80. Next thing you know somebody's on their ass and they're pulling your father off the court."

"That's enough, Jimmy," I said. We waited for the light at West Third.

"Terry, I don't say you play dirty. Gabby, I never seen your father start a fight. But," he chuckled, "I seen him end a few." Mango inched closer to me. "Does she know about the thing at the Garden?" he whispered.

"Enough, Jimmy," I said through gritted teeth. One punch and my scholarship was gone. Who's going to tell their kid about that?

The light changed. We waited for the last cab to run it, then proceeded.

There was a game under way at the Cage, and already there were about two dozen men waiting to play the winners. A small crowd milled near the fence; in an hour or so, it'd be three deep and men and young women would be craning their necks to see every deek and move.

"Terry, look," Mango said, "Automatic Slim. No chance for a run today."

On the court, a shirtless, razor-thin black sprinter was outplaying the taller man who was fumbling to guard him. Sun glistened on his lean back and shoulders.

"Bella, watch the guy with the pearl earring."

She handed me the ball and leaned against the chain-link fence.

Slim brought the ball over the yellow half-court line, paused to size up the situation, then stopped his dribble, held the ball over his head and passed it off. He clapped his hands and the ball came back; in one fluid motion, he caught it, sprang up and shot from just right of the key. The net barely rippled as the ball passed through. Several spectators nodded knowingly.

"Shit, Mills, stay wit' him," one player shouted, frowning, scowling. Sweat beaded his angry mahogany face.

"Watch your own game, Scoop," barked Mills, as he breathed hard.

I whispered, "Bella, keep an eye on Slim."

Scoop, the scowling guy who'd shouted at his teammate, handed the ball off to a third player, who looked to be in his late teens, about 15 years younger than the rest of the men in the game. The sinewy kid inbounded the ball to Scoop. When Scoop turned to dribble upcourt, Slim swept around Mills, swiped at the ball, knocked it loose, picked it up and kissed it off the backboard for an easy basket.

Scoop slammed the ball on the ground and started to yell at the kid, who had done nothing wrong.

"How'd you know that was going to happen?" Bella asked.

I pointed through the fence. "That guy Scoop was too busy thinking about himself. You have to be thinking about what's around you when you're playing."

"Slim ain't going to lose the court all day," Mango added. "These guys got him on a throne. They're afraid of him."

A burly black man on the other side of the fence turned and glared at Mango. He was about 6′9″ and weighed about 280.

"Who the fuck you lookin' at?" Mango snapped.

The big man thought about it, then turned back to the game.

"Bella, watch how hard they play defense."

"They're hitting each other."

"Technically, it's called hand-checking," I said softly, "but watch them work."

Mango said, "Terry, that young kid's got a game. File that away. We come back here one day and get him on our side." Pointedly, he added, "I'll put you up against some big stooge with his gut hanging over his shorts. You'll piss on him."

Behind the fence, the big man stiffened, then chose to ignore the little irritant.

I decided to relieve us of Mango and take Bella home via Seventh Avenue South and Varick. We could bounce the ball as we walked and talk about the game. We could go west when we passed Canal and stroll along the river, near its foam, amidst its salty scent. I wanted to tell her about Slim, whom I'd played against as a freshman in high school, who made all-city, who was on the cover of the *New York Times* magazine and in *USA Today,* who had earned a scholarship to Michigan, who worked harder than anyone on his game, who did seven years in Green Haven for armed robbery, who, remarkably, kicked his heroin habit while in jail. Who pushed a broom at the Bronx County Courthouse to support three sisters not much older than Bella was; who wound up in the *Times* magazine again, this time the subject of a "What Ever Happened to . . ." feature.

Now Slim pushed to the top of the key, ran Mills into a pick. Scoop switched off to take on Slim: Finally, the challenge Scoop wanted; he crouched and spread his arms like Spiderman. But Automatic Slim wouldn't bite. He simply passed the ball to the man Scoop had been covering. Layup; another easy basket. Slim tried to conceal a smirk.

Furious, Scoop kicked the ball. It flew over the top of the fence, over the adjacent playground, bounced on West Third and rolled under a Con Ed truck up on the curb in front of McDonald's.

"Go get the fuckin' ball," Scoop screamed at Mills. "Dumb motherfucker."

And with that, Mills blew. He ran at Scoop, got his hands on his throat, and seven other guys on the court dove in to break it up. The men waiting for the game shook their heads in disappointment, in disgust, and the gathering crowd laughed darkly, mocking the foolishness. Scoop had brought this good thing down fast.

"If Four-four was in the game, we'd be calling the morgue for that Scoop guy," Mango said.

Ignoring the tussle, Slim came over to the fence.

"Hey, Slim," I said.

He crooked two fingers through the diamond links. I shifted the ball under my arm, and tapped his fingers with mine. "Dog," he said.

"You doing OK, Slim?"

He shrugged as if to say "Why not?" His eyes were clear. He looked good, if older than he should have.

"My daughter, Gabriella."

"Hey, Gabriella. Nice hat."

"Hello," she said. "Thank you."

He looked at me. "You want in? Looks like I got game all day."

I shook my head. "I've got to run." I tilted my head at Bella. "Things."

Slim nodded and backed away. He winked at my daughter.

I leaned over. "Now you know somebody as famous as Diddio," I said.

"How do you know him, Dad? Did you play with him? Against him?"

The ball flew back over the fence. The sinewy kid had gone to retrieve it.

Mango chimed in, "Your father, Gabby, you put him and Slim on the same team, you don't need the other three guys."

Bella seemed impressed. "Really?"

I said to her, "We'd better get going. We'll come back another time. OK?"

I ran my hand across the back of her still-moist neck, and looked up for a newsstand so I could get us a couple of bottles of cold water. Behind me, the game resumed: the squeak of rubber on the asphalt, body banging body, the steady rhythm of the ball; trash talk, mild now since the dust-up. Scoop had been humbled, but not for long: You could tell by looking at him that he'd open his mouth again soon.

I glanced across the avenue, remembering a newsstand near the Waverly that had cold drinks. And there, moving steadily, was Sol Beck, heading for the All-American Diner, for his father.

"Oh, Christ," I said, louder than I'd wanted to.

"Dad, what?"

I thought quickly, then turned to Mango. "Jimmy, hold on to her." I said it sharply, and Mango nodded. He put his arm on Bella's shoulder. I looked at her; I tossed the basketball to her. "Bella—"

"Sol Beck is going into that diner," she said. "He looks mad, Dad."

I nodded. "I know. I don't want him to get hurt," I said. "You wait with Jimmy."

"I got her," Mango said.

And I turned and ran across Sixth, dodging taxis and cars rushing uptown, waiting on a stripe of white paint, inching sideways, heading south to go west; finally making it across the frantically busy street.

THE DINER WAS crowded this time, with people in every booth, and almost every sea-green stool at the counter was filled. They were all looking at Beck, who was screaming at his father.

As I came in, I saw that it wasn't too far gone: Sid, fumbling to remove his bifocals, had jumped in front of Beck. Rosenzweig was still in his seat. He seemed thoroughly unimpressed.

"Let him go, Sid," Rosenzweig said.

I bumped into a man who had stepped into the aisle to watch. Behind me, I heard flatware hit the floor.

"You coward! You God-damned coward!" Beck shouted. "You tried to ruin my show and then you attacked her. You bastard!"

I reached Beck, who was pointing at his father over Sid's shoulder. I grabbed the collar of his black jacket and yanked him back toward me.

"Ha!" Rosenzweig shouted. "Your bodyguard is here."

I tried to spin Beck around, but the aisle was too narrow. Instead, I grabbed his right wrist and held it tight.

"Cool down, Sol," I whispered.

He tried to shake free but it was no use. He was small and light.

"Don't hurt him," Sid said. The old man's round face was pale from fear, and he trembled from the sudden exertion.

To assure him, I nodded gently.

As they'd scrambled away from Beck, the people near the far end of the counter had formed a knot near the kitchen. A man in a white t-shirt, white slacks and a long apron, the one with the uneven mustache I'd seen days ago slumped at the cash register, emerged from the crowd with, of all things, a bullwhip. And he held it firmly at his side, as if he was going to crack it.

"Sid," I shouted. "Get back."

Sid turned, saw the man with the whip and jumped back into the booth across from Rosenzweig.

With a heavy Greek accent, the man ordered, "Get him the fuck out of here."

Rosenzweig stood. "It's all right, Alex." He put his right hand on the man's shoulder. "It's just some kid I used to know."

"I don't care, Chick," the man grunted. "Get him out."

I had my jaw near Beck's ear. "I'm going to release you now," I said, "and I'm going to walk you outside."

Beck snapped his head away from me in anger.

I continued, "Before I let you go I'm going to tell you something: You are wrong. You hear me? Your father has nothing to do with this, Sol. Nothing."

And I let go of his wrist, and took my hand from his collar.

He turned and looked at me. He was the saddest man in the world.

I stepped aside and let him pass. As we went down the aisle, I put my hand on his back, leading him past people whose looks of fear had turned to confusion and sympathy.

I led him through the last of the crowd and we went outside. Bella was there with Mango. She didn't seem frightened, but she was bewildered: She'd just peered through the glass doors to see her father drag Sol Beck, the brittle artist, away from a confrontation with a bull-whip.

I grabbed Beck by the shoulder. When he turned, he would not meet my eyes. "Stay here," I told him.

He nodded weakly.

I put my hand on his chest and gave him a gentle nudge. "Stay," I repeated. Then I turned to Bella and Mango.

"Nice going, Jimmy," I said. "Thanks."

"Fuck that," he replied. "I want in. Is that him, the guy they bombed?"

"You OK, Bella?"

"I'm fine. Are you?"

"Yeah. Sol's mad at his father." I put my finger on my temple. "He's not thinking straight."

"Stress," she said, as she looked past me at Beck. "It's natural."

"If you give me five minutes, I think I can help him." I looked up at Mango, at his ridiculous straw hat. "Jimmy, take her back to the court."

"Am I in? I'm in, right?"

"Later, Jimmy."

Mango nodded knowingly, as if we had just made some sort of pact.

Bella took Mango's hand when he offered it. Together, they went to the crosswalk.

I returned to Beck, who had turned his back on me. "Let's walk," I said, as I crooked my hand under his arm to turn him around. Behind him, people inside the diner were up and staring out the window.

He started walking, sliding under the Waverly marquee, moving toward his home.

"Lin-Lin tell you I visited her last evening? Sol? Sol, I need you to listen to me."

He sighed. It had all fallen down around him. He was defeated.

"Sol, you need to ask Lin-Lin what I told her. Sol?"

He muttered, "All right."

"I told her I know who arranged the bombing." We passed a pizza parlor and a vitamin shop. A thin man in a gray raincoat walked by with the aid of a cane.

Beck looked at me. "Who?" he asked.

"You'll have to ask her. She knows."

"You tell me, Terry," he said, frowning.

"I can't. She needs to."

"I don't understand."

We had reached Carmine Street. He took the curb gingerly, as if he feared he'd fall.

"Sol, you've got to watch your back. You've got to be alert. What happened to Lin-Lin could happen to you."

"She was mugged."

I said, "No, Sol. Remember, she wasn't robbed. They smacked her and ran off."

He repeated, "I don't understand."

We continued south, onto Father Demo Square, passing gangly trees and benches, several of which were occupied by older men and women who fed pigeons, read newspapers, sank into their heavy coats. "Sol, your father isn't in this thing. Understand that and you'll be able to focus on what's going on." We stopped and I turned him to look at me. "Sol, go home and calm down. Then go to the hospital and tell Lin-Lin we spoke."

He was nodding, but I wasn't sure he was hearing.

"You need to talk to your wife. You understand?"

He pursed his lips, and he closed his eyes. Then, he nodded as he opened his eyes. "I'll talk to her, Terry," he said.

"All right."

He started walking and he reached Downing. He waited for a car to pass, then he continued, slouching as he strode.

I crossed Sixth and trotted back to Bella.

TEN

MANGO BROUGHT HER NOT to the court, but to the playground, with its jungle gym, racks of rubber tires, plastic ponies on huge springs, scooting preschoolers and their contented mothers. Her back to me, off-white towel slung over her shoulder, Bella watched as two craggy-faced men in the corner hunched over a cement-and-stone chessboard. I knew next-to-nothing about chess and, fortunately for the two ancient men, neither did Bella or she'd be telling them what to do.

The contest in the Cage had found its flow, but from this viewpoint, it seemed a mass of scuffling black bodies surrounded by a diffident crowd. When the battered orange ball rose toward the basket, it seemed to come from deep in a pit. Then, cheering or recrimination, both shouted with insolence.

"She didn't want the swings," Mango said affably. He added, "I told her I'd push."

"She was probably afraid you'd throw her over the

fence. Christ, Jimmy, what the fuck did you let her see that for?" I pointed to the other side of Sixth, to the diner.

"What? You were a hero. Man, you was in there like Rambo."

I shook my head. "She doesn't need that."

He ignored my remark. "So, am I in or what?"

"In what, Jimmy? There's nothing."

"Hey, Terry, don't bullshit me, all right? You're looking for the guy who bombed the gallery."

"Who told you that?" I feared his reply. Did Bella tell his son, the little JJ Hunsecker, the Liz Smith of the fifth grade?

"Who told me? Tommy. Who the fuck else?"

I was going to ask him how his brother had found out, but I let it slide. Tommy was like an old-style beat cop: He seemed to know everything that went on in his neighborhood, and he had his finger in more than a bit of the action.

"What's the reward? Give me a ballpark. Five Gs? Ten?"

I looked over his head. Bella was sitting on the bench now, next to the man playing the black pieces. She had the basketball in her lap.

"No reward, Jimmy."

"So, what are you, fuckin' Robin Hood?"

I've never taken a dime for these things I do. I don't need to, thanks to Marina's success and my book. Nor do I want to: Something about the coin devalues the mission.

But try explaining that to one of the Mango brothers.

I said, "The woman who was hurt in the explosion was Marina's agent."

Mango took off his straw hat and held it over his chest. "God rest her soul," he said solemnly. "Your wife had real class."

I nodded. The old man explained his move to Bella.

"Somebody'll get that nut fuck someday, Terry, that fuck that did it."

Mango quickly returned the hat to his head, once again concealing his Larry Fine hairline. "So, I mean, to get back to my point. Money: There's always more than enough to go around, you know what I mean? This Harper broad: She's flush, right? She's got to have something stashed somewhere."

"Forget it, Jimmy. Judy's a friend."

He said, "Who's got your back, Four? And how can you do two things at once?"

"Two things?"

"You're trying to chase down the guy who killed the spook cabdriver."

Mango was like an incessant bug, buzzing near your ear. You either had to move away from him or swat him down. The problem was, if you tried to swat him, you had better succeed. Once in Big Chief's, Leo was tending bar when he saw Mango get into a thing with a smarmy, condescending guy about my height with a Schwarzenegger build. In a heartbeat, Mango was on the guy: He threw a left to the guy's temple, then a right to his jaw, before the big man could get his hands up. The guy went down fast, and Mango jumped on his chest, sat on him and punched him hard in the throat. Then he leapt up to watch the gagging, gasping man spasm, then cough up blood and bile. The whole thing took less than 10 seconds. Later, after EMS had gone, after Tommy the Cop got his brother out of the back of a squad car on Greenwich, when Big Chief's was empty, the lights were on and the restaurant staff was sweeping up, Leo found a rusted railroad spike under a table not far from where Mango jumped the big guy. Leo, who said he watched the incident from the start to its sudden end, never saw Mango pull the spike, never saw him switch hands with it, never saw him toss it away.

"You need a partner."

I looked at him.

"You're full of shit, Terry, you say you don't."

"Maybe I got something else for you," I said finally.

"I don't leave the house for less than two Gs."

"I'll give you $20 an hour."

"Done," he said quickly.

I gave him Amaral's address, the condo on 14th, not the place he lost way uptown. "Grease the doorman, find out what Amaral looks like and tail him."

"That's it?"

"That's it. Where he goes, when. Who comes to see him."

"I'll milk the shit out of this." Mango beamed.

"Don't dump this off. You've got to tail his ass, Jimmy."

"Got it, partner," he said. "The clock's running, ain't it?"

"Go take a fuckin' shower."

I left Mango and walked over to retrieve Bella. She was standing now, the fedora tipped to the back of her head.

As I approached, I said, "Give the man back his hat."

"We made a trade, Dad. Cool, no? How does it look on me?"

I turned to the man, 100 years old, curved over the board, his gnarled, bony fingers sliding a black rook. He looked up at me and smiled, revealing two long teeth. He raised his hand and tapped the beret.

I shrugged. "Looks great, Bella," I said. "Say goodbye to your friends."

She did and we walked toward the opening in the gate, toward Sixth.

"So I guess I got to know Jimmy Mango a little better," she suggested.

I held her hand. "He's nuts. Don't pay attention to him."

"You know, his son is different," she said. "They look the same, but he's different."

The light changed and we went across the avenue. "If the kid takes after his mother, he's lucky."

I ASKED DIDDIO to ease off the weed and take another late-night sit, and shortly before 1 A.M. I went directly to West Street and headed north, toward Little West 12th, where Aubrey Brown entertained his last fare.

The night had finally taken on a chill, and as I walked near the river I could hear the black water slap against rotted pilings, and I could smell salt and feel the bite of the bitter wind. Thick clouds had swept away the stars, and the dull glow of the flickering streetlights cast eerie shadows. The mottled blacktop, where during the day houseplants and macramé and woven baskets were offered by mobile vendors, where Rollerbladers shimmied and played, had been abandoned. I saw no one in front of me, and traffic heading south, toward the Battery, was sporadic and unreliable. In a mile or so, there would be gay bars and lovers on the tar slab called Hudson River Park, and the flow of pedestrians on Christopher Street. Then, as I continued north past the bus terminal, a few scruffy auto-repair shops and a car wash and, nearer to Ninth, steel-and-glass apartment towers, chic new restaurants, timeworn diners and the ghosts of Herman Melville and a livery-cab driver with vacant, haunting eyes. But now, with the Hudson to my left, and broken bottles and stubborn weeds under me, and parked cars—lifeless, hollow-eyed sentries—to my right, I was alone. As I shoved my hands into the pouch of my hooded black sweatshirt, I realized I was at least anxious and maybe a little bit afraid.

Diddio had turned up late—"She did four encores; what could I do?"—and he was toasted, of course.

"You really are the poster boy for pot, D."

"I had a rough day," he explained. "I had to do my laundry."

I checked my pockets: wallet, a little cash, keys, cell phone. "Yeah, it's brutal."

"You wouldn't understand. You got a machine in your basement." Suddenly, he seemed wistful. "That's living."

"Look, I appreciate you coming over," I said. "I know a critic needs to be out on Saturday night."

"Nah. I was going to check out a show at S.O.B.'s, but it's no problem. Sharon Stone, believe it or not, is cutting a live album, one of these Cybill Shepherd/Diane Keaton things. Big show-biz audience. I was thinking of pitching something to *Parade* magazine. Man, do they pay. It's, like—"

"D, you need to go to the show, go. I can do this tomorrow night." But I wanted to do this now.

"No, no," he replied, waving his hands. "I don't want to cut in on your action. I'm glad to see you got something going on." He stopped and sighed. "Maybe I'll get a date one of these years."

"D, what are you talking about? 'Date.' Do you think I'd go on a date like this?"

I gestured to my black running shoes, black jeans and gray t-shirt under my black sweatshirt.

"I would," he said.

I gave him a cold bottle of skunky beer and sent him

inside to watch TV. If Bella woke up, I told him, he should encourage her to go back to bed.

I locked the door behind me.

I'D REACHED WEST 10th, having passed Canal and West Houston and the Village, quiet factories, abandoned flatbed trucks in a litter-strewn yard, muscular men in leather on Pier 34, a rundown hotel. There was a burst of activity on the east side of the wide street: three, four people in a circle of animated conversation, others walking south toward the bars on Christopher, a young couple cuddling, teasing, pecking on the steps of an empty warehouse, the queue outside a nameless nightclub. I kept moving, and two blocks later it was suddenly quiet again and I could see no one on the street in front of me. And then I looked to my right, to the corner of Charles, and inside a black Lincoln, a woman in a fluffy faux fur eased herself onto the lap of a man who'd slid over to the passenger's side of the front seat, and she began to roll her hips and thrust her chest and the man threw back his head as he readied to shudder. A couple in their mid-30s, she with the early edition of the Sunday *Times* under her arm, he with a leash attached to a dog I couldn't see, walked casually by the car without peering inside, either not noticing or pretending not to. Meanwhile, when I looked back into the Lincoln, I saw that the woman had completed her task, and without ceremony, she opened the passenger-side door and walked away on shaky heels, patting down a silvery skirt that barely reached her thighs. Twenty-five dollars or so lighter, the sated man remained where he was, his head on the red pads of the big car's seatback, as he caught his breath.

Up ahead, the Gansevoort Market was silent. And once again I realized that on a Friday night, a man could be murdered on Little West 12th Street and no one would notice.

The hooker had disappeared, but I decided to follow and, hopping the divider, I headed across the empty highway to Charles and went into the hazy light on the corner, then passed the sagging man in the car. As I moved east, I heard the big roar of the Lincoln kicking in, and then the man drove past me and I watched him go. When I looked back toward where I was headed, I saw her out of the corner of my eye, in the shadows on a side street, and she saw me and she smiled. I imagined she thought she'd make $50 in five minutes. I rubbed my warm hands against my cold cheeks.

She leaned against the graffiti-covered brick of the squat building behind her. "You going out?"

"I think I'm looking for something different."

As I stepped closer, I saw that she was a hard case. Her speckled face was stretched tight over her skull, and black roots threatened to overtake the short-cropped, platinum-blond hair above it. Though her shoulders were wide, she was flat-chested; her legs were more sinewy than shapely, and her fingers, which rested on her thighs, were thick and her hands were large.

"What do you need, baby?"

In the distance, music, electronic and pulsing. The street was empty. "A boy," I said, perhaps too directly.

She slowly raised her hands along her thighs and slid her thin silver skirt up her leg, revealing a deliberate hole in her black stockings. And at the center of the hole, amid a tuft of dark hair, was a small, flaccid cock.

"I got what you need." His inner thigh glistened in the pale light.

I shook my head.

"You want a boy to suck, maybe. Is that right, honey? We can do that, baby." He started tugging on his penis, trying to make it jump to life.

"No, no, don't do that," I said, grimacing. "Christ, put that away."

He dropped the skirt. Suddenly, his voice was husky, at least huskier than it had been. "What's your fuckin' deal, man?" he barked.

"I'm looking for a boy. I told you that."

He came off the wall and started away from me, click-clacking down the barren street, toward parked cars and dented garbage cans.

"Wait—"

He turned. "I'm working. I got no time to play games."

I followed. "I'll pay. What do you get?"

He paused. "Fifty."

"Bullshit," I said. I dug into my pocket. "Here's thirty dollars."

He snatched at the two bills. I pulled them back and handed him the ten.

"This kid has got a big scar." I traced from above my eye to below my lower lip. "He's young, about thirteen or fourteen."

"You his father?"

I shook my head. "He's black."

"What makes you think he's here?"

His former friend Delroy Henry said he was living on the streets and working as a prostitute. You could get boys on the piers near Little West 12th, and underage girls, and a transvestite who could get you off by easing you between his scrotum and the petroleum gel on his firm inner thigh.

"He's here. They call him Montana."

"I don't know nobody's name," he said, "and I don't ever want to know."

"He's here," I repeated.

"There's a tribe in the abandoned building."

"Where?"

"Tenth, on the other side of market," he said. He had his eye on the twenty. "Go in on Jane Street. The fence won't hold."

"A couple more quest—"

"Hey, man," he snapped, "I've got to keep busy. Give me my money and get the hell out of here."

"Were you out here last Friday night?"

"I'm out here every night, Jackson."

"What do you know about the cabdriver who got killed?"

"Somebody gets killed every day, man. Sometimes it happens here."

"Anybody see anything?"

He smiled. He laughed.

I reached out and gave him the $20 bill. He snatched it and walked off, tugging at the collar of his cheap fur.

The rain had finally come as a delicate mist. In the distance, the top of the Empire State Building glistened in the haze.

I THOUGHT HE'D be on the piers, huddled in an old Sealand container or behind the Sanitation Department plant, or under Pier 34; he'd take a john behind the remnants of construction work—gaping, rusted pipes; pyramid piles of plastic tubing; mounds of broken concrete and soil; an overturned Portosan—or near the lapping water, or by the run-down shack where the tugs docked, and he'd lean back and let it happen. And that's how I would find him: I would position myself on the rotting planks near Little West 12th and wait to be approached, and I would insist on a black boy, a pretty one, with dreadlocks, and he would appear. As I pushed up Tenth, I told myself to focus, to be clear. It could still work, but I'd have to be alert as I went to Washington to come

around to Jane: I'd be in the shadows, isolated, surrounded by old, imposing buildings and thick walls, with
no easy way to break free. Once in place, I'd have to let
him come to me. I told myself, This is how it's done.

I came to the market: All blacktop and tainted brick, it
was empty, as ghostly as if it had been deserted years
ago, and there on the north side of Little West 12th was
the derelict building that the transvestite had mentioned:
battered, graffiti-scarred, silver metal plates over its windows, discarded tires, gangly weeds cracking the concrete that led to its foundation. In an attempt to make it
presentable, in another of Giuliani's cosmetic moves, the
city had painted its façade an odd mustard-yellow and
thrown up a cyclone fence. From Tenth, it looked like a
neglected building that the city had tried to make less of
an eyesore, somewhat passable; from the side street, it
was no different from the rancid, crippled structures in
the South Bronx that had long ago lost their tenants to
rabid rats and desperate junkies.

The new TriBeCa my ass, I thought as I turned down
Little West 12th.

Washington Street was hushed and dark; it was the
street, I realized, that the transvestite had walked down as
he left me, and I listened for the electronic music and the
edgy patter of his heels, but no sound came from the void.
And then, a car on Tenth, moving fast.

I headed toward Jane, walking along the cyclone fence,
bracing myself against the scent of stale urine. Near a yel-
lowed, crumpled newspaper and a broken Pepsi bottle I
saw a cat; I saw it before it saw me. I stopped. It gnawed
on the sinew of a chicken bone; then it caught me in its
gold, translucent eyes, and hunched its back to defend its
meal.

Then I turned and saw him and the blade flashed, and
he missed me on the first pass. But he brought it across

again with a high, backhand swipe and he caught me on the point of the chin. Blood spurted.

"Next one's your throat," he spat, as I turned my back to him.

He stepped up and pressed his body against mine.

I crouched, then stood still.

"I watch *you*. I find *you*," he hissed.

I spun and caught him square in the face with an elbow, and I knew I'd hurt him bad, stopping him for at least an instant.

He hunched over, his hands at his face. The switchblade was on the wet concrete. I bent and grabbed it, dizzy, from the blood, the rush, fear. I steadied myself.

"You broke my nose, fucker," he said, his voice muffled by his hands. He was small, a boy.

"Stand up," I said.

"Fuck you."

"Stand up, Montana," I shouted. I reached out and smacked his hands and they banged against his nose.

And he stood, slowly.

"You're not even bleeding," I said. "Wuss."

He looked up at me with disdain.

Meanwhile, blood was running down my neck, spreading on my t-shirt, my black sweatshirt.

"I ought to slice you up, you little shit."

He turned his head slightly, so I could get a clear view of his scar. "You think I'm afraid to be cut, man? Go ahead, I won't even fuckin' move."

He was wearing the same clothes he'd had on when I first saw him at Henderson's: red stocking cap atop his dreadlocks, black down coat, baggy jeans, stylish black high-top basketball shoes.

I pressed the heel of my hand against the wound. "Your name is Andre Turner. Your father is in prison, doing time for killing your mother. You were a student at Hurston Elementary, a good one, before he started abusing you."

He tried to remain composed, but his eyes revealed his surprise.

"See, I know you, worm." My hand was dripping blood.

"You don't know nothing," he replied calmly. "What you said is what was."

I wiped my hand on my jeans. "I came here to talk to you and you cut me. Damn it."

"Talk to me?" he repeated. "What for? I don't jeopardize."

"I want to know what happened to Aubrey Brown." I put my back against the red buttress of an old firebox.

"I don't know no—"

I cut him off. "Let's not fuck around here. You saw Brown get killed. Either you saw it or you did it."

He rolled his eyes and gave me an exaggerated wave.

"But you wouldn't risk coming to the funeral home if you killed him. So that means you only saw it," I said.

"You don't know shit."

"I got enough to have the cops bring you in."

"I been in jail before," he boasted. "It don't chill me."

"Not for manslaughter. You won't go to juvie."

He snorted in disdain as he inched toward the wobbling fence. "And what? Am I supposed to be shittin'?"

"Or maybe it'll be Family Court. You and your father, back in front of a judge."

He didn't like the idea of seeing his father or finding himself back in the system. For an instant, his bravado wavered.

"I can see it: You, your new foster family, upstate in some cracker town, milking the cows—"

He said sharply, "I didn't kill nobody. So I got nothing to worry about." He shoved his hands into the pockets of his down jacket. "Nothing."

"Except me."

"I can shake you any time I want," he said.

"No, I'll find you again. Montana."

He thought about that and he glanced at his switch-blade, which I held awkwardly, loosely, with the blade pointed at his chest.

"Help me put it together and get yourself out of this mess."

"I didn't take the wallet. I didn't go near the car."

"Not enough."

"What?" He shook his head stubbornly, insistently, snapping his long, twisted locks. "That's all I got."

"You saw it."

"If I did, there ain't nothin' I can do about it."

"Give him up," I insisted.

"Who? Give up who?"

I said, "Amaral."

And he registered genuine surprise on his scarred, fe-line face. He slumped, as if exposed.

"Whatever it is you owe him—"

"Yo," he charged, stiffening again, "I ain't no punk."

"You're bright enough to know about conspiracy after the fact," I said.

"Aw, get off with that." He waved the back of his hand at me.

"Not that I give a fuck," I said as I looked at my bloody fingers. "Your problems are your own, little man."

"I can take care of myself," he said. "Just give me my blade."

"Fuck that."

He paused. He wiped blood from his face with the side of his thumb. But he stayed quiet.

I turned and went north. The pretty boy was behind me, at the fence, calculating his move, but there was nothing he could do.

I kept moving, my hand under my chin.

"Wait," he shouted.

As I turned and started backpedaling, he came toward me. He reached up and grabbed at his cap. "I need that motherfuckin' blade."

"Trade," I offered.

He came closer. "What've I got to trade?"

I shrugged. "Suit yourself, little man."

I turned and kept going, kicking an overturned trash can. Crumpled fast-food sacks and cigarette butts lay on the wet concrete.

He shouted. "Go fuck yourself." It echoed off the abandoned buildings, the tattered cobblestones.

When I reached Horatio, I closed the blade and dropped it into a puddle in the gutter.

I could hear him scramble up the dark street to retrieve it.

I FOUND THE aluminum-and-glass tower at the center of 14th, between Ninth and Tenth. In the lobby there were potted plants, two soft chairs in teal with a cherry-stained coffee table between them and a big, circular cherry-stained security desk with video monitors. The middle-aged guard was reading a paperback novel through hornrims. A tall paper cup from Starbucks rested at his elbow.

The blood had stopped trickling and I dabbed at my neck with my sleeve, hoping to pat away red streaks. As I leaned over to examine my wound in a mirror on the side of a black Mustang parked across from Amaral's building, I heard a short bleat from a car horn. I looked up and saw a yellow cab at the curb. Jimmy Mango waved at me from behind the wheel.

I went toward Ninth to meet him. He had the cab parked at a hydrant. In the front passenger's seat was a young woman with close-cropped hair, a black top under an unbuttoned white shirt, a short black skirt. She wore black hose and had her shoes off. Her feet were in Mango's lap. She had a 40-ounce bottle of Colt 45 between her knees.

"Alice, Terry," Mango said.

"Alice," I said.

She nodded.

"We seen nothin'," Mango said. He pointed. "You got a hole in you."

Alice giggled.

I crouched down. "Cut the dome light," I said.

Mango reached up and killed the light.

"Jimmy, what's the deal here?" I gestured toward Alice.

He tugged at his dark turtleneck. "I need relief, you know what I mean, Saturday night. I been here since noon."

"Amaral," I said.

Mango shifted toward me, resting his elbow on the steering wheel. Alice pouted as she withdrew her feet.

"He went to the dry cleaner's. He bought a newspaper. Went to the deli. Nothing else."

"He see anybody?"

"Not out here."

"You sure you're on the right guy?" I asked.

"Definitely." He nodded. "By the way, you're out two hundred bucks with the day guard. Fuckin' thief. The night guard, that fuckin' librarian over there, he's a cheap date. Twenty-five bucks."

"Anybody go in?"

He shook his head. "The guards'll tip me if he gets a visitor."

As I stood, I saw a pizza box in the backseat. "Where'd you get that?"

"Alice is an angel," he replied and tapped her knee.

She smiled curtly.

"Jimmy," I said, "you've got to be alert now. This is the guy."

"I figured."

"You got a phone?"

He pointed toward the glove compartment. "But fuck the phone. Let's take him down now."

I said no. "Not tonight."

"Whatever. I'm on the clock. Better for me."

"Amaral moves, you call me. A kid with a long scar on his face comes to see him, you call me."

"No prob."

"You can't reach me, you call Tommy."

Mango smiled darkly. "Tommy don't give a shit, Four, about some spook driver. You oughta know that."

That sounded right. But it was after 2 A.M., my chin throbbed and I was freezing on the shadowy side street. It wasn't worth considering an alternative. "You can't reach me, call your brother. All right?"

Reluctantly, he agreed.

I tapped him on the arm and nodded good-night to Alice, who tiredly rolled her eyes up toward a heavy layer of mascara.

I started toward Ninth, then stopped and went back. Mango was taking a pull at the 40-ounce.

"Where'd you get the cab, Jimmy?" I asked.

He wiped his damp lips with his sleeve. "Aw, Four, you don't wanna know that."

Alice was giggling as I left.

ELEVEN

I FUMBLED WITH THE security code in the dull, tinted light outside my house, and silently swore at myself as I stood on the wet steps and punched the buttons again. I wanted to catch my breath, sneak in, slip into the half-bath off the kitchen and clean up before rousing Diddio, who'd be nodding in front of VH1, or accidentally waking up Bella and giving her a fright. In the morning, I'd lie to her: It'd be better than telling her I was cut by a boy who, had he been hard enough, would've raked the blade across my throat and left me gasping and bubbling in the rain as he watched me die. Another lesson learned, and a slice on the chin was a small price to pay.

I got the right four-digit combination, slid a key into the second dead bolt, quietly eased the knob around and stepped inside.

Bella and Diddio were at the kitchen table, drinking hot cocoa, toying with a multicolored Fisher-Price xylophone.

"She heard the door close when you went out, man," Diddio said immediately. "I didn't wake her up. I didn't."

Bella asked, "What happened to you?"

"I fell."

"On your chin?"

"I fell on my chin."

She shook her head, calmly, as if I were her child, exasperating her once again. I knew her: It was a preemptive strike.

"You are very lucky that you didn't get hit by a car," she said. "Why would you go out running at night wearing black?"

I looked at her, sitting there in her ankle-length cotton nightgown, her bare feet in her untied bowling shoes, jean jacket over her shoulders, a paper clip on her earlobe.

"I think it's time for a 'young lady' speech," I said.

"Uh, Terry," Diddio interrupted, "maybe you ought to do something about that hole in your face first." I noticed that Bella's fedora was perched precariously on his head.

I went into the bathroom to dry off and work on the cut, shutting the door behind me, twisting the faucet all the way open to get the water hot enough to soothe. On the other side of the door: tentative music, plink-plink. Outside, the rain continued unabated and I could hear it against the small window above the sink.

I studied myself in the mirror, under a bare bulb: streaks of blood caked on my neck below a ragged scab that had begun to form on my chin. I looked in my eyes. If I'd learned anything tonight, there was no evidence of it there. I saw the same eyes I'd looked into when I was adrift as a boy; a feckless, self-doubting teenager; a young man. The same eyes I'd seen when the world had blown apart.

My hair was wet and unruly, and rivulets of rainwater

and sweat ran down my cheeks. I needed a shave.

"Dad, hurry up," Bella shouted. "I want to show you something."

"Give me a minute," I said, over the rushing water.

I grabbed a towel from the bar behind me and ran it around my head. The peroxide was under the sink. Cotton balls? There, as well, near the Band-Aids. I set out to fix myself.

I CAME DOWNSTAIRS in a clean t-shirt and running shorts and found a cup of steaming hot cocoa in front of my seat at the table.

"Bella," I said as I sat to join them, "do you have any idea what time it is?"

"Sure. There's a clock on the wall over the sink, and one in the stove."

"Perhaps I should be more direct."

"Listen to this," she instructed. She picked up the plastic mallets and began to pluck out a familiar riff on the toy xylophone.

"Name that tune," Diddio said, as Bella continued.

"'Sunshine of Your Love,'" I offered.

"Right," Bella said. "Now, this one."

I waited. I recognized it, but couldn't come up with the name.

Diddio began to sing along. "'In-A-Gadda-Da-Vida, baby...'" He cleared his throat. "We're working on 'Voodoo Chile.'"

"Christ, Bella, those songs were old when I was a kid."

"Dennis says they're classics."

"She's a prodigy, Terry, I'm telling you. A regular Mozart. Or Steve Winwood."

"All right, enough creativity," I announced. "It's time

for bed." I looked at Diddio. "No sense in you going out in the rain. You take my room."

His eyes brightened. "A *bed*. Wow, I haven't slept in a bed in months."

Diddio had a futon, a purple thing. It was as comfortable as wet sand.

As she stood, Bella said, "I'm teaching Dennis to play chess." She withdrew two bills from her jacket. "I'm up six bucks."

She headed up the stairs, but not before giving Diddio a peck on the cheek, and not before she took back her frayed fedora, exchanging it for the paper-clip earring. I followed, watching her shoelaces flap.

I stood by the door frame as she hung her jacket in her closet and kicked her shoes off to slide them into their proper spot under the bed. She took a moment to stick the two bills into the trunk of her pink Barbie car, then bounced onto her floral down spread.

"I'm going to try to make it to 3 A.M.," she told me. "I've never been awake at three in the morning."

"You're very ambitious," I said. "Will I see you before noon?"

"Did you really fall?"

I hesitated. "It's a long story."

She pointed. "It seems unlikely that you could fall on that spot," she said. "Let me see your palms. Any scrapes?"

"I'll explain," I said, "but not at 2:46."

"Does it hurt?"

"Not as bad as cutting myself shaving, but yes, a little."

"Come here," she said. "I'll kiss you happy."

I leaned forward and she gave me a gentle kiss on the point of my chin.

"Mama used to say that."

"I know," I said. "'I'll kiss you happy.'"

She snuggled under the covers and smiled up at me. "I had a good day, Dad."

Somehow, we had succeeded in making it seem like it used to be, like it could have been, if only for a few hours.

I touched her cheek. Her skin was as soft as when she was a baby. I laid my finger on the tip of her nose, which was no longer the tiny bud it had been, and wished I could be as affectionate as I once was.

"Don't give Dennis his six dollars back."

I shook my head.

"More basketball tomorrow," she instructed.

"Maybe. We've got tickets for a play, remember?"

She nodded.

"You got Moose?"

She reached under the top sheet, rummaged around a bit and came up with the stuffed animal.

"Good night, Dad."

"Good night, little angel."

I cut the overhead light and closed the door behind me. As I walked down the hall, I noticed Diddio had already made his way into my bedroom.

"Thanks, man." A muffled, though grateful, voice from behind my door.

I went downstairs, bare feet on creaking wood.

PRODDED BY A stiff neck from the short night on the sofa, I woke up earlier than I might have wanted to. The comforter I'd pulled from the hall closet was on the floor, as was a cassette bearing Diddio's scrawl. The band's name was the Insolent Bastards. I guess they don't cover "Kumbaya," I thought, as I stood and felt for the bandage, which had stayed in place under my aching chin.

I headed toward the bathroom off the kitchen. It was a

little after nine, and still raining, though it was back to the weighty mist it had been before turning into a downpour around four, when I'd cut the computer and headed for the couch. Morning light seemed to be struggling to get through. Maybe it would clear; there might be time for basketball, before heading back to the Village and Minetta Lane for Shaw and his Raina and ridiculous Sergius and the ablest man in Bulgaria.

I brushed my teeth and washed carefully. I decided against shaving for now; I would later, when I was ready to change the bandage and examine the cut. The terrazzo floor felt cold against my feet and I felt a chill on my legs. October revealed the subtle flaws in this 150-year-old brick-and-wood house; I'd forgotten them over the warm summer. I'd have to put in the storm windows sometime next week.

The phone in the kitchen was a cordless model. As I went to the refrigerator for a bottle of Badoit, I punched in the number I'd gotten last night.

I decided to let it ring. If I woke her, I'd apologize.

She got it on the third ring.

"Hello?"

"Yes."

"Julie, it's Terry Orr."

"Terry, hi." She seemed pleased. "How did you get—"

"The Rosemont College alumni directory. You're on the membership committee."

"Right. The Web site."

I sat at the kitchen table, pushing the xylophone aside. "I hope I didn't—"

"No," she replied. "I was getting ready for church."

I imagined Julie Giada in a smart dress and black flats, her moon face solemn, though not enough to mar her bright eyes, her warm smile. Sharon Knight had told me she let Julie query the jurors they wanted to keep. Julie's smile swung them to the state's side before the first witness hit the stand. Sharon said, "She's a good girl. And happy."

"Julie, I need a favor."

"Sure, Terry."

"A tough one on a Sunday morning."

"Then I'll say I'll try."

I could hear her smile.

"I'm trying to find out if someone rented commercial space in SoHo. Or maybe uptown on Madison."

"I see."

I took a sip of the cold, sparkling water. "This'd be space for a gallery."

"An art gallery?" she asked.

"Right."

"Is it that woman who was hurt in the explosion? The one you know?"

"No," I said, "but close enough."

"Sharon was telling me. Sounds like something worth doing, Terry. To find out who hurt a friend."

I shrugged. "Feels that way."

"OK," she said, "give me the name. There's someone I can call. I'll have to get him out of bed, but..."

"Julie, I don't want you to use a chit you don't have."

"No," she replied. "Count me in. Like I said, sounds right."

I gave her two names. On the other end of the phone, pen scratching on paper.

I told her I'd call her.

"I'll be back by 11, 11:15," she said. "If you'd like to come by...Late breakfast, early brunch." She added nervously, "You know."

"I wish, Julie. I've got to work this now."

"Rain check?"

I hesitated. "We'll see."

It would've been wrong to say no. She's a good girl. And happy.

THE OFFICES OF *AbEx* magazine were in a building on the outskirts of SoHo, at the corner of Wooster and Canal, a short stroll from Chinatown. They were precisely as I remembered: musty, disheveled, comfortable, inviting. Years ago, I freelanced a piece for *AbEx*, profiling Sandro Chia, more as a favor to Marina than for the fee. The piece I turned in was breathless, a puerile display of pyrotechnics designed to impress my new wife. Arno Bloom took the overblown tripe and turned it into something presentable.

That I was standing in the open vestibule to the *AbEx* offices was no guarantee that Arno Bloom was inside. He'd been known to teeter out without closing up, head out for dim sum and a casual stroll to a gallery on Mercer or a meeting on Spring, and return to find a pair of homeless men asleep on the battered leather sofa that I stood in front of now. He denied that he offered this kindness by design, but his friends knew better, as did his neighbors in this old building, who made sure that no one walked out with his old Compaq 286. Arno kept his archives behind lock and key, so well-organized as to suggest that he knew what he had was of historical value. He'd founded *AbEx* during World War II and was the first American to profile in depth the abstract expressionists Marc Chagall, Max Ernst, Arshile Gorky and Yves Tanguy, among dozens of others. He championed Jackson Pollock, Willem de Kooning, Franz Josef Kline and Mark Rothko, and he created a diary of the downtown art scene at its height. It was said that the paintings Arno owned, all on loan to museums throughout the U.S. and his native Poland, were worth perhaps $100 million. Yet the 83-year-old man with the Einstein hairstyle and oversized glasses that made him look like a five-foot-high owl lived as he had since he arrived in New York shortly before the blitzkrieg—with a simplicity that revealed contentment.

I found Arno at work, his elbows on the dented gray Steelcase desk.

"A little early, Arno, isn't it?"

He looked at me and I could see him trying to place me. "Fiorentino," he mused as he stood. "Orr. Terry Orr. Chia. So many words. Alliterations. Do you control your enthusiasm now?"

I nodded.

The office was a mess: stacks and stacks of torn and creased manila folders and loose sheets and old newspapers on top of beat-up filing cabinets, and assorted folders and papers on the desktop; a big old TV and, sitting on it, a radio with its antenna extended skyward, and on the radio, more paper, at all angles. The crooked blinds over the long windows were speckled with dust and a ratty towel covered the air-conditioning unit. The Indian rug on the floor might've been beautiful, say, 30 years ago, but now it lay worn and faded on the linoleum floor.

"Your wife. Terrible, terrible," he muttered as he wobbled toward me.

I stepped closer and shook his hand.

"This was a woman with a gift," he said.

He gestured for me to sit, and he eased himself into the chair next to mine. A slight, knowing gesture with his head invited me to speak.

"Arno, I need to look up something in your archives."

"About your wife? Of cour—"

"Actually, about Bullethead. You remember?"

He wrinkled his nose. "A fraud. A successful fraud, but a fraud."

"I'm trying to track him down."

"A séance you'll need."

"He's dead?"

He nodded. "An overdose, though not so interesting as heroin and a model at the Château Marmont, if you will. Somebody dumped him on the Pacific Coast Highway, outside a Denny's. A very American death. A bit low-brow, perhaps?"

Christ. "When?"

"Two years ago, maybe," he replied. "This was, I think, about the time your wife and son were killed." He shifted in the chair. "Why are you asking about this guy? You're not going to write about him? You can't. There is nothing to write, nothing with Walter Pafko."

"Walter Pafko?"

"His real name. He took Vlad Smith from the Russians and David and Tony Smith." He frowned in distaste. "Don't waste ink on this guy."

"I'm trying to piece together what happened at the Henley Harper Gallery."

He smiled as if relieved. "Ah, yes. Judy. I hear she is better."

I shrugged.

"This crazy place..." He let his thought drift away. "You'll give my regards."

"Of course," I said. "I thought maybe Bullethead was involved in this thing. Just a random idea, I guess. Explosives, downtown, art."

He pushed off the wooden arms of the chair. "Makes sense to me." His back to me, he dug into his baggy slacks and withdrew the heavy end of a key chain, a ring with perhaps two dozen keys. "You'll see what you can find."

He went to a door with sturdy beveled glass and undid the lock. He snapped on the overhead light. Inside the small room, lining both walls, were high rows of old filing cabinets, dated from 1944 to the present. A wooden chair with casters rested against the wall.

"Every issue is in there." He pointed to a cabinet to my right. "Start with '84, maybe."

Arno stepped aside to let me squeeze in.

"Is there an index?" I asked.

He smiled and tapped the side of his head.

I WENT QUICKLY through the back copies of *AbEx,* skipping the issues I knew well; with Bullethead dead, I didn't know what I was looking for. There were only three copies of each magazine in each section, and I found myself turning the thin pages carefully, gingerly, as if I were holding a rare copy of *Frank Leslie's Illustrated Newspaper* from the 1850s; and rather than simply dump a copy on the floor when I was done with it, I put one back in its snug, proper place before removing the next.

Finally, I found a photo of Bullethead amid the back pages of the November 1986 issue. At a party at the Paula Cooper Gallery, he had his arm flung over the shoulder of Jackie Winsor, whom Arno described as an artist who "penetrated the anatomy of context" with her abstract sculptures. Scowling, tilting his shaved head in a manner that he seemed to think made him look menacing, Bullethead had a half-empty bottle of Jack Daniel's dangling in his hand. Winsor, meanwhile, looked like she hoped a trapdoor would open under him.

I looked closely at him, bringing the magazine under my nose in the stark light. His head looked more like the crown of an artillery shell than a cartridge. But "Bullethead" was close enough.

Ten minutes later, I found something. In the May 1988 issue, with a Mapplethorpe shot of a deadpanning Jasper Johns on the cover, there was a photo spread in back of a

Bullethead opening at the Carroll. Looking wan and soiled, his eyes sunken in black pits, Vlad Smith was sagging on a sofa, sycophants at hand. To his right on the sofa, looking as if she was responsible for keeping his head from lolling, was a young Edie Reeves. In the caption, she was identified as his representative.

I stood, chair creaking beneath me, and went out to Arno, who was proofreading an article the old-fashioned way: on paper, with a blue pencil in his hand. I slid the magazine in front of him.

"You remember anything about this?"

He looked at the cover. "Yes. I like this photo of Jasper. But this event? With Smith? Nothing."

"The girl?"

"She's pretty." He looked at the caption. "She is working now with Judy Harper."

"But she represented Bullethead?"

He dropped his finger on the glossy page. "If it says so . . ."

"No, I'm not questioning your reporting—"

Arno tapped my hand. "This is 1988," he said. "His time had passed. Who would touch him? She looks like a kid here. Her first job, maybe?"

"You know any of these other people?"

He shook his head. "They are interchangeable. Not to be cruel . . ."

I lifted the magazine. "What do you know about Sol Beck?"

"I knew Hopper."

"Beck's wife? Lin-Lin Chin."

He said no.

I went back into the archive room and put away the magazine. I cut the light and came out. Arno handed me his keys and I locked the door. I thanked him and offered to buy him a fresh cup of coffee.

He declined. "Work," he said. "I am alert until noon."

He stood to walk me to the door. "I don't know from spouses, Terry. Lin-Lin Chin. And you, I thought maybe you disappeared."

He put his hand on my back as we moved toward the open door.

He asked, "You are looking for work?"

"No," I replied, then added, to my surprise, "I'm still trying to settle in."

"I say this: Take forever. What's the rush?"

I said goodbye and I went toward the gray hallway and the fireproof stairs.

"WHAT'S UP?"

"You," I replied. "Is D?"

"No, he's still snoozing. But it's fine. I've got homework" she said. "Where are you?"

"Mulberry Street."

"Italian side or Chinese side?"

"I'm in the DMZ," I replied. "Now I'm on the Chinese side."

"That cell is clear, Dad. I can hear the cars."

I passed between cars inching impatiently toward the tattered rubber cones and flashing lights that signaled construction on the Manhattan Bridge.

"What are you doing?" she asked.

"I've got to see somebody," I told her as I reached the sidewalk. "Get D to take you to the theater. I'll meet you at 1:15."

"Can we ask him to lunch?"

"Whatever." I stopped. Lost in thought, in strategy, I'd just paced nine blocks. "Take the tickets. They're on—"

"The refrigerator. I'm looking at them."

"And Bella, I need you to do me a favor. I need the

phone number of a car service. I've got to do something and—"

"I'll call for you."

"No, you'll have to leave a credit card—"

"Dad, I know your Amex number," she huffed. "And your MasterCard."

That figures.

"Give me the address."

I did. "I need it in a half hour," I added.

"Can we keep it for the theater? Be cool to go to the theater in a limo."

No. "Maybe. Bella, don't do anything nuts. No white stretch thing."

"I was thinking that. Big, long, white limo, and I'll stand up through the hole in the roof and—"

"Say good-bye, Bella."

"*Arrivederci,* Poppa."

"Very cute."

EDIE REEVES HAD the third floor of an old cast-iron building on Watt Street, not far from West Broadway. Around the corner, a line snaked out of Starbucks.

"Terry Orr," she said. The modest exclamation revealed her British accent. She pulled back her front door and her bare feet padded the glistening hardwood floor.

Her nipples pressed against the thin fabric of her long, silklike orange robe. She tugged at her coal-black hair.

"You alone?" I asked.

"Sadly."

"We need to talk."

"Do you have an office—"

"Now."

She steeled herself to argue, then seemed to slump in sudden resignation. "Of course." She stepped aside.

* * *

NOW SHE WORE a shiny indigo top unbuttoned at the collar and black slacks above stylish flats, and she put a cup of coffee on the glass table at the center of her dining room. I looked through the glass at the bare floor below, my hands folded near the water she'd served me.

She returned with a small plate that held a stack of biscotti.

"Please," she said, as she offered me a cookie. "I know it's not Harrod's after Boxing Day, but..."

She tried to retain her customary reserve, but it wobbled hard.

I said, "We need to talk about Judy. And Bullethead and what you know, Edie."

She held up her hand. "Terry, please, let me explain."

Behind her, on the stark white wall, was a red sculpture, a diamond shape pierced by a red rod. Heartless arc-welding. It fit perfectly in this costly, soulless apartment.

"Let me get it out," she continued. "I should have come straightaway, I know, but it's hard."

I looked at her. If she expected a break, she wasn't going to get it from me.

"You were never cold, Terry," she tried. "Marina—"

"Let's not do that, Edie. You, Lin-Lin. Lay it out."

She brought her palm to her forehead, and closed her eyes. "Terry. Ambition, money... You know what I mean, Terry."

"No, I don't."

She reached for her coffee.

I said, "What I know is someone made a move on Judy. And did it with no class."

She wanted to say something, but she hesitated.

"You could be back in Brighton now, but you decided to stay," I led.

She sipped the coffee, then ran a warm hand on her thin forearm.

"I was going to come and see you, Terry. I was."

"Then let's do what we should."

She nodded. "How much shall I tell you?"

"Let's start with Bullethead."

"When I met Vlad— You knew Bullethead preferred to be called Vlad Smith. What a joke: He was too self-absorbed to have heroes and hadn't enough talent to have influences."

"But you represented him."

She shrugged. "I was ambitious. Nobody would handle him; the drugs, the arrogance. My beginning. His end. I was a kid. It seemed romantic."

She sipped the coffee, then held the cup between her tapered fingers.

"He was impossible. He wouldn't work. Couldn't. It was over. No one would touch him. And he was completely oblivious to it all. He thought he was brilliant. Really. All these people coming about and he thought it was because they adored him. The scene he created: He believed it was the Factory and he was Andy Warhol. It was one long party, completely out of control. You know, Terry. You were there."

"We were not," I said.

"No," she replied, as she let out a breath, "I suppose not."

"Bullethead . . ."

"I had to restore some form of order if I had any hope of making something out of the situation."

"And?"

"So I hired Just a Guy. The money was running low so I sent Bullethead to Laguna Beach to dry out and I hired Just a Guy."

"I don't get you," I said.

"After a while, he wanted to be called 'Just a Guy.' His real name is Zoran Vuk."

"And he did what?"

"He made Smithereens. He was a street kid who knew how to handle explosives and I showed him what Bullethead had done. He took to it in a heartbeat and he was spot on. Brilliant." She snapped her fingers. "And I had Vlad Smith back in business."

"Christ—"

"No," she interrupted, "I know. But it somehow seemed logical. There was all this money and so little genuine talent and it was exciting, Terry. I wanted to belong. It was all so alluring and, God, it was just bloody pieces of metal, after all. It wasn't like we were copying Rembrandt."

"Edie," I said impatiently.

"Justification," she nodded, "but at the time . . ."

I stood. To my right was a tall canvas splashed with pastels. Pollock goes Miami, I thought. There was more craft in the frame. "Tell me about Vuk."

"Zoran. Zoran was freaky, but compared to Bullethead he was very manageable. That is, until he began to understand."

"That he could make a fortune blowing up aluminum."

"Yes, I made a huge mistake when I showed him 'Angel/Angle.'"

"I'll bet."

"So we found ourselves with even more Smithereens, as he tried to replicate the box. We did well with the uninformed—a lot of uptown lawyers with trophy wives own faux Smithereens."

"Just a Guy originals."

She nodded.

"Then?"

"Then Bullethead died."

"We all agree: a very American death," I said. "Maybe Schnabel could direct."

"It made the papers."

"And your guy was out of business."

"Not immediately, but yes."

I came back to the chair. "What happened?"

"That's when he began to claim to be Just a Guy and he said now he had his own vision. But he was just absolutely awful. No sense of an aesthetic. No one could possibly take him seriously."

He started out with adaptations of what Bullethead had done, she said: He'd break bottles, old stained-glass windows; he'd find an old guitar sticking out of a garbage can, smash it and try to get Edie to sell the pieces. He had no idea. Little wonder: Why would shards of metal be valuable and not jagged pieces of stained glass? The difference wasn't in the art, but in the artist; not what he created, but how he behaved. Never mind style over substance. It was more about a uniform, about acceptance into a fractured fraternity.

"Then he began creating these monstrosities: mannequins with their nipples replaced by screws, for instance," she said. "Or a male mannequin with a Slinky between his legs. Awful. But by now, he was Just a Guy." She raised her hands to frame a marquee. "'Just a Guy. Guerrilla Artist.' A guerrilla who wants his money. Every bloody cent of it."

"You said he was freaky."

She nodded lightly.

"You and Zoran . . ."

"He was a pretty little boy, at least in the beginning, until the pierced tongue and the shaved head and spider tattoo. And he became possessive and he had a temper and . . . and—"

"And he beat you."

"I like to say that our disagreements became physical."

"Lovers' spats?"

"No, not after the Just a Guy thing. We were through by then. From then on, it was always about money. Selling his work and getting him the kind of money he made as Bullethead. What hubris, Terry. Fury and hubris."

"And this is the guy you trusted to go after Judy?"

"I?" She shook her head fiercely. "She asked me if I knew where she could find Zoran. Nothing more." She pointed at me and wagged her finger. "Terry, you couldn't possibly—"

"Lin-Lin."

"Lin-Lin," she repeated.

"It's all her? Her plan?"

"Yes," she nodded. "Absolutely. Completely."

I stood again. "We have to go somewhere, Edie."

"Why? I told you what I know."

"It'll be good for you." I ran my hand along the stubble on my face.

"Must I?"

I didn't reply.

She said, "I don't have a choice, do I?"

"You need fresh air," I replied. "Sunlight."

THE DRIVER IN his dark suit lazily strolled to the passenger's side and opened the back door. I let Edie slide in and I climbed in next to her, grateful that Bella had ordered a simple black Town Car.

When the driver squeezed behind the wheel, I told him to get onto Sixth. "Unless there's a parade."

"No parade," he grunted as he took the car away from the hydrant.

"Terry, where are we going?" Edie asked nervously.

I reached across her to tap down the door lock. As I

pulled back, I caught a faint scent of her perfume: orange, sandalwood.

"Relax, Edie. Enjoy the sights: Look to your right in a minute or two and you'll see Washington Square Park. All those plant shops on Sixth. Macy's. The Library: be interesting to see what's up at Bryant Park." If we had to go that far north.

"Terry, I don't understand." She adjusted her black raincoat, tugging it over her knees.

The driver looked at me in the rearview.

"You will," I said, as I pulled the cell from my jacket pocket.

I punched in Julie's number.

SHE KNEW. SHE knew before I asked the driver to pull over.

She tried a joke. "We could've come by subway, Terry. Your underground is—"

"I don't take the subway, Edie."

I haven't been on the subway since Marina and Davy were killed. Nor have I been in a subway station. Bella once asked if we could visit where her mother and brother had died, but I said no.

"No. Of course not."

We went north to 50th, hung a right by Radio City and passed the meandering tourists at Rockefeller Center. At Madison, we went left and pushed north on the avenue, which was characteristically and yet eerily empty on a Sunday morning. We passed the brownstone spires of St. James's, Breuer's granite cubes, then the white-and-gold awning of the posh Carlyle, and I told the driver to pull over at the center of 76th. He did, and Edie and I got out of the black car and walked past a frail tree, its earth moist, its fingerlike branches stretching toward the damp, lazy sky.

I pointed to the storefront. Behind its security gate, windows were splattered with hastily applied whitewash, its door with pages of the *Daily News*. Inside, the telltale signs of construction: yellow electric cords, collapsable work benches, buckets, a push broom, sawdust; disarray, promise, hope, aspiration.

"Explain," I said.

"Terry, I haven't yet spoken to Judy."

"How does an assistant afford to open a gallery on Madison and 75th?"

She put her thin hands into her coat pockets. "I have backers. A few."

I shook my head. "The lease is in your name, Edie. Your ambition's not going to let you share."

"I have saved. I can be frugal." She smiled uneasily.

"You can pony up $5,000, $6,000 a month?" I smiled in return. "I don't think so."

I came away from the storefront window, edging back closer to the car.

"I should speak to Judy," she said. As if that would make it right.

Pretending to tidy the glove compartment, the driver was eavesdropping through the crack he'd made in the passenger's-side front window.

"There's someone else you should speak to, Edie."

I leaned to open the back door.

TOMMY MANGO SAT in his spot at the bend in the Delphi counter, next to the wall nearest the dingy rest room and, importantly, the pay phones. Glowering, hunched, he had both elbows on the brown Formica and his huge hands surrounded an industrial-style porcelain cup filled with steaming hot water, lemon juice and a few drops of Tabasco sauce. Tommy the Cop liked his whiskey in quantity—Booker's, but would settle for Jim Beam—and tried to assuage his daily hangover with a near-overdose of acetaminophen and antihistamines; as a result, his nasal passages were as dry as parchment paper and he treated his head each morning to a mini-steam bath.

I nudged Edie toward Mango's corner in the railroad-car-shaped diner. Tommy was the physical opposite of his brother Jimmy, with the exception of a faint trace of similarity at the center of the face. Under a Sinatra-like silver toupee, he was strong and sturdy, without any evidence of fat on top of muscle. He preferred sharp-cut suits, silk shirts and a diamond-studded pinky ring, dressing more like a post-Gotti mobster than a detective. He wore an oversized .44 under his jacket and he allowed it to show when he leaned forward in his seat. He wore a small piece around his left ankle, one I'd never seen.

He saw us coming and he studied Edie up and down without much subtlety. With his pantherlike eyes and heavily applied self-confidence, he exuded a kind of controlled power that certain women found inviting. I could've told him Edie wasn't going to be one of them: She preferred Slavic boys with skullcap tattoos who could forge art and fire explosives.

"Tommy," I said.

"Terry Orr." He gestured toward Edie. "You back in the game or what?"

I introduced Edie to him. "The gallery explosion on Greene."

"The one you got my brother doing a sit on over on 14th?"

I said no. "About the gallery. She knows."

Mango tapped the padded stool.

Edie sat next to him, while I sat at her elbow on the near side of the bend, facing a glass case boasting seven-layer chocolate cakes and pies with yellow filling and towering meringue caps. From behind the swinging door to the kitchen came the faint strains of talk radio and the clatter of pots and pans.

"Ruthie," Mango shouted. "Two coffees."

The laconic, white-haired waitress, who had been serving the only other customer at the counter, poured two cups and delivered them.

"Terry Orr," he said to Ruthie. "His girlfriend Edie."

I let it go as the weary waitress nodded, then walked away.

"Thank you," Edie said, her voice thin, hollow. Mango patted her hand, squeezed it, then set it free.

I looked around the narrow diner. The Delphi could hold about 75 people and was nearly empty.

Mango said, "On the weekends, it's crowded at four in the morning, empty at eleven. Brunch is killing these guys."

I nodded.

He pointed to the wound under my chin. "My brother Jimmy give you that? I heard he took you for a half a yard at the courts. He says you still got game."

"I got shit, Tommy. But I got this." I pointed at Edie.

Mango snapped his fingers and Ruthie returned, pad in hand. "Give me a fresh cup," he said. "Plenty of steam." He looked at Edie and winked. "I'm going to take it easy someday."

She smiled uncomfortably.

"Tommy—"

He held up a thick finger and we waited until the waitress brought him his concoction, then he gestured for me to continue.

"It plays like this: Somebody wants to shut down the gallery," I said.

"Rivalry. Conflict. I like this," Mango said.

"Edie or Lin-Lin Chin, the artist's wife. Or Edie *and* Lin-Lin."

Edie said, "Terry, I tried to explain." Her voice quivered. "I thought you—"

Tommy the Cop looked at her; his glare shut her down. "Everybody gets a turn, sweetheart. Terry?"

"How's this?" I said. "Lin-Lin wants to take Beck from Judy, and Edie can represent him if they pull off the explosion and close down the gallery. Edie's got her own place uptown."

"No, Terry," Edie choked.

I nodded toward her. "She says it was all Lin-Lin's idea."

Mango asked, "That's how they do it in SoHo, with dynamite? You don't call a lawyer?"

"What if Beck doesn't want to go?" I said to Mango.

He turned to Edie.

She said, "Sol wanted to stay with Judy. He was excited about the opening. He's fond of that work, that sentimental work."

"You think he can do better?" I asked.

"I know he can. He has," she said. "He can be big, if he expresses."

"So if this Judy loses her gallery, this Beck goes with you," Mango said. "Cute."

"She's going to open her place with a bunch of new paintings by Beck. Maybe get a little boost from the publicity about the explosion."

I turned to Mango. "She's going to tell you nobody was supposed to get hurt."

Mango smirked. "So who smacked the Chinese broad? You?"

"No," Edie said sharply.

"You, Terry?"

I shook my head. "They hired a guy named Zoran Vuk

to do the bombing. When Judy got hurt, they wouldn't pay. So he took it out in flesh and bone."

Mango stared into the distance as I spoke. Then, he said, "So you think we ought to talk to this Vuk."

"Edie can tell you where to find him."

"I can't guarantee that. Lin-Lin made—"

Mango cut her off with a hard glance. "If he's legal, it's no problem."

"He is," Edie volunteered meekly.

Mango asked, "You know this guy?"

She hesitated. "I did, a while ago."

Mango nodded. He tugged at his ecru collar. "All right, Terry. Terry Orr, P.I. So what's the quid pro quo here?"

"None."

He slid his hand onto Edie's back. "You want her out of this."

"Fuck no. I want you to bury her ass."

Edie looked at me. She had a tear in her eye.

"You knew what was going to happen the moment Lin-Lin asked you to find Vuk," I told her. "Now I know why you stayed, Edie. You planned on dropping the whole thing on Lin-Lin."

"Oh," said Mango, dripping sarcasm. "When love goes bad..."

A haggard man in a GI jacket came up to the counter and asked for coffee. Ruthie complied. Mango waved to her and slid a dollar in her direction. The slouching, scruffy man nodded his thanks.

Mango withdrew his hand from Edie's back. "Honey, you and me, let's take a ride."

Edie looked at me, then looked away. "When can I call a lawyer?"

"Soon, sweetheart, soon," Mango cooed. He turned to me. "We'll pick up the Chinese broad."

"You have to, you have to." I gave him their address in the West Village.

"All right," he said, as he sat up and tugged at his suit jacket. "You want a call?"

I said no. But I knew I'd get one anyway, if not from him, then from Beck.

Without looking at me, he stuck out his hand and I shook it. "Maybe, Mister P.I., you got a future," Tommy the Cop said, as he adjusted his jacket. "Maybe I ought to keep an eye on you. You think?"

As I stood, he shouted, "Ruthie!"

When the waitress turned, he crooked his finger and she dragged her body over to him.

As I went for the door, I heard him say, "Ruthie, I'm ready for a little something. Toast, maybe. Four slices, no butter. And an egg cream. To go. Do that for me right away, all right, honey? All right."

Mei Carissima:

We have a change in policy now, a new rule. Bella is going to take a shower before going to bed, instead of first thing in the morning. "It just makes sense, Dad," she explained, as she dragged herself along Greenwich after a burger at Harry's. As a rule, no: Her hair will be a tangled mess when she wakes up. But in order to steal an extra few minutes' sleep after staying awake until 3 a.m., okay. She's upstairs, singing off-key, quoting Shaw: "Welcome our friend, the enemy?"

I saw Arno today, Marina, and I saw you, though I did my best to avoid you. But you were there, in a four-color photo, next to Susan Rothenberg, with your charm, your vitality, your smile. And you were there, in one magazine I did not have to open to see you: I remember what Helena Sing wrote: "She is mature, she is light. A strong visual experience gives way to an experience of the heart." I have that issue in my desk, in a drawer next to my knee;

I can see your photo when I want. And I often do. And it is merely an image on a page and I stare, and suddenly, I feel you in this small room and I expect you to run your fingers through my hair, or knead the back of my neck, or to say, "Terry..."

Marina, memories are so vivid tonight: We are in Bitonto. Do you remember this? Before you would agree to be married you insisted I meet your family. We flew to Italy on a crowded Alitalia overnight flight: that pinched-nose woman in front of me who insisted on reclining her seat from the moment of takeoff until we were about to land, pinning my knees to the seatback for more than seven hours; and the pudgy six-month-old behind us who cried for at least half of the flight as his parents quarreled about who was to blame for his wailing and tears. I was already anxious—I didn't want anything to ruin this very good thing I had, Marina, this life-defining thing. You know I worried that your family might disapprove. You told me Rafaela was very opinionated—and I came off the Rome-to-Bari leg of the trip limping and worn and in need of a shower and a shave and about 10 hours' sleep before I was ready to meet anybody I needed to impress. I told you that.

But of course, Benedicto and Rafaela were at the box-sized airport to greet us. Rafaela with the bouquet of wildflowers. As they hugged and kissed you, I realized I couldn't remember a single Italian phrase I'd memorized, and when the introduction came, I stammered, red-faced and forlorn. But as we stood in a small circle off the tarmac, human ebb and flow around us, your father and sister were thoroughly gracious, and immediately forgiving of my shortcomings, which I felt had tripled since we left Kennedy. Rafaela, cautiously, finger on dimpled chin: "He ees a tall one."

I remember this so clearly tonight: We left the airport in your father's—

"DAD."

I jumped. "Christ, Bella, you scared the shit out of me."

I grabbed at the water bottle.

"What are you doing?" she asked. "You're writing."

I reached and shut off the monitor. It hissed and hummed as it went dark.

She took the damp towel off her head. "You were writing."

"My diary," I turned toward her, swiveling the chair. "For the IRS, to be safe."

She wore a floppy t-shirt I'd given her and red sweats. "No, I'm sorry. You were editing. I was standing there a long time."

"Bella—"

"You did something today. You feel good about it and you're writing."

"An interesting theory, but—"

"So that's what's password-protected..."

"Bella, don't be so nosy, all right?" I said. "Sharon Knight told me to keep records in case something came back at me."

"Is it a book? An article?"

"Go now," I instructed. "Go watch TV. Double-check your homework."

She smiled triumphantly as she walked away.

My heart pounding, I took a long drink of cold water, then snapped on the screen to read what I had written.

TWELVE

I GOT AN EARLY start and, having tossed off Bella's clever, calculated advances—"Why don't you write something on Automatic Slim?" "A book on Slim." "Sure, yes." "A slim book." Thwarted, she pouted: "You want to waste a gift, Dad, that's your business."—I came back quickly from her school and went to it: Last night, I'd gotten the call I knew would come. I needed to get ready.

I took a short shower, shaved carefully and changed the bandage under my chin. I saw that I'd have a scar when the wound healed: a daily reminder of Aubrey Brown and Montana, who had scars of his own.

Knowing I needed to, I put on a pair of navy Dockers and a blue Oxford. As I slipped on my loafers, I punched in the number of Ellard Jackson, Brown's dispatcher. A young woman with a heavy Spanish accent answered, then passed me down the line.

"Yeah, I know who you are," Jackson barked. "Henderson said you'd call."

I told him what I wanted.

He asked, "You think everybody's going to come across?"

I nodded as I brushed the dust off the shoes, phone cradled between shoulder and ear. "If you tell them it's about Brown. It could have been one of their guys."

He paused. Behind him, someone else was working another phone, shouting out a terse traffic report. A problem on the Bruckner. The fuckin' Bruckner.

"All right," he said finally, "all right."

"I need to know if someone took a fare up to Fort Washington Avenue a week ago Friday late or early Saturday—"

"I know when Aubrey was killed, man."

I let it pass.

"You want to know if one of our guys picked up a man off Little West 12th and brought him to Fort Washington Ave."

"Right."

"And he's got to ID the guy?"

"At some point. . . ."

"You realize there are twelve thousand medallion cabs in New York City," he said.

"My bet is that a black man—a nervous, frightened black man—who wants to go to Washington Heights from Little West 12th isn't going to get a yellow cab to take him."

I stood and stretched. If none of Jackson's counterparts in the livery business could find out what I wanted to know, I'd ask Sharon to call the TLC. She was bound to have a tap there to pull. Whether the tap at the Taxi & Limousine Commission would be willing to toss 12,000 logs . . .

"All right," Jackson said again.

I gave him my cell number and thanked him. He hung up without another word.

I went to the closet. There's a blue blazer somewhere in here...

AS I WENT outside, I saw that the Monday morning sun was still bright, still defiant, as if it intended to repudiate the crisp autumn nip in the air. I sat on my front steps and blew into my hands, rubbed them together, then watched the steam rise as I exhaled.

I was thinking about Diddio, who somehow went home yesterday with only one sock. Diddio, who, in gratitude for a night's sleep, offered to walk the dog, "if you ever get a dog, I mean; you know, something little, like a Sparky or a Frisky, like. Yip-yip," when the nondescript black car with a steel-plated underbelly came the wrong way on Harrison.

I heard him throw the big car into neutral and saw him fling open the driver's-side door. I came down and slid in, careful not to bang my knees on the glove compartment, the short-wave radio under the dash or the bottle of Snapple Diet Peach he had in the cup holder. For some reason, he hadn't cranked up the heat, but it was warm enough inside, and I could feel the blood again in my hands and on my cheeks.

We bolted from the space near the yellow hydrant and flew onto Greenwich.

I drew the seat belt across my shoulder and lap, careful not to crease my jacket. "We're in some sort of hurry, Luther?"

"It's time to move," he grunted.

"I like to move," I replied, as we went west on Vesey, along the north rim of the World Trade Center complex. Scores of commuters, their faces blank, briefcases at the ends of their arms, emerged from the subway station and waited for the light to change. Others headed east, toward the sun, toward Wall Street, shuffling with little enthusiasm.

He ignored the red light and, sliding into the traffic flow, headed us north on West Street.

"Luther, if you're not going to talk, you might as well put on the radio."

"We can converse, Terry," he said coldly. "Always room for civility."

On the left, the New Jersey waterfront shimmered as if it were a mirage, and a crowded passenger ferry chugged across the calm water, coming toward the World Financial Center. I looked to my right and saw that we were passing the area I'd walked Saturday night: the car wash, the SRO flophouse, close-at-midnight garages, Superior Printing Ink, the Hotel Riverview, Charles Street. And then, the Gansevoort Market, alive again, with squat, refrigerated trucks crowding the sawdusted docks, and dozens of men with rubber gloves, sharp, threatening hooks and bloodsmeared aprons over soiled white uniforms handling huge sides of beef. Pallets of whole chickens waited to be loaded, as two men pottered with the stubborn engine of an outdated forklift, and a big, long truck sat idle as a man in heavy boots and a stocking cap used a thick hose to wash away the blood and marrow, if not the scent.

We waited out the red light.

"We stopping here first?" I asked.

He shook his head. "Just what do you think goes on in there?" He reached for the bottle of iced tea and nodded toward the activity.

"You don't want to know."

The light popped to green and we zigzagged onto Tenth Avenue, continuing north.

He put the nearly empty bottle back in the cup holder and he looked over at me. "I'm going to do you better than you're doing me."

"I'm not doing anyone. I'm doing what I do. And I told you that."

"You went to see Everett Langhorne."

"He wasn't going to keep that a secret," I said. "Harlem's leading educator calls the head of the Black PBA. Natural."

We reached the 20s on Tenth, passing orange cones, sentries around a crater-sized pothole.

I said, "And what did you tell him? 'Ignore that amateur.'"

"Didn't have time to. Your godmother called him."

"Sharon?"

He nodded. "She vouches for you. Told Everett you're a good man."

Though not happy, I thought. "So where are we?"

Traffic queuing for the Lincoln Tunnel spilled onto Tenth near Chelsea Park. Addison pushed the car to the right, put the wheels on my side up on the curb and got us around the gaggle.

"We picked up your friend Mangionella sitting on 14th." He shook his head and tapped the steering wheel. "Neighbors complained, him pissing in the street."

"When?"

"Yesterday. Noon."

"Great, Luther. You fucked up my play."

He snorted derisively and to himself said, "His play."

"Amaral. You know that now."

"Amaral went nowhere. In fact, he's at the school."

"You tell your buddy Langhorne we're coming?" I asked.

"Why?"

"If he tells Williams, Amaral is gone."

We blew past 42nd Street and headed toward John Jay.

"So you had Tommy Mangionella's brother sitting on Amaral and you went after the kid," he said. "And you found him." He gestured with his thumb. "That little Band-Aid on your chin could be a crude row of medical staples I'd be looking at in the morgue."

I said nothing. He hadn't told Langhorne we were going to his school. Addison knew about the thing between Amaral and the vice principal. He knew Amaral was worth talking to.

Sharon's call to Langhorne put Addison in a box. He had to check out how I saw it and there was a good chance he now saw it my way.

"It's a god-damned miracle your little man didn't go right to him," he said.

"No, he's smart. He knows somebody's sitting on the teacher." I drummed the dash with my index finger. "By staying away, the kid confirms that Amaral's involved."

"Or maybe he took off 'cause he's afraid you'll hang a frame on him. Maybe you've lost your only witness."

"Where's he going to run to? This kid knows nothing but here. He's uptown or over in Alphabet City. No, he's not gone."

We had passed the backside of Lincoln Center and now crossed in front of Martin Luther King High and the Red Cross offices.

"He makes his way as a prostitute," I continued, "and he's got a very distinctive scar. Your guys can pick him up in a heartbeat."

"So you admit you need my guys."

"Go bring him in," I said. "That's your job."

He hit the blinker at 72nd, and made the illegal left turn and sent us toward the entrance to the Henry Hudson going north.

ADDISON MADE A squealing U-turn on 125th and bounced the car onto the sidewalk in front of the squat, broad-shouldered bank that was now home to the Zora Neale Hurston Elementary School. Slamming the car's gears into park, he cut the engine and squeezed himself out.

"Don't mention Knight," he said over the roof of the black car. "We're in my house now."

"Luther, what are you talking about?" I said as he came around toward me. "You don't live in Harlem."

"All black men live in Harlem," he snapped. "You're about to find that out."

I followed him into the vestibule, under the "Education/Articulation" banner. He walked hard with a blend of élan and bravado, conveying a sense of confidence and authority, and a touch of intimidation.

He was marking his turf.

The security guard, Mabry Reynolds, was at his station. When I stuck out my hand, Reynolds shook it, and I let my gaze drift, first to the microphone pinned to his open-collared shirt, then to his Beretta nine.

"Mabry Reynolds," I said, "this is Luther—"

Addison interrupted, "Everett Langhorne, please."

Reynolds nodded, stepped back toward his area and spoke into a telephone handset. I heard him clearly: He knew Addison's full name and rank.

I peered into Reynolds's office, at the three small TV monitors that displayed the parking lot behind the building and the two entrances, back and front, where I could see a furry, black-and-white image of Addison's car shot from above.

"Your escort will be here in a moment," Reynolds said to the lieutenant.

I turned from the monitors to the immaculate corridor, its posters and other handmade tributes and decorations in autumnal browns and oranges, in anticipation of a young student arriving to meet us, one not unlike Delroy

Henry: well-mannered, attentive, studied, someone who had a sense of his own worth. As Andre Turner Jr.—Montana now; Scarface—may have had, until his father destroyed his family and his life.

I shoved my hands into the pockets of my slacks and turned. At the end of the hallway, coming toward us, wasn't a student but a man in his mid 60s with a narrow face and close-cropped gray hair styled into a sort of flat-top. The slender man wore a three-piece camel-colored suit, a dark brown bow tie and high-glossed brown wingtips.

As he drew closer, he smiled and said, "Luther Addison. As large as life."

"Everett, good morning," Addison replied.

The two men greeted each other warmly: shoulder taps followed double-clasp handshakes.

"A nice surprise, Luther."

"Everett, this is Terry Orr."

He looked up at me and nodded politely. "Yes, the young man we've heard so much about." Langhorne let his smile dissipate as he extended his hand. "I understand you have been diligent on our behalf."

I looked over at Addison as I nodded.

"Let's retire to my office," Langhorne offered, adding, "Mabry, thank you."

"Yes, sir," Reynolds said. He had his thick arms behind his back as he struck a military pose.

Addison and I followed Langhorne past Andre Watts, Shirley Chisholm and Luis Muñoz Marin, past classrooms of vigilant boys and girls immersed in education, fulfilling the promise that creates a new future, acting, not dreaming. They seemed content and proud, as if they already understood the liberating sense of satisfaction that achievement brings.

WITH A THIN finger, Langhorne held my business card against the blotter on his oversized, antique desk. His large, well-appointed office was tidy, so lined with awards and grip-and-grin-type photos with U.S. presidents and senators, familiar business leaders and the Harlem cognoscenti, that it appeared to be a ceremonial suite. Yet Langhorne had an undeniable presence that went beyond image, and it was clear that he knew how to subtly advance in his favor, and his students' favor, any discussion in which he participated. He had on his desk a silver marker that repeated the school's motto, and I understood by the directness of his questions and nuanced comments that, for Langhorne, articulation wasn't a matter of display, but a way to convey a trim intelligence while eliciting information that was essential to his position.

I sat in front of him with my legs crossed, feeling oddly ill at ease as Addison paced behind me. If I was finding Langhorne cryptic, he and Addison were thoroughly in sync.

"Curiosity can be a power ally," Langhorne said.

I'd told him how I came to find myself looking for Brown's killer, and how I found Andre Turner off Little West 12th.

"I have to say Terry has put more than curiosity into this, Everett," Addison said.

"Then I must confess to a certain confusion," Langhorne said. "Our great good friend Sharon Knight says Mr. Orr is determined, thorough. Dependable. And yet I've been told he is inexperienced."

"Dependable and inexperienced aren't mutually exclusive," Addison replied.

"Well, there may be a reason why the murder of Aubrey Brown didn't merit a formal investigation as determined, as thorough," Langhorne said. "I am not eager to offend your colleagues in blue."

Addison didn't bite. "At any rate, now I'll be speaking to Perry Amaral."

Langhorne kept his finger on my card. "I suppose someone should say a word about the students."

"Is it unusual for you to call a teacher to your office?" Addison asked.

"Actually it is, when classes are in session."

Addison turned to me. "Terry, you watch the door to the parking lot. Everett, your man out front, can we count on him?"

Langhorne closed his eyes as he nodded.

"You still having that problem with the kids on your roof?"

"Chained and locked, fire code be damned," he replied, adding, "And they weren't our children."

"No need to eye the roof," Addison said, as he came from behind me and rested his hands on the empty chair. "Everett, pull this Amaral's file. Let's get a look at this young man."

Langhorne nodded slowly and he used his phone as an intercom, asking Miss Oliver for Amaral's records.

As we waited, Addison said, "Terry, if he breaks your way, stay cool. Grab him and hold him."

I nodded. There was little risk: Amaral killed Brown with something he'd found in the cab. It was unlikely he'd be carrying a weapon now.

Addison added, "Don't let him get off school grounds."

"Do you think he'll run, Doctor?" I asked.

"I have to admit that I've had a very different view of

Perry Amaral," he replied. "My opinion has little merit, I'm afraid."

"Let's not get ahead of ourselves," Addison said. "Everett—"

The door to Langhorne's office. It was Denise Williams, not Miss Oliver, who carried the manila folder.

"As you requested, Doctor," she said.

Langhorne took the file. "Mr. Orr. This is Denise Williams, our vice principal."

"We've met," I said.

"Hello, Luther," Williams said, as she shook Addison's hand.

She gave me a short, wary glance and walked toward the door, past a narrow credenza on which sat an engraved silver bowl.

Langhorne passed the file to Addison, who, after a moment, handed me a color head shot of a light-skinned black man in his mid 30s. Despite a sheepish expression under tortoiseshell glasses, Amaral was a man who could be called attractive, more pleasing than handsome under a receding hairline, and the Windsor knot of his club tie was tucked perfectly into the gap in his white, button-down collar.

"Small," Addison said, as he peered over my shoulder.

"Could be swift," I said as I stood.

I passed the photo to Langhorne, who again picked up his phone's handset. "Excuse me again, Miss Oliver," he said. "Would you please ask Mrs. Williams to go to see Mr. Amaral."

"She already has," I said to Addison.

"I don't get you."

"Williams is tipping off Amaral right now."

"How..." Addison began.

"Let's go."

* * *

IT HADN'T GOTTEN any warmer, and the narrow parking lot was still marked with angular shadows and stark sunlight. I stood with my back against the front end of a yuppie wagon with Connecticut plates, a four-wheel-drive something-or-other that was forest green and beige and had big tires that someone had polished to a glow. If this thing goes off-road, then I'm Dennis Rodman, I thought, as I stared at the school's back door, its thick, opaque glass, its high-tech alarm box, its recent coat of black paint.

I looked at my watch: Ten minutes had passed and I'd figured if Amaral didn't appear in another minute or two, it meant he'd gone directly to Langhorne's office. I wondered if he'd break down, and how Addison would get him there, and I wondered about a man who could kill someone, then continue with his life as if nothing had happened; who would stand in front of his students with blood on his hands, offering lessons that in one way or another celebrated life, with hypocrisy dripping from him like so much rank sweat. These students were clever, I thought; would they know? And if not, how will they feel when they learn they've been deceived?

As I started to glance at the sweeping second hand of my watch, I heard the bar on the back door chuck and thud, and then the black door opened, and it was Reynolds. I went to him.

"He's gone," he said.

I put up my hand to shield my eyes from the cold, harsh sun. "How?"

"Boys'-room window, second floor, 126th Street side."

I looked left past the steel, spike-topped fence that opened toward the light on 126th. "I didn't see him."

"That means he went toward X. Or the subway at Frederick Douglass." He gestured for me to follow him. "We'd better go back inside. You'll want to see this."

WILLIAMS LAY ON the floor of the empty, second-floor classroom and there was a wide splash of blood under her head. She held a towel against the side of her face. A coffee mug lay in pieces near the open door.

When the vice principal went to adjust the towel, I saw that a thick shard of the white porcelain cup was lodged in her cheek.

One of her shoes rested at an odd angle on the light tile. Perfectly sharpened pencils were scattered by her legs. A few had rolled under the small desks in the front of the classroom.

"Christ," I said.

Down the hall, Langhorne comforted a small girl in a uniform. Crying, her shoulders shaking, she held on to the principal's legs. As she turned, I saw that she was about eight years old. Langhorne dabbed at her nose with his handkerchief.

"Terry."

I turned to see Addison. He was wiping blood from his hand with a handkerchief of his own. "Let's walk," he said.

I followed him to the stairwell. As we reached the landing, I saw Miss Oliver lead the two-man EMS team along the hall. Surprisingly—or perhaps not so, given the level of discipline Langhorne advocated—none of the students were at their classroom doors to peer at the unexpected activity.

"Where are the kids from Amaral's class?" I asked.

"In the auditorium. They're pretty upset, as you'd imagine."

"And the little girl upstairs?"

"That's Williams's daughter."

I followed Addison past the rushing EMS techs to the security station. Reynolds was back on post, one hand clasping a wrist behind his back, his Beretta nine still holstered.

"Can we get it?" the lieutenant asked without stopping.

"I'm waiting for a call back, sir."

From the stairwell behind us, a walkie-talkie echoed and squealed.

Addison made a sign to Reynolds that told the guard to contact him as soon as information arrived.

As I went outside, Addison said, "They might be able to pull some tape on Amaral's escape. There's a security camera on the gate at 126th."

He went to the driver's side of his car.

"What the hell happened in there?" I asked.

"Amaral knew what she wanted. The kids say they argued briefly and when she insisted, he picked the mug off his desk and slammed her upside her head."

"Got her good, didn't he?"

"Your man is strong," he replied, "and he's violent."

He likes that move to the head, I thought.

Addison slid into the front seat. I waited and opened the passenger door. He signaled for me to get inside.

As I sat, I said, "Guy jumps from a second-story window has got to be lucky not to break an ankle."

"He's fucked," Addison barked. "Everett's good people."

"And Williams?"

"I've seen her, here and around. If Everett likes her, that's fine with me."

I didn't reply. Denise Williams was a racist. But that didn't mean her little girl had to see her with half a coffee mug jutting out of the side of her head.

"Now listen to me, Terry," he began. "You had some amateur-ass luck here. Or you did a good job." He was looking straight ahead, toward the thick trees at the General Grant Apartments. "I'll give you some credit for your work."

I knew where he was going. I decided to let him go.

"And maybe you don't care if you showed me up with Knight and with Everett," he snapped. "But now you're out of it. I don't want to hear you, I don't want to see you. If I do, I'm going to run your ass. I'll lock you the fuck down until Gabriella turns forty. You hear me?"

He turned to look hard at me.

I met his gaze. He was boiling.

"Sure, Luther. No hear, no see. Got it."

"Terry, don't fuck around. Your way is not how it's done."

I shifted and put my back against the passenger door. "What are you going to do?"

He looked at me and he told me, but only after he was able to turn down the flame.

"We've got a man at his apartment—"

"A guy who doesn't piss in front of the neighbors."

"Amaral doesn't have a car, doesn't have a license," he continued. He flicked an index finger against the five on the other hand. "That means the airports, Port Authority, Penn Station—"

"I got one other place for you to check," I said as I took out my cell.

"WHAT HAPPENED?"

Jackson said, "I can't find your number."

"Well?"

"I got something for you. May not mean much."

I could hear the dispatcher flipping pages. In my

mind's eye, I saw a clipboard and notes scribbled on the back of a form.

Addison looked at me. Anger had given way to curiosity.

Jackson said, "Over at Dyckman Livery they say a guy picked up somebody on 14th and Seventh at 12:45 on Saturday morning. Took him to Riverside and 165th."

Fort Washington Avenue was a block east of Riverside Drive. "Close enough," I said.

THIRTEEN

THE SUN HAD DROPPED behind the office buildings on the Jersey palisades. A red-orange glow burned the horizon and, above it, the sky was a dull, muddy gray.

On West Street, the cars that were headed north toward the Lincoln Tunnel, the GW Bridge, were in an orderly line as if parked three across, and on the other side, more cars slithering toward the Brooklyn Battery Tunnel. A typical rush hour on the south end of the island: No one was rushing, all accepted their fate. Headlights on the west side, taillights on the east. In two hours, the parking lot would be a highway again. Now, under violet streetlights, the blacktop was a study in inertia.

I squeezed past a white Olds and a burgundy Toyota hatchback, straddled the divider, then waited until a UPS truck rolled by. Then I made my way to the cracked sidewalk on the west side of the wide highway and started toward Little West 12th. Behind me, a car horn rang out, and others on both sides of the road joined in. Then a sudden silence and I could hear the river, its relentless ebb and flow, its persistent slap against the rotted piers, against stone retaining walls.

I'd been waiting near the abandoned building at Jane Street, my back flat against cold brick, tucked in the shadows near a hissing hydrant, accompanied by the smell of rust and motor oil, of decay and abuse; by the memories of the edge of the blade against my chin. To ward off the cold as the sun began to tumble, I went west to Greenwich, pacing, trying to stay clear of trucks on the way to the Gansevoort Market and taxis circling west to go uptown. Then I buried my hands in my pockets and went back to Jane. From noon to now, I had waited and I watched.

I knew Amaral wasn't going to Fort Washington Avenue: By now, he knew he didn't live there anymore. And he wasn't going to take it out of town: He had unfinished business here. When Addison returned my cell phone, I left his car and kept walking until I could flag a cab.

If Addison wanted to stand on Fort Washington Avenue with his thumb up his ass, fine. Who gives a shit?

I went home, threw on old black jeans, sneakers and a hooded sweatshirt, asked Mrs. Maoli to stay through dinner and came back out. And I went where I knew Amaral would be. I wanted to be there to finish it.

He had tried to save Montana. Then he killed for him. I wanted to know why. Then I wanted to end it.

When I was huddled on Jane Street, shivering and shuffling, I had time to think. I stared at the mustard-colored building and I thought.

I'm going to get this done.

I embarrassed Addison. So be it. Pushing me away brought me back hard.

What kind of man will be so easily discouraged from doing what he really wants to do? *Has* to do.

I hadn't been paying enough attention to Bella. If that was true . . .

The best thing I can do for her is to find out how to take down the man who killed her mother and brother.

A daughter without a baby brother, without a mother.

A boy wears a scar his father gave him as he tried to save his mother's life.

A sad-eyed painter, rejected by a heartless father, finds solace in a brutally ambitious wife.

There's a moon up there. It's cold, it's lifeless. An empty, mottled ball in the sky.

I needed to do this thing and I needed to do it by myself.

On West Street, I went toward a break in the fence. Twilight, and I knew where Amaral would go.

IT WAS ALMOST six when I got to the Sealand container that sat abandoned on the crumbled pavement by the pier. And then I came around to its back doors: one was off its hinges, the other was closed—an ineffectual guardian of privacy for hookers and their johns, for junkies. On the soil that had erupted from under the splintered concrete, used condoms and crack vials testified to the container's sordid utility. Ready to look inside the box, I had my back to the thumping, slapping river, to the vanishing strip of light at the horizon, and I moved carefully. And I came out from behind the door and looked in and I saw Amaral.

He stood at the far end of the container, 40 feet away. I ducked to enter and stared at him. He stood straight, his eyes wide behind his round glasses.

He wore a dark blue suit, a white shirt, and his conservative blue-and-yellow tie was at half-mast. I stepped inside the long, narrow box.

"I'm—I'm waiting for someone," he said.

His voice echoed in the container and a metallic ringing remained after his words had disappeared.

"I know. Andre. Andre Turner."

He tilted his head. "Who are you?"

"I came to talk to you."

"I'm not—I'm not who you think I am."

"I think you're Perry Amaral," I told him. "I was at the school today."

"You—" He stopped. "Denise. How . . . ?"

"She's not dead." Unlike Aubrey Brown. "Stitches."

"I didn't know."

"You didn't know what?"

"I can't believe I—"

"Hit her? Sure you can. That's your move. The whack in the head."

He said no.

"Somebody saw you," I lied. "Not far from here."

"I—I live in the neighborhood," Amaral offered.

"At 455 West 14th."

He frowned and his small voice tried to rise up to challenge me. "Who are you?"

"I was at the school today. And I didn't call him Montana, did I?"

He seemed to realize that he had placed himself in the container's corner and he shuffled toward me, dragging his shoes across the soiled wood floor, hugging the tattered wood on the walls.

"Tell me," I said. "A divorced man, his son taken away. He finds a child who needs someone . . . Is that why you moved downtown? To be near Andre?"

Amaral hesitated. "Better conditions."

"No, not really. I think it's Andre. He's here."

Amaral didn't reply. Then he said, "My student. He's my student."

"Still?"

"No, I mean he was my student. He had to leave us."

"Why?"

Amaral touched his glasses. "Several—different reasons. He couldn't keep up."

"Because of what he experienced."

"Yes."

"You tried to help."

"I did."

"But..."

Amaral looked at the dank floor. "I failed."

"Happens."

Amaral shrugged.

"But he still needs you," I said.

"He doesn't have anyone else."

"I spoke to him, you know."

Amaral looked at me. "How is he?"

I said, "He's the same. He's working. You know what I mean?"

He nodded slowly.

A short snap of wind off the river pushed the container.

"There's nothing wrong with you knowing. A friend would know. You are friends, right?"

"I would say so."

"Good friends?"

He hesitated. "OK, yes."

"He's like a son?"

Amaral shook his head. It was a slow, deliberate denial. Or a painful affirmation.

"He comes to your apartment?"

Amaral didn't reply.

"That's natural. The streets are a hard way to go."

Amaral interrupted. "Yes, he comes to my apartment."

"You let him use the bathroom?" I led. "You feed him?"

"Yes."

"Does he spend the night there?"

"Almost never," he said.

"Once a week? Twice?"

"Not so often." Then he added, "All right. Maybe twice a week."

"He comes to you when he needs you," I said. "No problem there."

For a moment, Amaral seemed to drift, then he straightened up, his back now taut against the container wall. "I don't want to do this."

"Why not, Perry? We're almost there."

I looked at him. There was nowhere to run. Despite inching forward, he was still some 30 feet from the door, where I stood.

He said, "It's not fair. To be judged."

He was chasing the thoughts in his clouded mind. His eyes rolled up into his head, then he opened them wide, then blinked several times, exaggerating the gesture.

I listened to the river, to the car horns on the highway.

"You do what you did, you get judged, Perry."

"No one asks why."

"I'm going to. I will. But I need to know."

"Need to know what?" he snapped. An attempt to be firm again; he was becoming agitated, more agitated.

I said, "Something that might explain why." I held up my empty hands. "Let me try something, all right? All right?"

"Yes, all right."

"When Andre stays with you, he sleeps in your bed, doesn't he?"

"You can't ask me that."

"I am trying to understand, Perry."

"No. That's not a question. You want to judge—"

"Perry, it's a question. Andre sleeps in your bed, doesn't he?"

"You want—" He suddenly stopped. Then he closed his eyes.

"You and Andre have been lovers. Haven't you?"

He looked at me. He was confused. There was nowhere to go. It was out now, the darkest secret.

"I don't—I don't know how it started."

Suddenly, his agitation abated and his false bravado vanished, and Amaral put his hands in the pockets of his suit jacket and edged into the shadows. "I don't know how it started."

"Tell me about last Saturday morning, Perry."

"I went to see him. I mean, I tried to find him. And I did ... find him."

"All right," I said. "Where?"

"Near the piers. Behind the buses."

He'd gone north of Little West 12th, up by the yellow brick terminal, the buses shut down for the night, sand in mounds for the inevitable snow, the faint scent of gasoline, dark, restless water.

"That's where he goes," he added.

"Was he alone?"

"No."

"Was he with Brown?" I asked.

"I didn't know the man he was with," Amaral continued. "They came. They came to ..." He came off the wall and faced me. "This one was white, my age. He was ... servicing Andre."

"What happened?"

"Andre mis—he misunderstood. He said I was messing up things for him. He said I was invading him."

"'Invading him'?"

"He misunderstood. I wanted to see if he was all right. Safe. That's all. I wasn't spying on him. I was looking—"

"You were lonely," I said.

Amaral nodded. He sighed, "I'm always ..."

"But you argued. So you left."

"I left," he agreed.

"And then?"

"I saw the car sitting there, the taxi. I just wanted to get away."

"And, Perry? What happened?"

"I got in. And he was looking at me."

"Aubrey Brown."

"He was staring at me. His eyes, in the rearview mirror."

I'd seen Brown's eyes. Penetrating. Ghostly.

"He told me to get out," Amaral added.

"Why?"

"He thought I was on the piers with Andre. He thought I was . . ."

"A john?"

". . . scum. Those eyes— He accused me. Like everybody, when they . . . when they think they know . . ."

"You hit him, didn't you?"

He didn't respond.

"Perry, you hit him."

"I hit him." He opened his mouth and tilted back his head to choke off a cry.

"You hit him with what, Perry?"

"The steering-wheel lock. It was on the floor, under the seat."

"Then?"

"I—I don't know. I ran."

"You killed Aubrey Brown, Perry."

"It was a mistake. He was accusing me. I just— It gets worse and it gets worse—"

I said, "What are we going to do now?"

He frowned severely, shook his head and then he looked at me. " 'We'?"

"You and me. We."

"No, no. That's—I'm alone." Then his voice grew softer. "Alone."

I watched him as he struggled to continue.

"It all fell apart," he said finally.

"I unders—"

"One thing, another thing," he mumbled. "My family. All of this . . . I lost myself. It's unfair."

I watched him. He let his head fall back, as if he wanted to study the box's dented ceiling. "What will happen?"

"I think, Perry—"

He looked at me. Then he took several small, lurching steps toward me. Then he seemed to stagger.

And he pulled his hands out of his pockets.

In his right hand was a small gun, tarnished silver, black.

"It's unfair."

He lifted the gun.

"Perry, think this through," I said quickly.

He slowly brought the small gun to his chin.

"Nothing now," he said as he slid the gun up his chin and pressed it against his lips.

"Perry, wait." I came off the door.

"No family. Disgrace."

I was about 10 feet away.

"Nothing now," he repeated.

He jammed the gun into his mouth.

He closed his eyes.

He pulled the trigger.

The sharp crack gave way to a muffled blast. Amaral pitched forward, collapsing at my feet, the gun skidding out of his hand.

The ugly sound reverberated in the box and, as the red mist settled, I could smell blood and death.

Above the metallic echo, I heard the flapping wings of a flock of pigeons bursting from their perch.

I looked down.

I thought I was going to be sick.

"Christ." I turned away.

I ASKED THE Midtown dispatcher to put me through to Lt. Addison. The mention of Amaral's name made it happen.

I was standing outside the container. The cracked pavement seemed to undulate under me.

The cold, sobering air felt good on my face.

I watched a small plane float above the palisades. Early stars were pearls in the night sky.

Addison answered the call.

"You want him," I said, "he's on the piers near Little West 12th. In an old Sealand container."

"What did you—"

"He's dead," I interrupted. "I'll wait ten minutes."

I cut the line, then dialed my home number.

"HEY, DAD. GUESS what?"

"Bella—"

"I signed up to try out for the basketball team. Dad?"

"No, that's great, Bella."

"What's the matter?"

"Oh, you know . . ."

"Rough day."

"That's a good way to put it," I said.

"Come home, Dad," she replied. "I'll kiss you happy."

I told her I'd be right there.

FOURTEEN

SINCE I WATCHED A man kill himself I'd spent the day doing next to nothing. I worked out hard. I lay on the couch and watched an oddball Elliott Gould festival on TCM, picked up an anthology of Hegel's lectures and immediately put it back down. I made a call to Sharon to let her know, but she already knew. "I was going to call you," she said. "You OK?" After that, I called Julie to thank her. "We're worried about you," she said, and I knew it was true: Julie Giada is incapable of telling a lie, an admirable trait (though likely a handicap in her profession). Addison called me, but I let the machine take it. After talking to him on Monday at the pier, again two hours later on my front steps and at the Midtown Precinct yesterday morning, I'd had my fill of Luther Addison. The high point of our second talk, as the wind off the river kicked up behind us: "Lieutenant, I don't give a fuck if you believe me."

I snuck into Bella's room as she slept, took Moose

from under the covers and put my old basketball near her pillow. Before I could leave the room, she wiggled, found the ball and, frowning in her sleep, slapped it away.

Yeah. Well.

I returned Moose to her arms and put the ball on the chair by her desk.

This morning, I decided to get away, to try to banish thoughts of Amaral, his terror, his body at my feet, the stark photos Addison thrust in front of me in his squat, stuffy office, and I went uptown to Modell's at Herald Square and bought Bella a few pairs of shorts, socks, a couple of t-shirts. (I stood before the sports bras much as Champollion must have first stared at the Rosetta Stone: *What the hell . . . ?*) To compensate for not getting her that piece of equipment—the female equivalent of a jock, I guess—I tossed a couple of pairs of wristbands into the basket. Then, knowing my daughter, I threw a headband in there, too.

I decided to walk back on the shady side of Broadway to let my mind go, and though I saw in the distance the early yellows and reds of the trees in Madison Square Park and, as I drifted to Fifth, NYU students going by in packs, cops in blue-and-whites monitoring Washington Square, I was doing nothing more than thinking. I was trying to understand what I had learned.

The Madman Weisz, I knew, wasn't going to fold as easily as a heartsick elementary schoolteacher or an assistant in a SoHo art gallery. When the time came for him to take form, a diamond glint in his empty eyes, it wouldn't be as a confused, despondent man or a pretty woman with money on her mind. That I knew.

And I knew that when I went in after Weisz it wasn't going to be with Tommy the Cop out front or with Crazy Jimmy at my back. Or with Addison hectoring me, offering an odd form of support and protection. (He'd had his shot at Weisz.) No, I was going in alone: The diamond glint in Weisz's hollow eyes would be trained only on me, focused with feral intensity or the cleverness of a man who once was and, I believed, was still brilliant. His savagery had shown itself when he killed a mother and child; his brilliance when he managed to slip away without a trace.

I wondered if he knew that the day when I would summon him from the ether was closer now. I wondered if he knew that I was learning what it would take to bring him down. I had the option of hoping he did not, so that one day I would take him without warning and do what had to be done; or of hoping he did, so that he lived now filled with dread and uncertainty, in constant trepidation, peering around corners, with the sense that the hot blade was poised inches from his pale skin. I wondered if I had become his obsession, as he had become mine.

When I pulled back from these festering thoughts, I saw that I'd blown past Canal and was back in TriBeCa. I thought about stopping off for lunch at a Korean-run salad bar on Hudson that served Mongolian stir-fry alongside the requisite pork fried rice, stuffed cabbage and macaroni-and-cheese, but decided instead to drop off the Modell's bag and see what Mrs. Maoli had on the stove. Or eat the cold *braciole* that was in the refrigerator, a remnant of last night's splendid dinner.

On Harrison, the sun cast an uneven light onto the cobblestone, bleached and diffused. I crossed Greenwich, moving toward the silver river, passing a delivery truck filled with bok choy, cabbage and pea pods for Chinese restaurants west of Mott.

And then I saw him, in front of my house, moving back and forth, with intent and yet meandering, his hands buried in his pockets, his slouch made more pronounced by his ambling. I stopped and watched him, and though the long bill of his strange baseball cap cast a shadow across his face, I knew he was troubled, again. Still.

As he turned around to begin another small, lurching lap, Sol Beck saw me and stopped pacing and, without looking at the flow of traffic, ran onto Greenwich toward me. He made it across, oblivious to a barreling yellow cab that nearly took off the heels of his paint-splattered sneakers.

He grabbed at me. I easily deflected his clutching hands.

"I called you," he said. The quick dash across Greenwich had hastened his breath.

"I know," I replied. "There's nothing I can do. I warned—"

"He put a bomb in my house."

This time his hands made it to my sleeves and he held on as if he feared he'd fall. He was pale, despite the pounding panic. "We have— We have to run."

"Did you call the cops?" I asked.

"I can't. Lin-Lin said—they'll think she had something to do with it."

"She did have something to do with it, Sol. That's why they picked her up."

"They didn't keep her."

"Sol, she and Edie hired Vuk."

His eyes wouldn't meet mine: The averted glare, perpetual for Beck, when confrontation flared. He muttered, "There's a bomb now and she's home."

I pulled away from his grip and put my hand on the shoulder of his worn, sagging blazer. "Sol, call the cops and get her out of there."

"Find Vuk," Beck countered. "Make him take it away."

"Where?"

"You can find him, Terry."

He grabbed at me again and started tugging me up

Harrison, toward Hudson, toward the West Village. "We've got to hurry," he panted.

"Sol, hold it," I protested. Yet I was going along with him, back past the delivery truck with its fresh vegetables, toward the lace curtains of Chanterelle, then to Varick near where Vuk had attacked her.

"She's there, saving the work." He slapped at my arm. "Everything will—everything will be all right if we hurry."

Sol Beck started to trot. The tail of his frayed white shirt flapped between the vents in his coat. He turned, beckoning me to follow, an oddly hopeful glow in his sad eyes.

I deliberated, though not for long, and then hustled to catch up, running toward a bomb.

WE MADE IT to King, running under rusted fire escapes, dodging cars at Canal, and murky puddles from Sunday's rain, and up the block, there was Lin-Lin, in a long, black sweatshirt and jeans, stacking paintings in front of a neighboring brownstone. Her orange cat played a comedic sentinel, peering suspiciously at us as we scampered up the block.

Lin-Lin saw us and she seemed angry; then she immediately disguised her temper, cramming it back into the box, and her battered face instantly took on a calm but not quite serene appearance, as if emotion had been muted in favor of a better focus on the task at hand.

Beck was gasping heavily, and beads of sweat turned to thin streams that ran along his sallow cheeks. He removed his hat and raked his sleeve across his forehead. "There," he managed, as he pointed.

Lin-Lin went back toward their brownstone without acknowledging him.

About two dozen canvases were propped against the gate; wooden frames and stretched canvases against black cast iron.

"You do those?" I said.

Panting, he said yes.

Paintings Edie and Lin-Lin would build their new businesses around. Businesses that excluded Judy.

"Sol, where's the bomb?"

"I saw it. When Lin-Lin hung up, I—" Beck gasped for air. "I went downstairs. In the beams—it's there."

"The bomb is in the basement?"

"Putty and a wire; I don't know. Maybe more. I couldn't— I panicked when she told me."

Lin-Lin emerged with two more paintings and, ignoring us, added them to the stack. The cat circled warily. On Sixth, midafternoon traffic flowed steadily and, above us to the east, a helicopter hovered over the Manhattan Bridge.

"Sol, call the cops," I repeated.

"No. You find Vuk. Make him take it away." He was a boy, full of abstract optimism, brimming with fragile hope. Deluded, he wouldn't allow himself to understand.

"Listen to—"

Beck looked at his wristwatch. "You've got twenty-five minutes."

"Sol, forget it. You need the bomb squad, not me."

He said, "Terry, he said if we call the police, it'll go off." He started to backpedal. "I've got to help Lin-Lin." He turned and ran toward her.

Once again, I followed, this time hesitantly, warily, passing a motor scooter chained to a "No Parking" sign-post and a silver, nondescript delivery van in the center of the long block. Lin-Lin exited the brownstone with two more canvases, and Beck ran by her and skidded into their house.

As I moved closer, I saw the marks on her face, the thin

bandage over the stitches, the bruises, bumps and sickly purple swelling. Red scratches marred the bridge of her nose.

Continuing to ignore me, she put down the two works and began to walk away.

I called to her; I called to her again and she didn't respond. I reached out and grabbed her long, shining hair and yanked, snapping her toward me.

She hissed in pain until I let go.

As she turned, I said, "Give this poor bastard a break."

"It is you who has caused this," she replied flatly.

"You hired Vuk. Pay him and shut him down. Put an end to this."

"I have things to do," she said dismissively. "I'm protecting the work."

The cat curled itself around Lin-Lin's ankle. It purred coyly.

"Is it really a bomb?" I asked.

"Yes. A precise one." She turned away from me.

I went after her.

She stopped and said, "That was your word. 'Precise.' So there is a precise one here now. It will destroy his work. It will damage the house."

As she gestured, I turned to the stack of paintings. They were modern, if not contemporary: angular; beiges and pale ochers; weak, unsteady slivers of greens and blues. Faint colors behind heavy black lines. A touch of Mondrian, a bit of Klee. As derivative as his Hopper reproductions at the Harper Gallery, with little display now of his craftsmanlike technique.

"Was the idea to destroy the paintings at Judy's?"

"I will not confirm what you believe is true."

I stepped closer to her. "Look at him. Look how fuckin' earnest he is," I said, pleading almost. "How's he going to be when this is over?"

"I cannot help you."

"Christ, how heartless can you be?"

"Oh, Terry," she moaned as she closed her almond eyes. "Edie was right about you. You are an innocent."

"Vuk is going to get his money," I said. "He won't let you make a dime off this work."

She tilted her head and gave me a look of cold, bottomless contempt.

Beck emerged from the brownstone, carrying other canvases to add to the hoard.

"Vuk will get nothing. And no one will believe I was involved. Edie and her boyfriend tried to hurt my Sol." She smiled darkly. "I am so easily misunderstood."

Beck, straining, said, "Terry, you've got to get going. Find him and bring him back here and make him take it away." He wasn't yet wild-eyed, but he was getting there. "Lin-Lin," he added, "you can talk to Terry later. He's going to help us."

"Yes, Sol," she said as she turned and walked away.

I watched Beck place the paintings next to the others. "Terry," he commanded, in a low voice. "Go."

I nodded and I went, leaving Beck to help stack his paintings on the street, to protect them so they could be taken from him. I knew where I had to go. It was a long shot, but it was the only thing that made sense to me.

I went to Sixth and then north. If Beck was right, I had about 20 minutes to get it done.

I KEPT MOVING, trotting now, squeezing by lazing pedestrians and a lanky mailman with his canvas bags on rollers, and I bounded into the All-American Diner. In front, a fresh-faced young woman entertained a small boy with ketchup-soaked french fries as she scanned a fashion magazine. I slid down the aisle, between revolving stools and empty, four-seater booths, passing faded clippings of soccer stars, Athenian landmarks, the torpid teenager burning toast, frying onions on the grill. In his customary spot in the rear, back to the wall, sat Chick Rosenzweig in a brown sweater-vest and white shirt; his friend Sid was examining his eyeglasses, cleaning the lens with a paper napkin.

"Look who it is, Sid," Rosenzweig said, looking up from his *Daily News.* "The bodyguard."

Sid turned, and a splash of fear crossed his round, aged face.

"Your son needs you," I said directly, as I sat on the revolving stool nearest Rosenzweig's sidekick.

"Son?" Rosenzweig mocked. He looked down at his paper. He put his index finger in the ring-handle of his coffee mug.

"Solly's in trouble?" Sid asked.

I nodded. "It's the wife."

Rosenzweig peered up at me.

"She hired the guy to plant a bomb in the gallery. She wanted Sol to leave his agent and when he wouldn't, she set out to damage the gallery so he'd have to make a move."

"The kid's got loyalty? Don't shit me, bodyguard."

"Now your son's got nobody."

"That's right," he nodded. "He wanted it that way."

"Chick," Sid said, "Solly's a good boy."

Rosenzweig didn't argue.

"The bomber's after him now," I said. "He planted a bomb in his house."

"There's a bomb in his house? Get the cops." With scorn and a sneer, he added, "I'm retired."

I came off the stool to coax him and I slid in next to Sid, who inched over to give me room. "Put it aside, Chick."

"Think it goes that easy, bodyguard?" he asked as he shook his head.

"Blood's thick," I said.

"Chick, it's Solly," Sid added. "He needs you. Solly, he needs you."

Rosenzweig was about to challenge his compassionate friend, but he cut it off. He turned to me. "The place on King Street?"

I nodded. He knew where his son lived.

"You see the thing?" he asked.

"The bomb? No, but your son did."

"What it is? RDX? Pentolite? Slurries?"

I shook my head. "He said putty and wire. In a beam in the basement."

"Did he see a timer?"

"He didn't say."

"See, no timer means the guy is there. The guy is there to set it off." He paused. "What do you think, Sid? I go save his ass?"

"It's Solly, Chick."

"Yeah. Solly."

I said, "Come with me." I withdrew my cell. "I'll call the cops and we'll head over there."

"The kid don't want the cops," Rosenzweig said as he pushed up against the tabletop. "I got to save his ass again. Just like when he was a kid. Couldn't fight for shit. Sid," he intoned, "give me my hat."

Sid reached to his right and pulled two berets from the seat. They were identical: brown, worn, neat. Sid looked at both, then passed the right one to Rosenzweig, who, with a deliberate flash of bluster, placed it on his head.

"Sid, go call Marion. Tell her you're gonna get her something at Carvel's," he said, as he reached into his pocket and tossed a $5 bill on the tabletop. "I'll be back in a few minutes."

Rosenzweig walked past me and, with shoulders thrust back, headed down the aisle.

WE PUSHED SOUTH on Sixth, passing the drugstore, the bakery, the old folks huddled in Father Demo Square, a lone, sagging tree and pigeons pecking at birdseed. I told him about the deadline; by my watch, we had 15 minutes.

Rosenzweig shook his head. "No timer means no deadline, kid. The guy's there with his finger on a button. The bitch lied again."

He was walking fast, with a gait that, while not at all limber, displayed his cockiness.

We crossed Houston, hopping down from the high curb. I said, "There's no way to dismantle it if he's sitting there."

"I got to get in through the back or from next door," Rosenzweig said thoughtfully. "This guy, he know you?"

I shrugged. "He might." Lin-Lin might've described me to him; and if he was nearby, he'd have seen me tagging along with Beck, arguing with Lin-Lin near the pile of paintings. Or maybe he saw me years ago with Marina: the tall guy with the beautiful, gifted Italian woman.

"I gotta go my own way then," he said. "He sees you go to the house, he'll let 'er rip."

"I don't think you can get in any other way," I offered.

Rosenzweig said, "I'm a super, kid, remember? I can make anybody think I'm coming in to fix their pipes."

We reached King. There was no time to argue with him. Without a toolbox, a man in a natty brown sweater and matching beret, no matter how long he's been a janitor, isn't going to fool anybody in this part of town. I was certain now: I undid the cell and punched 911 to get the Bomb Squad.

The operator had a hoarse voice, as if she'd smoked

since childhood. I told her about the bomb and I gave her the address. When she asked for my name, I reminded her that she had my cell number and could track me down in minutes. Then I cut the connection.

"I'm going in," Rosenzweig announced.

"Can you handle something over your head?"

He thrust his left arm in the air, as if to demonstrate that it was fine, that he was ready to save his boy.

"Hey," he said, as he brought down his arm, "there's Solly."

Beck was adding an armful of paintings to the growing pile, which now numbered about 35 or so.

"He looks like shit," Rosenzweig added.

Lin-Lin was entering the brownstone, her bruised face knotted in determination.

"Tokyo fuckin' Rose," Rosenzweig muttered. He jabbed me with a bony finger. "I'm going to Charlton. You look out for the guy with the trigger. He's—"

And suddenly, it went off: a muffled roar, a sonic implosion, molecules rupturing; orange light, then sounds of destruction, of collapse: cracking wood, flying glass, raw release. The explosion tore through the bottom half of Beck's building, spewing debris onto King, onto parked cars on both sides of the street. Thick black smoke snaked into the air.

"Holy shit," Rosenzweig shouted. "He killed her."

Beck had frozen, mouth agape in shock. The paintings fell from his arms.

At the center of the block, the door of a silver delivery truck flew open and a man bounced out. Spry, spindly, he had a spiderweb tattooed on top of his bald head.

Vuk ran around the back of the truck, flung open the back doors and went toward the stack of paintings. Before I could break toward him, he had several in his hands and was hauling them to the truck.

I went forward, hard down King, through the cloud of debris, running in the center of the street, passing Beck, who, wobbling, bewildered, went toward his brownstone. Eyes wide, he brought his hand up, inadvertently knocking his cap off his head.

I came up along the driver's side of the truck, as Vuk, determined, moving willfully, had dumped in a second batch. He had his back to me when I jumped him.

He was quick and he was capable, and he wriggled free of my grasp as we hit the sidewalk. He kicked at me, grazing my outer thigh, as he scuttled backward along the rough cement, trying to find room to leap to his feet. But before he could bounce away, I was on him again and I punched him hard just below the sternum and the air flew from his lungs. He pawed meekly at me, and I grabbed his head near the ears, near the green-blue veins of his tattoo, and I drove the back of his head hard into the pavement, and then I did it again. And then I did it again, and his expression moved from anger to pain to confusion to surrender, and I did it again and I saw the blood on the sidewalk and I stood. And I kicked him and I saw he was about to lose consciousness and I grabbed him and lifted him. But he was out now, so I let him fall. In the distance, the wail of sirens.

I turned. Neighbors had begun to collect on the street. They were in jeans and work shirts, and the older women wore housecoats. They were frightened, concerned.

Traffic—a yellow cab, several small cars—piled up on the block. Horns honked, rubbernecks craned.

Stunned, wretched, Beck was in his father's arms.

The tinkling of falling glass. Smoke rising toward eternity.

A police car barreled down King. Red lights, a piercing wail.

I looked at Vuk. Blood ran from his scarred head.

Beck sobbed. Rosenzweig ran his fingers through his son's thin hair.

The helicopter hovered above us.

I SAT, ELBOWS on knees, on the steps of a brownstone near the construction scaffolding that extended to Varick, away from the police activity, away from the EMS personnel who were turning it over to a team from the coroner's office. Another emergency-services team had repaired the gash at the back of Vuk's head, and now he was on his way to the precinct house.

I watched a cop in blue wave off the crowding, nudging traffic that demanded to turn onto King. I watched as a pert blonde did her stand-up for her station's cameras; she shifted sideways to allow the camerawoman to frame her with the damaged building over her shoulder, and she dramatically stole a glance at a clipboard that held a blank sheet of yellow paper.

I watched as Rosenzweig tried in vain to console his son. The old man argued with detectives in dark coats who tried to talk to Beck, and he gave the finger to news photographers who had ignored the hastily arranged wooden sawhorses on Sixth.

Beck howled at the fading sun, at its platinum rays. He tore off his worn blazer and threw it on the sidewalk and he kicked at it.

I thought, That'll be on the cover of tomorrow's *Post*.

Beck accepted his father's embrace.

Fifteen minutes had passed since the explosion.

They were leaving me alone. A man in a red flannel shirt with a small dog had seen me pummel Vuk; he pointed to me with a sense of accomplishment, as I watched Beck's paintings. When the cop approached me, I gave him my name and I told him to call Tommy

Mango. "I'm not going anywhere," I said, "until you guys get all these things off the street."

The least I could do now was keep an eye on Beck's paintings.

I watched Beck sink in his father's arms.

I shifted on the slate and hung my arm over the thick railing. I was trying to gather my thoughts. I saw that there were splatters of blood on the side of my right hand.

I realized I'd better call Judy, to save her from hearing about this from TV, a breathless *Special Report* from a woman who read from a blank sheet of paper.

And then I remembered that Mrs. Maoli watched the late-afternoon soaps and trailer-park confessions. If Bella was home, and if the camera panned King Street, and if she heard the name Sol Beck . . .

I left the brownstone and, keeping an eye on the paintings, went west.

FIFTEEN

IT WAS A WINDLESS morning with a high sky that had been cleansed by last night's obstinate rain. After I deposited Bella amid her cackling friends, I ran south along West, swinging east around the Battery through Bowling Green to South Street, past bustling, briny Fulton Street and the upscale shops of the Seaport. And then I thought, what the hell, and went over by Pace University and up onto the Brooklyn Bridge. I did the bridge, but passed on tacking on a couple more miles by challenging the Promenade and its view of the backside of Wall Street. Instead, I hung a huey and came back on the north side of the Roeblings' span. The East River shimmered like glass beneath me, and bobbing ferries crisscrossed as they headed toward the old piers or uptown on their way to LaGuardia. I felt good, I felt fine, but I did not reach up and grab low clouds, I did not hear Copland's "Fanfare," and I did not feel a validating sense of accomplishment, of triumph, of, Christ, vindication. I kept running, and when a stitch caught me on my right side, I walked, passing the ass end of City Hall, then on Chambers to Greenwich.

After a shower, I dressed, threw down an orange and some flatbread and went via Hudson to Sixth, stopping first at an ATM on Worth. When I reached the courts on Houston, I found him where I thought he'd be. He was hustling a short, muscular man half his age. From a block away, I saw he was playing him nice, flicking the handball to let the wobbling guy make an easy return volley. After losing awhile, Jimmy Mango would turn his wrist, throw some backspin on the ball and Li'l Hercules would sprawl onto the cracked concrete.

I came up just as Mango lost his second game. He saw me and skidded away from his opponent who, between gasps, seemed on the verge of cockiness. "What the fuck, at least I'm learning, Howard," Mango said. "Another shot, I think maybe, I don't know, I could take you."

Howard shrugged impudently. No way the little guy with the bony knees and the straw cowboy hat was going to beat a man who could bench-press 350.

"Guy's got a set of guns," I said to Mango.

"Howard? His arms ain't long enough to scratch his balls." He ran his thumbs under the waistband of his sagging shorts. "I'm trying to get him up to $50 a game."

"You're down what?"

"Forty. At worst, I walk home with sixty. Best, one-ten."

I dug my hand into the pocket of my jeans.

Mango grabbed my wrist. "Hey, hey," he said urgently, "don't produce here, Four. What the fuck's wrong with you?" He shook his head. "I don't want nobody thinkin' I took Terry Orr for a couple of yards here. Man, you'll kill my play."

"Jimmy, here's the 750—"

"You're short," he said.

"I'm giving you $20 an hour for 36, which is generous."

"It was $50 an hour."

I shook my head. "Plus the cops made you. You and that fuckin' cab," I said.

"That cab is a tank, man." He smiled. "It's got a backseat and a half. Know what I mean?"

"Take the 750, Jimmy. Go back to Macho Man."

"Leave it in your mailbox, Four." He started to backpedal.

I told him to ring the bell. Mrs. Maoli would make the handoff. She'd serve him espresso and pignoli cookies. He'd be more entertaining than the tube.

LEO HAD THROWN on a couple of pots of coffee, and when I entered the Tilt, the aroma seemed to beckon me, welcoming me as an old friend, as clearly as if it could crook a finger and dispense a smile.

"Mr. Media," Big Leo nodded as he ran a damp rag along the bar. "With a bounce in his step." This morning's *New York Times* was spread open near his half-filled cup, atop an old *Times-Picayune*.

Diddio was hanging out of the jukebox, the worn soles of his black, high-top Converse All-Stars arched and nearly off the floor.

"D," I said, "you missing a sock?"

He backed out of the machine and shut its twinkling, starburst lid. "No, but somehow I got an extra one. I think they breed or something, pop out a little brother now and then."

He came toward me, dusting his hands on his already-dusty black jeans. His eyes were clear: too early for a joint, I guess. "Terry, Gabby's right: You got to get a better P.R. agent for yourself. Two things in the paper, and your name isn't in either of them. I know this woman, used to work at Polygram, got a little mustache on her, you know, but she wouldn't let that happen."

Metro Section readers were greeted with "Explosion in West Village Brownstone Kills One" on page one above the fold. Plenty of speculation, but nothing yet about the late Lin-Lin having hired Vuk, and not a mention of Edie. Detectives at the First made Vuk do a perp walk, and there he was in the *Times,* hands cuffed behind his back, head bowed; in the color shot, his green-black tattoo seemed to jump from the shiny dome, as if in 3-D.

On Tuesday, Amaral's suicide got a box on B-8. I expected a follow-up this morning, with some healing words from Everett Langhorne. But nothing, at least not today.

"I ain't met too many folks called Zoran Vuk," Leo commented. He pointed to the side-by-side coffeepots. "Decaf?"

"High-test," I said. "Let's see what happens."

"You must be tired."

"I am tired," I said. Whatever reservoir of adrenaline had been driving me had dried up. Bella's pounding on my bedroom door had woken me from a deep, dreamless slumber.

Leo put an empty cup on the bar and I sat in front of it as he filled it. Behind me, the sweep of a steel brush against a cymbal, the easy chugging of electric guitar; a slow, steady blues, a baleful moan. Diddio joined in: "'Wednesday's worse and Thursday's oh so sad.'"

He had a horrific singing voice that didn't prevent him from detonating it whenever the inclination struck. "'The eagle flies on Friday,'" he screeched, contorting the melody, bellowing like a sea lion.

"Don't be breaking my glasses, D," Leo grimaced and

pointed to the overhead rack. He went over and cut the volume.

Diddio went silent. A critic immune to criticism, he didn't complain.

And Leo returned to the *Times,* and Diddio drifted toward the pool table in back, and I put my elbow on the bar, and my head in my palm, and we settled in, killing time together, in silence except for the occasional wheeze of the coffeemaker and music that had been shifted to the background. On the overhead TV, a man seemed very serious as he read something that required a panorama of Herald Square, where a pigeon sat on Horace Greeley's head.

I started to drift away, and in the gray light I saw her. We were in Peschici, with Rafaela. She had something to show us, she said, and this delighted Marina, because she had chosen this silver day to tell her sister that she was pregnant with a daughter, and that it was fine.

I'd fallen behind; they were up ahead, blue sundresses shimmering above sandals as they walked on the cobbled streets. We were weaving our way to the church, Chiesa Parrocchiale, to see the Pacecco De Rosa paintings, but I was craning my neck to examine the coarse white stones of an ancient castle, ruins that had stubbornly refused to surrender to salt air and time. And when I looked up, Marina and Rafaela were bickering. I couldn't understand the bursts of Italian: something about a fire. Or flowers. *Fiori, fioraia.* And father; that I understood: *padre.* Some sort of sisterly squabble, I thought. Let me stay out of—

"Terry?"

I opened my eyes to find Addison, in black and white, a diamond shape woven into the center of his thin tie.

"What's wrong?"

He replied with a shake of his head.

I turned to Leo, who was slowly working his way through the Science section, examining a drawing of what appeared to be a kangaroo with wings. "You got iced tea back there?"

Addison interrupted, "No, it's not necessary. I won't be long."

I stood. "Something up?"

"Let's talk."

I gestured to the back of the musty bar, where two padded vinyl booths sat under dim lights near the pinball table and a column of empty beer bottles in reinforced cardboard cases.

I followed Addison toward the red booths, past Diddio, who was asleep on his stomach on the pool table. He took the side facing the bar, with his back to the Tilt's only rest room and Leo's cramped office. I slid in across from him.

"That's the rock critic, isn't it?" He pointed to Diddio.

I nodded.

"I suppose somebody might think that's cool," he said. "If she was fifteen."

"Leave him alone," I replied, thinking he was off by a few years. "He's a good guy."

He frowned his disapproval. "The chin?"

"Fine." I touched the new round bandage I'd put over the scab after I returned from my run. "What's up, Luther?"

"I don't want you to read about it." He dropped his hands on the old, Formica-coated table. "We've got a few complications."

"Really?"

He nodded. "You know how the thing he hit him with was wiped clean? Whoever wiped it left traces of semen on it."

"And..."

"The semen belonged to a man whose blood type was B positive."

"And it's not Amaral's type?"

"Not according to the school's record," he said. "But it's Andre Turner's type."

"And how many other people?"

"About one out of every ten."

"That's 800,000 people in Manhattan alone."

He brought up his right hand. "No need to get defensive, Terry."

This kind of cautious logic, this hedging, conveyed reasonably, paternally: I'd heard it before from Addison. Weisz, he told me several times, many times, "is a suspect, Terry. Nothing more. You seem to want to forget that." Twelve people saw him standing next to Marina as she screamed, saw him staring at Davy, who was trapped in his stroller. But Weisz is only a suspect.

I said, "Amaral confessed."

"To you."

"He confessed," I repeated.

"Explain the semen."

I shook my head. "I don't know. How about this: Turner saw Amaral kill Brown and tried to help by wiping the Club down."

"With something with his semen on it?"

"Amaral said an old guy was doing Turner. All right, so the kid cleans off so he can go back to work. He comes up to West Street and he sees Amaral smack Aubrey Brown. Something tugs at his conscience and he tries to help his teacher. But he uses the same rag he used on his woody."

"An interesting theory," he muttered. "Maybe Turner will tell it another way."

I shifted on the sticky plastic. "You haven't found him yet."

Addison sat back. "You know where he is?"

"Little West 12th. The piers," I replied. "Somewhere."

"Loose ends, and it's not done until Turner comes clean." He slid to the edge of the booth and he stood. "We'll find him. Here, somewhere."

I followed as he started toward the door.

He stopped at the pool table, scooped up the cue ball and dropped it near Diddio's ear. When Diddio failed to react, Addison said, "Pot coma."

"Probably," I lied.

We reached the front of the bar.

Addison stopped, reached over and extended his hand to Leo. "Good to see you again."

"Yeah," Leo said, taking it. "Likewise."

"Terry, say hello to your godmother," he added dryly. Sharon.

I said, "Why not?"

I looked through the dusty blinds. Addison's car was on the sidewalk, all four tires on gray cement.

He bounced into his seat and slipped the key into the ignition. As he looked back at the bar, he tapped the side of his head with a finger, telling me, once again, to be smart.

"HE GONE?" DIDDIO asked as he sat up on the pool table.

Leo told him yes.

Diddio swung his legs around and jumped down. "Man, that guy gives me the heebies and the jeebies."

"You carrying?" I asked.

"It's not that," he replied as he nodded. "He's bad times. You know, with Marina. I don't know how you can hang with him. I see him, I remember I won't see her. I don't know."

"All right, D," Leo cautioned.

I sat on a stool at the crook in the bar. I was thinking about a walk around the Village or over to McSorley's for a dark ale and a liverwurst-and-onion sandwich with their tart, spicy mustard. (Colman's, made fresh, then aged.) Then maybe a trip to the Guggenheim's SoHo branch to see what hadn't been sent to Bilbao—the Rauschenbergs, perhaps, or Max Beckmann's work— and avoid inanities in flashing lights, someone's trite attempt to turn something like the news zipper in Times Square into art. I debated whether to go home first to drop off the bankroll and leave a note for Bella and Mrs. Maoli.

And I thought of Turner, of dirt and grime and blood and semen, and an alley cat in search of marrow; where philosophy gives way to a blow to the head, and a job not done until everything is in its place.

He hadn't gone anywhere. He might be streetwise, he might be as hard as a hammer, but he's 14 and a lifelong New Yorker. With no coin in his pocket and no time on the run, he had to stay here. There was nowhere else for him to go.

And no one for him to go to.

They'd squeeze him hard. Until he gave them something that put him in the middle of it.

"Leo, let me have the .38," I said, remembering Turner's speed with a knife.

Without hesitating, Leo went between the taps and dug with his hefty hand for the piece. I heard the tape pull away from the bar. He brought it out and handed it to me. I shoved it into my jacket pocket.

"You free tonight?" I asked Diddio. "Early?"

"I guess," he shrugged. "I got John Scofield at Birdland, but I'm cool 'til midnight."

"Dinner," I instructed.

I looked at Leo, who nodded. We had a deal: If I use it, I toss it. Neither of us were licensed for firearms.

I tapped the bar with a knuckle.

DIDDIO FOLLOWED ME outside. The sun had made its way above the brick towers, and Hudson was bathed in a dull, wan light. Across the street, on the corner of North Moore, a UPS truckdriver chatted with the florist; under his brown jacket, he wore shorts, despite the midday chill. She wore a green apron and smiled as he joked and tucked his clipboard under his arm.

"Terry. We OK? I mean, maybe I shouldn't mention Marina?"

"No, no," I said quickly. "I'm thinking of something else." I tapped his slender arm.

"You know, we never talk about her."

I hesitated. "I don't, D. But it's all right. If you want to, I mean."

"Gabby asks me all the time," he said.

"I imagine she would." Behind him, a gray Volvo missed the yellow and ran the red.

He thrust his hands into his pockets. "Terry, I read that story and I heard what you've been saying," he began, his voice soft, almost whispering. "The one kid gets abused by his father and is out on the street. The other guy, the painter, falls in with a wack crowd, probably because he needs someone to tell him he's not a dweeb. You know what I mean? Like, if his dad was solid, he would've done better?"

He squinted as he looked up at me.

I said, "I'm with you."

"Gabby says you're happy you did good and all..."

"Well, I wouldn't call it happy, D."

"No, I guess I'm saying . . . I mean, tonight is the third time I watched Gabby this week—"

"Hey, D, if you're busy—"

"What I'm saying is maybe you should think about her, Terry."

I felt my stomach tighten. "I think about her all the time, Dennis," I said sharply.

A scrawny cat, eyes wide, head cocked, stood before me. He was frightened yet oddly defiant. "I ain't saying nothing, Terry. But the one you got to save is her."

"A little melodramatic, D, no?"

He shrugged as he looked down at his black sneakers. "Maybe. But my point—"

"I get you," I told him, as the fire started to die down. "Look, D, I'm clear on this thing."

"She's five stars, Terry, you know. And Marina was my friend."

I nodded. I took a breath. "I appreciate the advice. I do."

"I don't want you coming home dead, man."

"Me neither," I said.

"And now you got a gun."

"To back me up. Nothing more."

He said, as he shook his head, "Us losing Marina fucked up everything."

"I know, D. Believe me."

We stood in silence as a short young woman with an oversized black portfolio walked by, leaving behind the scent of her raspberry shampoo. Her braided ponytail hung halfway down the back of her peacoat.

"All right. I had my say," Diddio announced.

"You did good, D," I replied. "I'm with you."

"I'm still invited for dinner?"

"Anytime you want."

I stuck out my hand, but he came forward and hugged me awkwardly. His head pressed against my sternum.

As he stepped back, he said, "You get yourself killed and everything's doubly fucked."

"Sure, D," I said.

MRS. MAOLI HAD baked a chicken with a sprig of fresh rosemary and we ate it with a hearty side dish of panfried potatoes with black olives and a gentle sprinkling of red pepper flakes. Diddio and I sipped a black-cock chianti from Tuscany, Bella Yoo-hoo from the bottle. The radio offered a series of dances by Wernick, and I ignored their demands to change the station, refusing to eat a succulent chicken breast and tangy Ligurian olives to the sounds of Steppenwolf and Moby Grape.

"Dad. A word, please," she said as I pulled on a hooded black sweatshirt.

Diddio was hunched over the kitchen sink. "Doing the dishes," he'd said. "It's so Alice Nelson, man."

I followed my daughter to the back of the house. We stopped in the living room, tidy now; Mrs. Maoli is a whirlwind on Thursdays.

"I got a 105 on my French test," she began.

"As you said."

"And I already finished my project on Descartes."

I replied, "Well, you wrote about how he wasn't Fermat. To irritate Mr. Bannister."

"He's a *putz*," she muttered. "But"—she held up a finger—"the point is, I did it. Almost a week early."

"OK."

"And I'm watching Dennis again."

"A profitable endeavor," I said. "Don't hustle him in chess tonight, Bella. Stare at the TV or something."

"Whatever." She waved her hands impatiently. "I think you'll agree I'm doing well in school."

"Bella, what is it?"

Quickly, she said, "Glo-Bug is having a party Friday night. I have to go."

"You have to?"

"Well, if I can't go, she won't do it."

"I see."

She inched toward the arm of the sofa and leaned her hip against it. I could see the anxiety in her pretty face.

She began to knead her hands. "So . . . ?"

"Will there be boys?"

"Little Mango. Some others."

"What about Mrs. Figueroa?"

"She's got a date. But it's not a make-out party or something like that, Dad. We'll just watch MTV, go online, listen to music. You know."

"What time?"

"I'm going to help her get ready. From six to about midnight?"

"Midnight," I said.

"I have to help her clean up."

"Of course."

"So . . . ?"

"Sure," I said, "why not?"

She sprang toward me and threw her arms around my waist. "Thanks, Dad. Really."

"Sure, Bella. You deserve a good time."

She hugged me, then looked up. "You'll be all right?"

"When? Tonight?"

"No. Friday night," she replied. "Do you have something to do?" She stepped back. "I mean, we haven't been apart on a Friday night since Mama and Davy died."

"I'll come up with something, I'm sure," I said.

"And we'll play B-ball on Saturday?"

"Absolutely."

I put my hand on her head as I walked by. I went toward the stairs, past Marina's sea-arch of Vignanotica and cliffs at the Gargano coast, the lake near Campobasso.

From upstairs, I could hear Bella squeal in delight as she used the kitchen phone. I slid into my leather coat and dropped the .38 in my side pocket.

I DECIDED TO head north along Greenwich, and to stay on Greenwich, and I stopped to see if Addison had someone on me, and when I saw no one, I moved on.

I reached Jane a little before nine and I set up on the corner, outside the white halo cast by the streetlight, across from the leaking hydrant, the abandoned building Montana and his crew used to get out of the cold, to hide away. "Back again," I thought, as memories of Amaral returned. In the distance, the clamor at Little West 12th, refrigerated delivery trucks coming and going; a horn honks, brakes squeal, the groan and rush of a heavy engine. The scent of salt from the Hudson, the rank odor of rotted food and waste from the wire basket to my right; old newsprint kicking up Greenwich, caught in temperate wind. Someone had pissed in a Colt 45 bottle and left it at the curb.

And I stood for an hour, counting passing cars and Postal Service wagons; and I listened for boats on the river, but heard only the rush of traffic on Tenth and a siren blare as the blue-and-white headed uptown and the rattle of an old truck as it found a pothole hidden among the cobblestones. I shifted and tried to find house lights on the Jersey palisades. I leaned against the cold brick, I counted the cracks in the sidewalk. Thin magenta clouds seemed translucent.

I went toward the building.

SIXTEEN

INSIDE, MURKY DARKNESS WAS offset by the tinsel strands of moonlight that oozed through the back of the old tenement, and the floor buckled and creaked as I groped my way to the stairs to my right. I continued, guiding myself by using the dirty banister, taking the steps one at a time, catching the soles of my running shoes on the chipped linoleum. Incomprehensible graffiti covered the cracked, dust-coated walls.

The earthy scent of human sweat, of cobwebs that had been brushed aside but not removed, surrounded me as I went on, and I thought I heard the rustle of rodents well above me or far below me through gaping holes in floor-boards, the insistent scraping and gnawing of rat's teeth on paint chips and waste.

I stopped on the first-floor landing. It was littered with old beer cans, cigarette butts and fast-food wrappers, and I nestled in the dark corner and waited for the sound of breathing, of people moving softly, stealthily; and when I was sure the place was vacant, when I thought I heard silence, I looked for a place to go. The door to the apartment to my right had been removed and replaced with a tin sheet that had been peeled away; now it hung limply from the frame, and I decided to step into the blackness that lay beyond the portal.

I inched inside and went carefully toward where I thought the center of the room would be, on my way to the dots of cloudy light that trickled through pin-sized holes in the tin that covered the windows on West. As I dragged my feet along the decayed floor, I felt something against the side of my shoe. I kicked; a mattress.

I moved along the edge of the mattress until I felt against my shin what I'd expected to find, and I bent down to turn it on, groping for the small plastic switch. A bare bulb in a cheap lamp clicked on, casting a coarse glow into the room.

I stood up and looked around. The floor was littered with crack vials and spent matchbooks and used condoms and crumpled wrappers and an old rag of a towel; the mattress had been soiled with urine and semen. At the edge of the light's rim, there was a makeshift table, a splintered spool that had once borne cable at some nearby construction site. On it was a tin that had held takeout food, a plastic fork; and a cat with yellow eyes who'd been interrupted as he pecked at the remains. He hunched his back and stared at me defiantly, as if daring me to go for the tray. Instead, I leaned over, killed the light and shuffled backward for the black corner of the room.

TWENTY MINUTES LATER, they came up the stairs and there was giggling and a man's voice, coarse and throaty, full of lust and excitement and a vague sense of discomfort as he asked, "Where are we going, baby?"

"Easy, easy," a girl replied. "This is where we are."

I heard the cat bound from the table and scurry away from his visitors.

And then they came into the room and she told him to wait. I heard her scamper expertly across the mattress and reach for the lamp.

"Where are you, baby?" the man asked.

She snapped on the light.

He saw me before she did. "Hey, what the fuck—"

I had the gun raised and pointed at him.

She was young, no more than 16, and she had on too much eye makeup and, under a short fluffy coat, a red tube-top that surrounded her small breasts and revealed her ribs and a sunken stomach. She wore a black miniskirt and her legs were like frail sticks that extended into her cheap stiletto-heeled boots. Her pasty skin was dotted with blemishes. She tried to stay calm, but she was confused and that frightened her.

"Toss me your wallet," I said to the man.

He was stocky and his red-striped tie was away from his unbuttoned collar. His dark suit was disheveled.

He dug into his back pocket and did as I'd asked.

"You bitch," he spat.

As I opened the wallet, I heard a smack. The girl spilled onto the mattress.

"Hey," I shouted, "asshole. Back off."

"She set me up. Pimp."

"Shut your fuckin' mouth." I looked at his driver's license. "Eugene."

I threw his wallet toward him. When it landed on the filthy floor, he bent over to pick it up. He wobbled as he stood, the rush of alcohol throwing him off-balance.

"Go back to Port Chester, Eugene," I said. "Be a good boy and maybe I won't call Mrs. Eugene."

He tried to glare at me, but his eyes kept drifting to the .38 in my right hand.

"And give her what you owe her," I added.

The girl on the mattress looked up at me.

The man fumbled and came up with a twenty. He crumpled the bill and tossed it down.

She scrambled to grab it.

"Go," I told Eugene.

He went.

THE GIRL WAS staring at me.

"Get up," I told her.

"Who are you?" she asked.

I shoved the gun into my pocket. "Batman."

I reached out to help her up, taking her small hand in mine and lifting her without much trouble.

"I'm looking for Montana. The kid with the scar. You know him?"

"You're a cop."

"Where's Montana?"

"He didn't do it," she said as she backed off the mattress.

"I know."

She looked at the small bandage under my chin. "Oh, you're the guy he cut. You *are* tall. But not seven feet."

I said, "He needs to come in. He needs a lawyer and he'd better tell it straight."

She ran her hands along her thin forearms. Her costume jewelry jangled. "He's got nobody now," she said sadly.

"One thing at a time..."

"Cherry."

Of course. "Cherry, let's help him with this first."

She looked at me. "Your aura. It says you're all right."

"I'm all right," I said.

She hesitated. "He's not the only one who needs money."

"We'll settle up after we see him, Cherry."

She nodded. "Let's go," she said. "I've got to get back to work."

I FOLLOWED HER south on Greenwich and she led me to a brick warehouse that butted up against West. On the narrow side street, the scaffolding held up a walkway that went the length of Charles at the second-floor level. A blue tarp hung off the silver rails and flapped in the wind off the river. The broad building's ground-floor windows were boarded with plywood and the plywood was covered with bills for movies, rock shows.

"He's in there," Cherry said.

I looked up, following a battered, snakelike cylinder used for funneling heavy refuse from the upper floors. "It's a big building." The sky was a black dome dotted with flickering stars.

"He's in the basement. He's been there since Sunday."

I shook my head.

"I'm sure he is."

I said, "Call him."

"No, no. I'm not with this, mister. And don't you tell him I was here."

"Tell him there's money to be made."

A FedEx truck came up the street and continued on. A Toyota passed us for the second time, its driver no doubt searching in vain for a parking spot.

"I've got to go," she said, as she shuffled to ward off the cold. She held out her hand. I slapped a twenty into her palm.

"They tell you to get off the streets, don't they? City Services."

She replied, "Where am I going to go?"

"Go home."

"Shit," she said, "it's better out here." She tugged on the tube top and slid the bill between her tiny breasts. "Don't tell him you saw me."

She turned and went between parked cars to the other side of Charles and headed toward West.

I waited until she turned north on the wide avenue, then looked for a way inside the warehouse. Behind me, closer to Greenwich, there was a break in the scaffolding and I moved toward it.

A sturdy wooden ramp led to makeshift front doors held together by a thick chain and a lock. I noticed that the chain hung loose between the door's square handles and when I went up and tugged on it, the doors moved apart. It was enough space for a small boy like Montana to squeeze through, but I couldn't fit. Instead, I used the chain for a boost and I went up on the scaffolding, pulling myself up on the cold bars.

Crouching, I crept along the runway on tottering planks in search of another entrance, along a row of windows boarded from the inside. About a third of the way up the block, I found a loose board and pressed against it. It gave, but didn't come away from its mooring. I worked it with the heel of my hand until it was away from the frame, then worked my fingers in until I could hold the top to prevent it from falling. When I leaned against it, it started to give way at the side. I twisted until it peeled away, and I slid in the opening, my hood catching for a moment on the sharp corner of the plank.

The floor was freshly poured concrete and the beams were exposed. Yellow-plastic cages protected the light-bulbs, some of which glowed timidly. I went toward where the makeshift entrance had been, guessing that there might be a stairwell. There was, and it was sturdy, reinforced cement from when the old building was new. I took it down, going slow.

As I reached the first-floor landing, I could hear two male voices in animated conversation, as comfortable as two friends over cocktails. I could smell burning wood, and as I reached the entrance to the basement, I heard the wood crackle, snap and hiss.

I hung back. Montana had his hands out by the flames that danced above an oil drum. His wavering shadow was cast long and thin behind him to the far reaches of the concrete basement. The other guy, his back toward me, was talking, scuffling; and Montana was watching, taking in his tale, and then he let out a high-pitched laugh.

I came out and stood in the door frame and Montana didn't see me. But then he did. His expression dropped and he let his hands fall to his sides.

I stepped up.

"What?" his friend asked as he turned. He was a red-head and his face was splattered with freckles. He had thick arms, unlike Montana, who was small, sinewy. He looked hard and like he knew how to use his hands. I made him for 17 or 18; he'd been on the street longer than Montana had been.

"I cut your ass," Montana barked at me.

"You've got to come in," I said. "They're going to find you and hang it on you."

Montana came around the flaming barrel and pulled out his knife. "I told you to fuck off."

"Your semen was on the Club," I said. "They think you're in on it."

"Fuck that," he said. "Amaral did it. Everybody knows."

"Only I know."

Out of the corner of my eye, I saw the redhead grope for a piece of wood that stood above the spitting flames.

I moved to my left, closing toward Montana, but out of reach of the redhead if he swung the plank.

"You tell your friend if he pulls that, I'll cram it down his throat," I said.

The redhead put his hand on the wood. As Montana came closer, he said, "What we're gonna do is fuck you up."

"I'm bringing you in, Andre," I said.

The redhead looked at Montana. "Andre?" he asked.

And I bolted forward and sent the redhead against the barrel. It tipped over and I stepped back, squared and, as he recovered, I caught him flush on the jaw. He went back and stumbled against the bottom of the hot barrel and he let out a yell.

I turned and Montana moved toward me, his arm extended as he loosely fingered his switchblade. "Come," he gestured. "Come on."

I put my left arm in front of me, to use the leather sleeve in case he took a quick swipe at me before I could pull the .38.

"Don't make it happen like this," I warned. "It's different now."

"Let's do it, then," he said as he crouched down. He had the blade pointed at my waist.

I brought my right hand around the grip of the gun.

Suddenly, a horrifying, high-pitched scream ripped the room. I looked to my right. The redheaded kid had rolled into the fire. His oversized jacket was ablaze.

"Christy!" Montana shouted. He dropped the knife and grabbed for his friend, latching onto the bottom of his jeans and tugging him away from the burning wood and debris.

I slid Leo's piece back into my slacks and whipped off

my jacket. I used it to beat against the kid until the flame died.

I saw that his jacket had quickly burned through and the back of his neck and hair had caught fire. The skin on his right hand had already begun to bubble and blister.

"Call somebody," Montana shouted, as Christy moaned as he tried to stand.

I grabbed the cell phone from my belt and I hit speed dial. As I waited, Montana went to his knees. He looked at me, then went back to Christy.

Addison answered the phone on the fourth ring.

When I finished, I looked up. Montana was gone.

I FIGURED HE would bolt for the front exit. It was the right move, if he was swift about it: He'd be able to squeeze through the narrow gap between the steel doors; I couldn't and he'd be gone by the time the cops came. But as I ran toward the stairs, I heard scuffling above me and I realized he was going up, where it was crowded with construction material and debris. There'd be places to hide and maybe there was a way out I hadn't seen.

I figured I could outrun him and, with a longer stride than his, I'd catch up fast. I heard the slap of his soles echo on the stairwell's concrete walls and the ruffling of his down jacket as he turned hard on the newel posts. And then there was silence: He'd chosen a floor. I quickly calculated, took the stairs and followed into the dull light. We were on the eighth story of the building.

As I entered the floor, I saw him dart sideways and duck behind a dented Dumpster. There were similar heavy containers throughout the room and I slid behind the closest one to my left. It was tipped tight against a round column.

A caged lightbulb hung among the distended cables in the exposed ceiling, and I could see clearly despite its weak glow. Star-speckled darkness entered through the circular opening where the hollow trash-cylinder hung.

I was secure where I was. If the little man had nothing more than his blade, I didn't have to move until he did.

There was silence and then it was split by the wail of sirens along West.

"Andre," I shouted.

No response. I could see his feet near the Dumpster's wheels.

"They're coming," I said.

"They come here they get nothing," he replied. His voice was high-pitched yet confident. "I got places."

I said, "Don't let them hang it on you."

The sirens grew closer and, through the cracks in the tin sheets on the windows, I could see faint traces of blue-and-red lights.

"Andre—"

Suddenly, he bolted to his right and I came around the post, around the container.

He was going to the trash cylinder. He was going to try to slide down the side of the building.

He ran frantically across the dusty floor, through the dim, scattered light. Far below, sirens howled.

I quickly cut the distance between us, but he made it to the rubber cylinder before I could and, with an acrobat's agility, he leapt feet-first into the dark hole.

I skidded toward the opening and I saw his dreadlocks rattle as he began his slide.

Then he vanished. I stopped.

And then he screamed.

I looked into the black cylinder. Turner was caught on the jagged rods and harsh nails that held the cylinder together; his left arm was pinned above him on ragged steel against the thick rubber tube. And that had saved him: Had he not been caught, he would have tumbled eight stories through the razorlike shards and jutting edges of the industrial trash that was caught in the cylinder. He would have been shredded as he tumbled toward the debris down below.

He quaked and screamed again, in pain, in terror. The slice in his arm told him what would happen if he came loose and went down.

He was eight feet below me. I kneeled to reach in and I could barely touch the fingers of his left hand.

He started to twist.

"Don't," I shouted. "Don't shake loose."

He hissed. "It's *in* me, man," he said, "a nail! Something." Looking over his right shoulder, he peered directly into my eyes.

"See if you can brace yourself with your legs," I said.

He spread out and pressed his right foot against the rubber.

I leaned in, grabbing on to the outside of the cylinder with my left hand. "Give me your right hand," I said.

He tossed up his right arm and I caught him by the tips of his small fingers.

I inched forward. I was in the space now, eight floors above the hard street; only my left forearm, hand and leg were beyond the cylinder. The opening was wide enough to send us into the abyss.

His fingers crept up my right hand until he grabbed my wrist.

There was a glimmer of hope in his eyes.

"We've got to get you off the spike," I said.

"It's in me," he repeated fearfully.

"Come up my arm," I told him.

He tried to slither up, but could only get to my elbow.

"Hold on tight," I said.

My left hand trembled as I stiffened.

I looked into the blackness beyond him.

"Brace hard with your legs," I said.

When I saw him push against the cylinder, I let go with my left hand. Now he was supporting me, with his legs and the tight clamp above my forearm. My knees were pressed hard again the outer edge of the cylinder.

I reached under him with my left arm and lifted him, keeping him flat against the cylinder so that the jagged shard would go out as it came in.

He screamed again. It echoed eerily in the tube.

But he was loose and he knew it. He tried to snake up toward me. I had him tight and, with a heave, I pulled him to me.

I tumbled backward onto the floor and he fell on top of me.

The left sleeve of his down coat was shredded and his left hand was slick with blood.

"Don't," I said. "Don't run." I scrambled to my feet.

"I ain't," he muttered as he looked at his bloody hand. "I'm not."

I gasped for air. "Tourniquet," I managed.

"I can't feel—I can't feel it," he said. "But it's all right."

He was flat on his back. I reached down to lift him.

I thought, Someone's son got saved.

I listened for footsteps in the stairwell. Sirens continued to wail.

THE EMS AMBULANCE had only one bed, and Christy McMahon was on it, his raw skin being treated quickly for the short ride to the emergency room. I sat on the wooden ramp with Andre Turner under the streetlights and stars. I'd tied his belt around his thin bicep. That seemed to halt the blood flow.

I told him I knew a lawyer who'd help him and I told him to keep his mouth shut until the lawyer told him to open it. And I told him he could do a lot worse than having his lawyer get in touch with Langhorne.

He kept nodding. He might've been listening.

I stood when I saw Addison's big black Buick sweep onto Charles and ease in next to a blue-and-white. "Stay put," I said.

Turner reached down and put his finger into a drop of blood on the ramp. He muttered something under his breath.

I went over to the curb as Addison stepped from his car and I pointed to Turner, who was now hunched inside his shredded down coat. He had his collar up above his dangling dreadlocks.

"That's your boy," I told him. "He needs help."

I watched as Addison went over and talked to Turner. Then he led him to the patrol car and ushered him into the warmth of its backseat.

The EMS ambulance pulled away, its bright lights whirling, its harsh siren blaring. Another blue-and-white came along West from the south. Addison beckoned to one of the uniformed cops and she came to him. Then she went to join Turner, who sank with resignation as she came toward the car.

Addison came back to me. "Don't tell me you knew where he was all along."

"Have a little faith, Lieutenant," I replied.

"And I thought I told you to be careful."

I pointed to the blue-and-white at the curb. "There he is," I said, "ready to tell you all about Amaral."

He nodded.

"And I'm going home."

I went east to Greenwich and turned south on familiar cobblestone, heading toward the silver Twin Towers, their crowns hidden in low-lying clouds.

SEVENTEEN

I SAT ON THE long sofa in the airless waiting room, my knees drawn more closely to my chest than I'd preferred but not so tight as to warrant a complaint. The *Business Week*, *National Geographic*, *Weekly Reader* and *Wired* magazines on the nearby table were testimony to the diversity of Harteveld's clients, and to the conceit that neurosis knew few boundaries. To my right, from behind the white counter, John kept a wary eye on me, as if I might suddenly turn either violent or conversant. I tried to ignore him and went on reading Nagel's biography of John Quincy Adams as I leaned against Bella's overcrowded backpack, with its patches and symbols and scribbles done in fluorescent yellow Magic Marker: Someone had penned a swearword on the bag and Bella had converted it to Puck, adding in parens, A Midsummer Night's Dream by Billy Shakes.

Earlier this morning, after I'd learned from Tommy the Cop that Vuk had given up Lin-Lin and Edie, I went over to the Strand and was caught up in the endless stacks, the packed shelves, the vast array of titles on tables, on the floor and in the aisles, and the musty smell of printed paper and bound books, and the lurking browsers, studious yet assertive. I wound up with six books in a flimsy shopping bag, including the Nagel, a Paul Auster for Bella and a coffee table book on Ghirlandaio that she and I would give to Judy when we went to see her tomorrow night at her place in Gramercy Park. Her son and his fiancée were staying with her; she sounded fine, despite Edie's betrayal, and was threatening to expand the gallery rather than merely repair it. A bit of bravado, no doubt, but so characteristically Judy Henley Harper that I took it as a sign of a proper recovery.

On the way back to TriBeCa, I stopped in Washington Square Park and sat on the lip of the dry fountain, and I thought for a moment about Andre Turner. Everett Langhorne had gotten him a bed at Harlem Hospital, not merely to fix his wound but to buy time to figure out how to convince Turner to turn his life around. As a surprisingly harsh wind pushed in and the sun went behind angry clouds, I thought about Langhorne. A persuasive man, I told myself. Maybe he'd find someone to take Turner in. As I left the fountain, I allowed myself the illusion that it would work out for the little man.

Now I came off Harteveld's waiting-room sofa, standing to stretch my legs, coincidentally, at the moment that my daughter bounced down the hall. She was all smiles, her burden, if not lifted, at least lessened.

"You're up, Pops," she said. To John, she added, "My word for today is 'conflagration.'"

I said, "Bella, I'm not up." My next connection with Harteveld would wait. "Play a quick one with John and let's rip, OK?"

She sighed and went for her coat.

John said, "Fax me."

WE HEADED WEST on 60th, going toward the park, and I thought of mid-October, when there would be a kaleidoscope of colors, an unimaginable splendor that belies the inevitable surrender to November winds, to age, to the relentless logic of nature's cycle: bare trees; thin, knotty branches that seem to grope for the sky; brown leaves ground to dust. With winter yet to come, it was too soon to think of new leaves, buds that blossomed and a warm, lustrous sun. A pleasant afternoon in the fall doesn't suggest summer, only the burden of the days ahead.

Bella held my hand as we passed the Pierre and the Sherry Netherland hotels and their uniformed doormen, who blew their hot breath into their white gloves to gain a moment of added warmth.

Across the street, steam rose from the rickety cart that carried chestnuts and pretzels.

"You hungry?" I asked, as I shifted her backpack on my shoulder.

"No," she replied, "I don't want to eat before I go to Glo-Bug's. I'm not cold either. Because I am properly dressed. Dad, you have to get a winter coat. Something long."

"Maybe I'll get a cape."

"Get one of those things Sherlock Holmes wears. It's like a cape."

"The word 'pelerine' comes to mind, but I'm not sure why."

We stopped at the cart. I asked for two bottles of water and placed the bills in the squat man's calloused hand.

I gestured to a bench in front of the thick brick retaining wall. As we sat, I pointed to the crowd across from us that poured from F. A. O. Schwarz.

"Maybe you ought to take some of that money you've got stashed away and spend a little bit of it," I said.

"No, I'm saving for something."

"What?" I asked.

"I don't know yet. But I want to be ready when I see it."

The tip of her nose was red and I reached to cup it, to make it warm.

"You washed your hands at Dr. Harteveld's," she observed.

"Yes. How do you know?"

"You smell like Dial soap. She has Dial soap in the ladies' room, too."

"Pretty clever, Bella."

"The cut is healing," she said, pointing to my chin.

The body heals, I thought.

"Tell me again how you fell," she continued. "Or admit it was something else. Like it had something to do with you saving that kid. Admit it."

We cracked the plastic caps on the water bottles. I took a drink: The water was cold and crisp.

"Well, I'll admit this, Bella: My feet are frozen."

"Now it's you who's being clever. Get good shoes like mine and you won't be cold. A good hat and good shoes: that's the secret to staying warm."

"Bella, you're wearing bowling shoes Diddio stole for you and an old man's fedora."

She stood and pointed to the Plaza. "We can get a cab over there."

I hoisted the backpack as I left the bench and took another long pull of water to finish the bottle. I spun the white plastic cap back on, spotted a trash can near the curb and tossed the clear, thin bottle toward it. The bottle hit the rim and bounded away.

"Dad, you're losing your touch. I think I'll take you tomorrow."

"The wind took it," I said, pointing to the threatening, steel-gray-and-blue sky.

"'The wind took it.'" She repeated as she picked up the bottle and dunked it in the can. "Somehow, I can't imagine Automatic Slim saying that."

We started toward Grand Army Plaza, where jittery pigeons pecked at birdseed and bread crumbs laid out by a hunched woman in a floral scarf who carried empty aluminum cans in a baby carriage. Two men in African garb made their way around the flock of bobbing birds as they walked toward the east side.

"Bella, I've been meaning to ask you something: How's Mordecai Foxx doing?"

She hesitated. "Pretty good."

"You didn't think I knew."

"Who told you?" she asked.

"And you've got him there with Tilden and Tweed and Riis and Slippery Dick?"

"Right with them," she said, looking ahead, toward the yellow taxis and hansom cabs and the many national flags that fluttered aggressively over the hotel's entrance. The new one by Merchant-Ivory was at the Paris Theater.

"Bella, you know there was no private investigator working for Tilden called Mordecai Foxx."

She stopped, but did not face me.

"You made him up."

"There could have been a guy like him," she offered.

"I think I would've known. I mean, some people say I wrote a pretty good book about those guys."

"Maybe you should write a book about Mordecai Foxx," she said. She reached up and adjusted her hat, pressing it down to keep it from flying away in the wind that ripped across town.

I turned her toward me and I looked down at her red cheeks, her dark eyes. "Maybe you ought to. Let's see if you can write a book."

"I did it for you, the research."

We held hands as we crossed 58th Street.

"You *have* been writing, Dad. Admit it."

I decided to tell her. "I write letters, Bella. To your mother."

She looked at me, her expression somewhere between shock and surprise. "You do? Can I see them?"

"If you let me see your journal..."

She paused, then said, "I don't think I'll do that. But will you tell me?"

"About what I write? Sure. Why not?" Then I said, "By the way, nice name. Mordecai Foxx. It's got a ring of authenticity."

"You think so?" she asked. "I thought so too."

"Do something with it," I challenged.

She said, "I could write a book."

"Sure."

"I *could.* I'm disciplined. I'm smart."

"In two weeks, you won't even remember that you said you could."

"Hah," she barked.

"I'll give you three-to-one for all the money in the trunk of your Barbie car that you can't write one chapter of a mystery featuring Mordecai Foxx."

"Make it $100 at four-to-one and you've got a deal," she said.

I stuck out my hand and we shook. "One chapter by January first," I said.

"I'll give you one by Monday," she replied.

We turned to walk on, and she draped her arm around

my waist and I felt her head against my ribs. She looked up at me and she smiled.

We went on toward the cabstand. We would slip inside a warm taxi and a driver with an unpronounceable name would head south down Fifth, passing St. Patrick's and the crowds at Saks and the Library. And I would offer Bella my shoulder and she might take it, or she might not. She might pull a book from her bag, the Salinger or the Auster I'd gotten her, maybe; or she might talk to me about something Diddio had said, or she might point to some strange man on the street with a green Mohawk, or a woman in Versace with a Vietnamese pig on a ruby-studded leash, or a pop star. Mrs. Maoli, she might say, said something funny today, imitating her Italian accent to demonstrate how she abused the English language. As she told her tales, Bella would bubble, Bella would exude life, would radiate life.

I held open the taxicab door for her and she squeezed by to jump inside.

I slid in beside her. For now, thoughts of revenge, of atonement, of justice, of vindication were set aside.

In the moments before twilight, we were on our way home.

The following are the disks that Diddio placed in the jukebox at the Tilt the day the *New York* magazine reporter visited:

The Best of the Animals	*The Animals*
Music for Six Musicians	*Don Byron*
Def Trance Beat (Modalities of Rhythm)	*Steve Coleman & Five Elements*
Saved	*Bob Dylan*
Then Play On	*Fleetwood Mac*
The Very Best of Aretha Franklin, Vol. 1	*Aretha Franklin*
Extensions	*Dave Holland Quartet*
"The Hot Spot" Soundtrack	*John Lee Hooker/Miles Davis/Taj Mahal*
Hate to See You Go	*Little Walter*
At Last!	*Etta James*
The Anthology (two disks)	*Curtis Mayfield & the Impressions*
Shakill's Warrior	*David Murray*
Southern Exposure	*Maceo Parker*
Sticky Fingers	*The Rolling Stones*
Come On Home	*Boz Scaggs*
A Go Go	*John Scofield*
The Best of the Staple Singers	*The Staple Singers*
Hard Again	*Muddy Waters*
Jumpworld	*Cassandra Wilson*

He removed all but *Then Play On* two days later.

New York Times bestselling author

NEVADA BARR

BLOOD LURE

An Anna Pigeon Novel

"All is not well in Grizzly Country...
Barr's red herrings and sly twists culminate in one
huge payoff."
—*Entertainment Weekly*

❏ 0-425-18375-0

**Available wherever books are sold
or
to order call: 1-800-788-6262**